"How much time?" Trip asked.

"How much time do Hoshi and I have?"

Neesa frowned. "That's hard to say. There are a lot of factors involved."

"When we first found out about all this, you said months."

"I know."

"We're not talking about months anymore though, are we?"

She shook her head. "No. Certainly not for Hoshi. For you . . . if these test results are right . . . if the rate of depletion continues to accelerate . . . if—"

"Neesa."

She looked up at him.

"Just tell me."

She shut her eyes a second, and shook her head.

"Six weeks," she said, sighing again.

In a month, they'd be dead.

For a complete list of
Star Trek books log on to
www.simonsays.com/st

— STAR TREK —
ENTERPRISE

DAEDALUS'S CHILDREN

DAVE STERN

**Based on *Star Trek*
created by Gene Roddenberry
and
Star Trek: Enterprise
created by Rick Berman & Brannon Braga**

POCKET BOOKS
New York   London   Toronto   Sydney

An *Original* Publication of POCKET BOOKS

POCKET BOOKS, a division of Simon & Schuster, Inc.
1230 Avenue of the Americas, New York, NY 10020

STAR TREK is a Registered Trademark of Paramount Pictures.

ISBN: 0-7434-7646-8

First Pocket Books printing May 2004

10 9 8 7 6 5 4 3 2 1

POCKET and colophon are registered trademarks of Simon & Schuster, Inc.

Manufactured in the United States of America

For information regarding special discounts for bulk purchases, please contact Simon & Schuster Special Sales at 1-800-456-6798 or business@simonandschuster.com.

For Margaret,
who wanted a good story . . .

The events take place just prior to
Captain Archer being taken by
the Tellarite bounty hunter Skalaar on
March 21, 2153

DAEDALUS'S CHILDREN

One

JONATHAN ARCHER CLENCHED and unclenched his fist. Once, twice, several times . . .

There was definitely something wrong with him.

An ache in all his joints, not just his fingers. A weariness in his bones, an exhaustion that just wouldn't go away, no matter how much he rested during the day, how many hours of sleep he got at night. It went beyond a simple adjustment to prison life, he was certain of that, even though Rava One's doctors dismissed his complaints as bellyaching.

"Archer!"

He looked up from the cot he was sitting on.

Tomon, one of the prison guards—Archer's least favorite guard, in fact—stood outside his cell.

"Up!" he yelled, brandishing his weapon, a long, thin metal rod akin to an old-fashioned Taser. Primitive, but highly effective. If he touched you with it, you got a debilitating electric shock. Archer knew this from hard-earned experience—the first time he'd been a little too slow in obeying Tomon's commands, he'd gotten a taste of that shock. It had left him twitching on the ground for what felt like hours.

It had left Tomon with a nasty smile on his face.

Archer remembered that smile as he rose from his cot and locked eyes with the guard. Tomon was small and slight—almost half a meter shorter than the captain, a good twenty-three kilos lighter—with a nasty streak Archer was sure he'd adopted in an attempt to compensate for his size. Over the last couple weeks—since the crew had first been imprisoned here on Rava One—he'd turned that nasty streak on the captain more than once.

Archer was looking forward to a little payback—sooner, rather than later.

Some of that attitude must have shown in his eyes.

"You want some more of this?" Tomon asked, raising his weapon.

"No," Archer said with as much humility as he could muster, gazing down at the ground.

"Then wipe that look off your face. And fall in." Tomon stepped to the side of the cell doorway and deactivated the ion field.

The captain of the *Enterprise* shuffled forward, stopping just outside his cell.

A metal wall rose before him, stretching up a good three stories. High at the top of that wall, a single porthole—a piece of glass perhaps two meters square—looked out onto the stars.

Rava One was a satellite—location unknown. Archer and his crew had been trapped here for two and a half weeks.

"Eyes front, Archer," Tomon snapped.

The captain lowered his gaze and stared at the blank wall in front of him.

"Good."

Tomon moved on to the cell to the captain's left.

Archer risked a quick glance to his right.

O'Neill stood there, hands clasped behind her back, in front of her cell. She wore a drab, gray, one-piece coverall. The same coverall Archer wore. Beyond her the captain saw Dwight and Carstairs and Duel.

The captain nodded briefly to all of them.

Dwight looked worse, he saw. Pale, thin, hunched over like an old man. Archer frowned and shook his head. The young ensign had been in the infirmary most of the last week, unable to keep down any of the food the Denari were giving them. He wasn't the only one, but he'd been by far the most seriously affected. An allergic reaction—anaphylactic shock, Phlox had called it—had almost killed him the first day. Dwight had been sick almost every day since. More than the rest of them, he'd had to be very careful about what he ate. The captain knew his last meal had been almost nothing.

Archer locked eyes with Dwight now, and offered what he hoped was an encouraging smile.

Hang in there kid. D-Day—D for deliverance—is coming soon.

"What did I say, Archer? Hey?"

The captain heard Tomon's yell and felt the jab of his weapon at the exact same second.

His brain exploded in agony.

He was vaguely aware of falling, the back of his head slamming to the floor, his hands and feet, arms and legs, twitching spasmodically, over and over again. Mostly, his world was pain. White-hot daggers of it shooting up and down his spine, through his nervous system as the electrical impulses from brain to body overloaded.

"Back!" the captain heard Tomon yell. "Or you're next!"

Archer had no idea who exactly he was talking to—one of the crew, obviously—but he silently urged whoever it was to do what Tomon said. No incidents. That might mean a lockdown—no exercise period. They couldn't afford that now.

The thrashing subsided. Archer got control of his body back and lay there a moment. He tasted blood in his mouth—he'd bitten his tongue again. The backs of his hands were bruised where he'd slammed them into the hard metal floor.

He looked up and saw Tomon looming over him.

The guard pressed the rod, deactivated—for a second Archer had been certain Tomon was going to shock him again, and he'd tensed up—against Archer's chin, forcing his head back against the floor.

"Now. Why don't you get up, and do what you're told. Captain."

As usual, the Denari guard put a sneer into that last word.

Archer forced himself not to react.

"I will," he said, and climbed to his feet.

All around him, he sensed his crew watching. Four to his left, thirteen others to his right.

Stay calm, everyone, he willed silently.

Tomon stepped back then and ordered everyone to form a line. Then he marched them down, in formation, to an open space by the exit door, where he lined them up again in a single row.

Archer heard the rest of A block fall into formation behind them.

Two more rows of eighteen prisoners. Blocks A-1 (his) through A-3. All *Enterprise* crew. B block, next to them, held the rest of them. C and D blocks—the remainder of the prison satellite—held other prisoners. Denari prisoners. With whom *Enterprise* crew was not allowed to mingle.

Nonetheless, the captain had been able to learn a few things about them. Most of his information came from Doctor Phlox, who, out of all of them, seemed to be having the easiest time adjusting to life in Rava. Not physically—he suffered, albeit to a lesser degree, from the same problems as *Enterprise*'s human crew, an inability to (as the doctor put it) "tolerate" some of the Denari foods, a general malaise, a growing stiffness and soreness in his body that he attributed to certain chemical deficiencies—but mentally. The doctor seemed, by and large, to be his usual, good-natured self. Though the captain knew that with Denobulans, appearances could be deceiving.

Phlox, who had one of the two universal translator modules the prison authorities had allowed them to keep (Archer, had the other), had managed to convince those authorities to allow him to work with the medical staff on Rava to help figure out what exactly was affecting the *Enterprise* crew. And while he'd spent the vast majority of his time in the prison infirmary doing just that, he'd also managed to find time to speak with some of the other prisoners—the Denari—and glean a few pieces of information that Archer had found more than helpful.

Rava held some two hundred prisoners, *Enterprise* crew included. Most of them had been there for years—more than a decade, in some cases. They were political prisoners moved off-planet to avoid any rescue attempts. Control of the prison and the system were held by the same person, who apparently had ordered the attack on their ship: General Sadir, a dictator who ran Denari with an iron fist. He was in the final stages of a war designed to crush his remaining opposition, a group of former government officials and miners collectively known as the Guild.

The prison was run by a minimal staff—forty guards, all equipped with the Taser-like rods Tomon so eagerly used on him, as well as hand weapons eerily identical to the old Starfleet laser pistols; half a dozen administrators; three medical workers; and a Colonel Gastornis, a military man whom Archer had never met, in charge.

No one had ever escaped from the prison satellite.

But almost since the day they'd arrived, two and a half weeks ago, Archer had thought of nothing else. Escaping, and getting back his ship. After talking with the crew in B block, he'd put together the guards' schedules. After a week, he thought he'd spotted a weakness in the system.

Another few days, and he'd come up with a plan. Not a perfect plan—he'd had too few opportunities to speak, unobserved, with his crew, for that—but a plan that could, should work, if . . .

"All right, everyone. March!" Tomon and the other guards stepped aside, and the huge door leading from A block to the central prison complex beyond opened.

It was the same door they'd marched through that first day, when they'd been led out of the transport to their cells. Archer had still been in shock then, or something close to it. Everything that had happened from the moment the explosion had crippled *Enterprise* right up until then had seemed more like a dream, a nightmare, than reality. One minute they were cruising toward the anomaly, everything going according to plan, everything on schedule, T'Pol and Lieutenant Duel ready to board the cell-ship for a week-long scientific study—and the next minute, there was a hole in the bottom of the saucer section and they were being boarded by two dozen ships whose existence, according to T'Pol, was "an impossibility."

There had been so many of the Denari troops—hundreds, he'd guessed—that their presence, the sight of them swarming every deck aboard his ship, had seemed like a bad dream as well. His and his crew's helplessness—the ship was crippled, the armory inaccessible—had only added to that feeling of unreality.

They'd been escorted off *Enterprise* and onto a single crowded transport vessel. A day's journey that had ended here, where they'd been marched off to identical, featureless cells.

Only then had the realization of what had happened sunk in. *Enterprise* was in enemy hands.

Archer and his crew were prisoners of war.

* * *

They stepped from the cell block proper into the corridor beyond.

It was slightly wider and significantly taller than those on *Enterprise*. The additional height was for a pair of walkways that ran at shoulder height, and to either side of the main corridor.

The guards proceeded down those, toward the door at the far end of the corridor. Five on either side, weapons drawn, eyes glued to the prisoners on the path below.

Archer heard the door behind them slam shut.

He coughed.

Up ahead, Ensign Dwight suddenly stopped and bent over double.

The prisoners behind him came to an immediate halt. Those ahead continued to march.

"Halt! Everyone!"

That was Tomon, up above them, to their left and almost directly parallel with Archer.

"You!" He pointed to Dwight. "Stay in formation! Keep moving!"

The ensign gasped and let out a moan. He waved a hand at Tomon.

"Oh God. Please. Give me a minute."

He sounded like he was in agony.

"Keep moving!" Tomon said again. "Now!"

"Here—let me through, please. Let me through."

That was Phlox, coming up behind the captain. Archer turned and saw the crew making way for him.

"Stop!" A guard on their right yelled and raised his laser pistol.

Phlox froze, steps behind Archer.

The captain tensed.

8

Dwight moaned again and collapsed on the ground. All eyes went to him.

Phlox took another step forward and passed the captain.

As he did so, he slipped Archer a hypospray he'd stolen from the medical ward.

"Stop!" the guard on the right yelled. "No more warnings."

Phlox glared. "Let me see what's the matter with him."

The guards exchanged reluctant glances.

"All right," one of the guards on the right said. "Quickly. The rest of you, keep moving."

The prisoners around Dwight began to back away from him—a movement that rippled through the entire line.

The movement, subtle and precise, put prisoners near every one of the guards, save for the two farthest away.

Archer jumped into the fray.

"Let me through," Archer said, and began walking forward.

"You stay where you are," Tomon hissed. "Captain."

Archer froze in his tracks.

Right next to Tomon.

He craned his neck and looked up at the guard.

Tomon had his shock rod out. The captain saw the weapon was charged and ready.

But so was he.

"You have to use that word," Archer said, "with a little more respect."

Tomon's eyes blazed fire.

He jumped down to the main corridor and advanced on Archer.

Predictable, the captain thought. *So predictable.*

"You're going to need a week in the infirmary," the guard said. "Captain."

He jabbed the shock rod at Archer.

The captain might have been weak, a little tired, not entirely up to snuff, but the day hadn't come when he couldn't outfight a twerp like Tomon in his sleep.

Archer dodged right.

The weapon—and the guard who held it—slid harmlessly past him.

As Tomon tried to recover, Archer's right arm shot out, and he jabbed the hypospray into the guard's arm.

"Hey!" Tomon stopped moving and rubbed his arm. "What—"

His eyes rolled back in his head, and he passed out.

That was A block's cue.

The prisoners who had maneuvered next to the guards above them attacked. Archer heard rather than saw them move.

He was too busy pulling Tomon's laser pistol from his belt.

The guards at the end of the corridor were already moving too. One of them toward the fray—the other, obviously more savvy one, toward what could only be an alarm button on the wall.

Archer targeted him first.

A single shot from the laser pistol—it was uncanny how identical these were to the ones Starfleet had stopped using a dozen years ago, right down to the colors and feel of the hand grip—and that man went down. A second shot, and the other guard followed.

And when the captain turned around, it was over.

The ten A-block guards had all fallen—as had some of his own crew, though a quick check by Phlox revealed none of them were seriously injured—and Archer's people were gathering the guards' weapons. Some of them were changing into their clothes for the next phase of the plan.

Archer nodded as he watched, a grim smile on his face. It wasn't an escape yet.

But they were well on their way.

The captain found Dwight and clapped him on the shoulder.

"Nice work, Ensign. You should have been an actor."

The young man smiled. "It wasn't entirely an act, sir, but I appreciate the compliment."

Archer nodded. No, it wasn't entirely an act. The ensign's illness, and the sickness the rest of the crew were suffering from, were all too real. Not the least of the reasons they needed to get back to *Enterprise* was to get Phlox to sickbay and his equipment, so the doctor could get them all well again.

But first things first.

Archer turned to the door at the end of the corridor.

The main complex, where they'd find the rest of the crew—B block—waiting to take their exercise.

No, the captain corrected himself silently.

Not the rest of the crew.

Not Trip, nor Hoshi—who'd never even made it with the rest of them to Rava. Archer didn't know where they were; Reed had been of the opinion that they'd taken the cell-ship and escaped. The captain thought that likely at first, but as the days passed, his certainty waned. He knew Trip. *Enterprise*'s chief engineer would have come looking for them—would have found them by now. If he could.

So something had happened along the way. Either that, or . . .

Archer wouldn't think about the "or" just now.

Other members of his crew were missing as well. T'Pol. Reed. Travis. Hess and Ryan from engineering. They'd all come to the prison, been on A block until the third day after their arrival. Then all had been marched away, and not heard from—or of—since. Archer had only a rough idea of the prison complex's size, but it was certainly big enough for them to still be here, somewhere. He intended to find them, if they were here.

"Captain." O'Neill, dressed in one of the Denari guard uniforms, approached. "We're ready."

Archer nodded. They had to move quickly.

"All right, everyone."

He looked around at his crew.

"You know the plan. Let's move."

They took up positions—the "guards" on the walkways above, the prisoners on the corridor below—and began to march.

TWO

TRIP COULDN'T GET used to the beard.

It looked strange on him, like a bad prop from a high-school play. The kind teenagers wore when they had to play grown-ups. Obviously fake—even more so considering the tiny flecks of gray that had come in with the dark blond. Gray hair? Him? He was thirty-two. It wasn't possible. He rubbed it with one hand and shook his head.

Snap out of it, Tucker, he told himself. *After these last few weeks, you should know anything is possible.*

Trip—Commander Charles Tucker III, late of the *Starship Enterprise*, currently residing aboard the Guild ship *Eclipse*—stepped back from the mirror and frowned.

Shave it, he thought. *And then . . .*

No. He'd grown it for a reason. Looking at himself in the mirror, he saw that reason still held. He saw it in the way the green and orange Guild uniform hung off his shoulders, in the tendons that stood out in his neck. If he didn't have the beard, he'd see it

13

even more in the thinness of his face. He was losing weight. A lot of it—more than he could afford.

Losing weight? Ha. Why gild the lily?

He was dying.

Someone knocked at his door.

"Come."

The door swung open, revealing a man—a human, though dressed in the Guild uniform as well, medium height, square build, in his early seventies, with a halo of frizzy white hair—standing in the entrance.

"I hope I'm not disturbing you," he said.

"Not at all. Come on in."

The man obliged, smiling and making eye contact as he did so.

Trip met his gaze for a second, and then had to turn away.

He still didn't know how to deal with his visitor. Who went by the name of Victor Brodesser, who was the exact image of the Victor Brodesser Trip had known a decade ago, the Victor Brodessor who had been a father figure to Trip while the young Lieutenant Tucker had served on the *Daedalus* project. The exact image physically, but nonetheless . . .

A different person altogether.

At first Trip had chalked up those differences to the time that had passed since he'd last seen Brodesser. The day of *Daedalus*'s initial test flight more than ten years earlier, when its experimental ion drive had exploded, and the ship was presumed lost with all hands on board, including the professor.

Now he knew better.

Now he knew that he and this Brodesser were strangers. That they had no previous relationship of any kind, hadn't even met until Trip had helped the Guild rescue the man from an isolated prison outpost two weeks ago.

It made for a certain awkwardness between them. And a lot of small talk.

"I was in the launch bay," the man said.

"Heading there myself in a few minutes."

"I've been working on the cloak, of course," the man said. "Still trying to stabilize the initial field states."

Trip nodded. The man was talking about the cloaking device on the Suliban cell-ship—the device that had enabled Trip and *Enterprise*'s communications officer, Ensign Hoshi Sato, to successfully flee the Denari forces that had captured *Enterprise*. Brodesser—this Brodesser—had managed to duplicate that device more than a week ago. Or so it seemed at the time.

Over the last few days, however, problems had arisen. Problems with the particles emitted by the cloaking device, normally harmless, light-refracting particles that were somehow being transformed— albeit on a very limited, very random scale—into superenergized, highly radioactive, very, very lethal ones. Marshal Kairn—*Eclipse*'s commander, as well as the Guild's military leader—had forbidden the device's use until Brodesser ironed out the problem.

"No luck?"

"In actually replicating the field states? No, I'm afraid not. Very discouraging."

"I'm sorry to hear that." Which he was, but he didn't know why the man had come here to tell him about it. Was he expecting Trip to offer suggestions?

Insight? That just wasn't going to happen. This man might not be the Victor Brodesser Trip had known, but he was still a genius. Head-and-shoulders above where Trip was, especially when it came to things like advanced field theory. Just like Trip's Brodesser in that respect. In others, though . . .

He was indeed very, very different.

It had been on another mission for the Guild—an attempt to kidnap Denari's leader, the dictator General Sadir—that Trip had learned the reason for those differences in the man's behavior, his personality, his very memories of the *Daedalus* project and its tragic outcome. Trip now understood why he was so like—and yet unlike—the man he had idolized.

On that mission Trip had discovered a book—*The Song of El Cid*—which he and *Daedalus*'s engineers had given Brodesser. But as he had examined that book closely, he'd seen that in fact it wasn't the same copy they'd presented to the professor. There were subtle differences—Trip's own inscription among them. How was such a thing possible? The answer had come to him in a flash—parallel universes.

Quantum theory held that the space-time continuum was filled with all possible realities. The explosion that had crippled *Enterprise,* that had led to its capture, had also catapulted the starship into an alternate universe. One where Victor Brodesser and *Daedalus* had survived, where that vessel, crippled by the explosion of its ion drive, had arrived in the Denari system only to be seized by then-Colonel Sadir, who then used Starfleet technology to overthrow his planet's government.

A reality, more importantly, that Trip and his shipmates were physically unable to tolerate. One that was responsible for the wasting away of his body and would soon be responsible for his death and the death of everyone else who had crossed the boundary between universes with him.

Trip needed to find *Enterprise* and escape this reality before that happened. He'd been spending every one of his days—and many of his nights—over the last week in *Eclipse*'s launch bay, in the war room that had been set up there, trying to find a way back. He needed to get back to that search right now.

He didn't have time to waste with Brodesser.

"Something I can do for you, Professor?" he asked.

The edge in his voice must have come through. The man glared at him momentarily, and for a second Trip thought he was going to respond in kind. That was what the real Brodesser—*his* Brodesser—would have done: given Trip his attitude right back, and spoken exactly what was on his mind.

Not this man, though. This man was more political. Calculating. More concerned with getting what he wanted than having his say.

His glare softened, and he spoke.

"Yes. I hope so. I hope so indeed." Brodesser clasped his hands behind his back and began to pace.

"I know you have plans for the cell-ship, Trip, once you find *Enterprise.*"

"That's right." The second he found news of his ship, in fact, he and Hoshi were going to take that little vessel and find a way to rescue her.

"But in the interim . . ." Brodesser looked up and met his eyes. "I was wondering if I could have your permission to disassemble the cloaking device entirely."

"No." Trip didn't even need to think about it. "Absolutely not."

"Trip, it's the only way for me to find out what I'm doing wrong. Compare my device to the original—at the component level."

Trip shook his head. He understood the professor's problem—knew on one level that the man was absolutely right. Every device aboard the cell-ship, cloak included, was black-box technology to them. They knew what it did, could even access and control its functions through the cell-ship software, but as far as understanding the principles behind its operation . . .

They were all entirely in the dark. It made sense to try and penetrate the mystery behind the cloak's function to figure out what they were doing wrong.

But Trip was afraid that if he let Brodesser pull the cloak apart, the man might not be able to put it back together again.

"I'm sorry," he said, meaning it.

"Trip, that cloaking device, if we can get it working, could make the difference between the Guild's survival and defeat."

"And it might also be the only way Hoshi and I can get to *Enterprise* and rescue her."

"Perhaps," Brodesser said, a slightly condescending smile on his face that all at once made Trip angry, "but think about it this way. A working cloaking device could enable the Guild to actually win the war. You'd have no need to rescue *Enterprise*. It would be yours—ours—by right of victory."

"After how long? Do you know how many ships

Sadir's army has? Even with cloaks on every functioning Guild ship"—which there weren't that many of anyway—"it could take months to win a war. Me and Hoshi and the *Enterprise* crew, we don't have months."

"All right." The man nodded, tight-lipped. "Then help me. You must know something more about how the ship functions. If I understood the relationship between the cloak and the ship's power source better, how the device's initial field states are generated . . ."

Brodesser looked to Trip expectantly.

Trip just sighed.

What could he say to that? That the function of almost every component on that vessel was a mystery to him, that it was technology hundreds of years in advance of Starfleet science, that it had come to them courtesy of time-traveling aliens who hadn't bothered to provide an instruction manual?

No. He couldn't say that. He couldn't even let on that such a thing as time travel was possible. And he didn't want Brodesser to start pulling the ship apart trying to understand its power source, because if the man found out the vessel ran off an ion drive . . .

Trip's permission or not, he'd crack that ship open in a flash.

"I can't help you."

"I see." Brodesser's expression was still unreadable, but Trip could hear the tension in his voice. "Perhaps I should speak to Marshal Kairn about this."

"You think he'll give you the go-ahead to rip the cell-ship apart?"

"He might."

Trip met Brodesser's eyes, and frowned.

There was a chance, he realized, that the professor was correct. If Brodesser presented the idea to Kairn the right way, the marshal might indeed decide that the prospect of a working cloaking device for his forces overrode all other considerations—even given all that Trip had done for him and the Guild over the last few weeks.

The Guild was in the middle of a war, after all. Trip couldn't say for sure he wouldn't order exactly the same thing, were their positions reversed.

He sighed. "All right, Professor. Let me think about it. Okay?"

"Of course." Brodesser nodded, but didn't look as happy about his little victory as Trip would have thought. "We're on the same side in this, Trip. I wish we could find a way to work together again."

"Again? We never worked together before." The words came out before Trip could call them back. Came out harsher than he'd intended them to as well.

For an instant, anger—and perhaps, a touch of indignation—crossed Brodesser's face. Then it was gone.

"I'm sorry," Trip said. "I didn't mean that the way it sounded. It's just—"

"It's all right." Brodesser's expression was again opaque, unreadable. "I know you're under a lot of pressure."

He walked to the door and paused.

"I'll look forward to talking to you again—shortly."

And with that, he was gone.

Trip frowned after him.

I could have handled that better, he thought.

Brodesser was right about the pressure he was feeling. It wasn't just that though. These last few nights, he hadn't slept well at all. Cramps in his stomach, and last night in his legs as well. He'd talk to Neesa about it later, after he checked this morning's intercepts.

He'd taken two steps toward the door when the com buzzed.

"Trant to Commander Tucker."

Trip smiled. Speak of the devil . . .

He punched open a channel.

"Doctor. It's good to hear your voice."

Trant was Doctor Trant Neesa, *Eclipse*'s physician. In public, he called her "doctor," and she called him "commander." In private, they'd been lovers for two weeks now.

A fact they were hiding for a number of reasons, not least of which was that Trant was married. Normally that would have stopped Trip from getting involved in the first place. Except in this case, her husband—a former government official named Ferik Reeve—was no longer aware that the two of them were man and wife. Was no longer aware of much of anything, in fact. Ferik had been tortured by General Sadir, his mind and memories sifted through until he was a shadow of his former self. Neesa couldn't be expected to live her life celibate because of what had happened. As for Trip . . .

His time with Neesa was just about the only bright spot in his world right now. He was too busy enjoying it to feel remorse.

"I'm glad I found you as well, Commander," Trant said. "Can you come to the medical ward?"

Trip frowned. She sounded anything but glad.

"Why? What's the matter?"

"Nothing. I just want to run a few tests."

"More tests?" Trip sighed. "Didn't we just go through that?"

"We did. Just a few discrepancies I'd like to clear up."

"I'll come by later. I need to go through the day's intercepts first."

"Later when?"

"This afternoon."

"Early this afternoon."

"All right. Early this afternoon." He paused a second. "Are you sure nothing's the matter?"

She hesitated before answering. "I'm not sure. That's why I want you to come back in, do those tests. You're eating the *pisarko*, aren't you?"

His eyes went to the refrigerator in the corner of the room. It was filled with an odd-tasting, odd-smelling grain product called *pisarko* that, more than anything else, resembled burnt scrambled eggs.

Trip shuddered at the thought of it.

"I had some for dinner last night." He'd had some, in fact, for every meal this past week. And with the last of the ration packs from *Enterprise* gone, it was all Trip would be eating until he got back to his ship. Because he was violently allergic to almost every other food aboard the Denari ship. Not to the foods themselves, actually, but to certain compounds within them. A specific class of proteins that his body couldn't absorb. Proteins that were an essential part of the basic building blocks of life in this universe.

Pisarko gave him calories to live off, fuel to burn,

but none of those nutrients. Without them, his body was breaking down. Hence the weight loss, the cramping in his legs, and other, less visible—for the moment, at least—indicators of malnutrition.

Which Trant would no doubt enumerate for him later.

"What about breakfast?" she asked.

"No. Not yet."

"Trip . . ."

"All right. I'll have some."

"Good. I'll see you in a few hours. Trant out."

He closed the channel and turned to the refrigerator.

For a second, he thought about the stasis units aboard *Enterprise*. The steaks Chef had stored in them—he'd given Trip a tour once. Row upon row of meat. Grade A. Top choice. And then Chef had shown him the cheeses—a wheel of cheddar the size of one of the antimatter pods. His mouth watered. Food. Honest-to-God food.

Another reason to find his ship as soon as humanly possible.

It was all he could do to force down two bites of the *pisarko* before setting down his spoon and heading for the launch bay, where he could continue his search.

Three

"Good," Archer said, his laser pistol still pressed firmly to the side of Gastornis's head. "That was well done."

"Thank you." The colonel—Rava One's commander—swallowed visibly. "So you can lower your weapon now . . . yes?"

Archer locked eyes with the man.

He didn't want to lower the weapon. For what Gastornis had done to T'Pol . . .

He wanted to squeeze the trigger and exact a pound of flesh. But they might need the colonel again, to do something similar to what he'd just done—broadcast a very convincing SOS to the nearest military vessel. Tell them that all was not well inside prison satellite Rava One—systems failing, repairs impossible, send help ASAP. A task the man had performed quickly and convincingly. Gastornis was an excellent liar.

"It wasn't my idea, you know," the colonel said. Archer could see the fear in his eyes. "To do those things to your crewmate. The Vulcan. The order came from the Kresh—from General Elson himself. Find out what she knows."

"I see." Archer's gaze bored into the man. "And that makes it right?"

"Yes. No. I don't know—I was just trying to explain why . . ." Gastornis searched for the word.

He was babbling. Archer saw a useless, babbling coward.

Reluctantly, the captain holstered his pistol.

"Tie him to the chair. Tightly," he told Duel and Carstairs.

The two men, both ensigns aboard the *Enterprise*, did as he'd ordered, handling Gastornis none too gently in the process. Archer smiled thinly at the man's discomfort.

They were all in Rava One's com center, a small room at the top of the prison's administrative tower. They'd brought Gastornis here after breaking into his office and removing the man from where he'd been cowering behind his desk, the last act in the day-long rebellion that had now left Archer in command of the prison. The first act in his struggle to find and regain control of his ship.

"If he tries anything," Archer said to Ensign Duel, "hurt him. If he suddenly doesn't feel well. If he apologizes for what he did. If he complains about—"

"I won't say a word," Gastornis said hurriedly. "I promise."

Archer ignored him and looked to Duel. The ensign, normally the picture of the dispassionate scientist, looked every bit as angry as Archer felt.

The young man nodded. "I understand, sir. I may hurt him anyway, if that's all right."

"You have my permission," the captain said. He knew Duel was just talking. Gastornis didn't. The colonel went an even paler shade.

Archer turned to Carstairs.

"You have an ETA on that vessel yet?"

The ensign had resumed his seat in front of the com center's sole console. The sensor display was on his immediate left.

The young com officer, normally Hoshi's second when they were aboard *Enterprise,* shook his head. "No, sir. Nothing yet."

"Keep me posted," Archer said. The vessel in question—the military ship that had responded to Gastornis's fake SOS—had said they would proceed at top speed to the prison. Top speed in the asteroid belt, however—where Archer had learned Rava was located—was dependent on a number of factors. His ETA was approximately two hours. Gastornis had also assured them the ship had warp drive. Fast enough, the captain had to assume, to get them to wherever *Enterprise* had been taken, once they had control of her. Archer doubted taking command of a military ship would be as easy a task as commandeering this prison, but he also had little doubt of the end result.

They would capture the Denari ship. They would find *Enterprise,* and then . . .

He would discuss the consequences of an unprovoked attack with Denari's military commanders.

The captain left Duel and Carstairs in the com center and made his way through Rava's tunnels to the infirmary.

The beds were filled with *Enterprise* crew members. A great many of the crew—Archer included himself in the number—had been taken sick since arriving at Rava One. A reaction to something in the food the Denari were giving them, Phlox had told the captain. Certain people were more sensitive to that something than others. Dwight, for example, who'd been the point man on their escape earlier in the day, had been violently ill on more than one occasion.

Right now the young ensign was sprawled on one of the infirmary beds—asleep or unconscious, Archer couldn't tell which—looking pale, thin, and worn.

The captain stood over him a moment, feeling guilty—he'd known Dwight was on the edge of collapse when he'd assigned him a prominent part in the escape, but he felt the needs of the crew—the need for escape—had to outweigh any other considerations. He hoped the young man wasn't now paying too harsh a price for his part in the day's earlier events.

Archer went in search of Phlox to find out.

He found the Denobulan—the other nonhuman aboard *Enterprise*—in the intensive care section of the prison's infirmary—a separate room with two beds. T'Pol was sitting up in one of them. Phlox stood over her, reading something off a medical sensor.

"Captain," T'Pol said, "I gather from your appearance here that the colonel did as you asked."

"That's right. A military transport answered the SOS. They're on their way." He studied his science officer a moment, doing his best not to let his eyes dwell on the burns along her right arm. "How are you feeling?"

"I am fine," she said immediately, in a tone of

voice that implied there was no reason for her to be anything but. "Anxious to return to duty."

Archer looked to Phlox and raised a questioning eyebrow. The doctor shrugged.

"Vulcans," Phlox said, "have a remarkable ability to compartmentalize pain. Had you or I been subjected to this sort of treatment"—he nodded to the burns on her arm—"we would undoubtedly need to remain hospitalized for several days, hooked up to an IV of very strong pain-killing medication. However . . ." He shrugged. "Provided Sub-Commander T'Pol feels capable, I can see no reason for her to remain in the infirmary."

"Thank you, Doctor," T'Pol said.

"With the understanding, however," Phlox continued, "that she will check in with me periodically— every six hours, let's say—to make sure the burns are healing properly and that no infection has set in."

T'Pol frowned. "I am capable of monitoring my own condition, Doctor. And you are quite busy here."

Phlox shook his head. "Every six hours," he said firmly.

"T'Pol," Archer said, "let's do as the doctor suggests. All right?"

"Yes," she said. "As you wish, sir."

He could see she wasn't happy. But he knew she would do what he asked.

"Good. Then you're cleared to return to duty."

"Thank you." She swung her legs out of the bed, stood, and—

Took a very, very deep breath.

Archer reached out a hand to steady her. She held up one of her own to forestall him.

"I am fine, sir." She exhaled slowly. "I doubt I will be capable of taking part in any tasks requiring extensive physical activity for some time. But my desire to return to duty is mainly prompted by—"

"There's no need to rush this," the captain interrupted.

"On the contrary." T'Pol shook her head. "As I was saying, my desire to return to duty is prompted by a need to finish a series of observations I began while in Colonel Gastornis's custody."

"Observations?" Archer frowned. All he'd known about the time T'Pol spent after she'd been taken from them was that Gastornis had held her in isolation, had tortured her in a vain attempt to force her to betray secrets relating to Vulcan technology. This was the first he was hearing about any observations.

"Yes, sir. Observations. I feigned cooperation with the colonel over the last few days, in order to be allowed access to the prison's auxiliary sensor systems. During that time, however, I found . . ."

She paused, and took another deep breath. "I found some anomalies which I am at a loss to explain at the present time. That is why it is imperative I continue these observations."

"Astronomical observations." Archer shook his head. He was tempted to ask Phlox if the stress T'Pol had clearly been subjected to could have affected her judgment.

"Captain," she said, her voice taking on a sudden edge, "I cannot stress enough how critical these observations may turn out to be. It will take me approximately eight hours to complete them. At that point—"

"All right," the captain conceded. "Go. But T'Pol—every six hours. Sooner, if you feel weak."

She looked from the captain to Phlox. "Every six hours. Yes, sir. Ensign Duel—"

"He's with Carstairs in the com center."

"Can I request his assistance in my work?"

"By all means. Have Lee"—Archer was talking about Chief John Lee, security's second-in-command—"pick someone to take his place."

T'Pol nodded. "I will."

Archer and Phlox watched her leave the room.

"You think she'll be all right?" the captain asked.

"As I said, you or I, under the same circumstances—we would be in agony. T'Pol's system is certainly stressed at this moment, but it appears to be nothing she can't handle."

"All right." The captain gestured to the main ward. "I saw Dwight out there. How's he doing?"

"As well as can be expected. Weak, but in no immediate danger."

"I don't suppose you've had any time to—"

"Find out more about what's causing all this?" Phlox shook his head. "Unfortunately, the equipment here"—the doctor spread his arms to take in all of the infirmary—"it's simply inadequate to perform the kind of analysis necessary. All I can do is mitigate the allergic symptoms—though one of the medicines itself seems to have caused a reaction. In Lieutenant Bellars."

"The medicine caused a reaction?"

"Yes. I've never heard of such a thing happening. The entire situation is most puzzling."

O'Neill—Lieutenant Donna O'Neill, the ship's

third-shift commander—chose that moment to poke her head inside the isolation ward.

"Carstairs just checked in, Captain. ETA on that ship is forty-eight minutes."

"All right," Archer said. "I'll be back to you soon, Doctor. D.O., let's get moving."

Three-quarters of an hour later, they were standing in the cargo hold. Four of them, all dressed in the black uniforms they'd taken from the prison guards, all armed to the teeth—Archer and O'Neill, Crewmen Scott and O'Bannon. All had their communicators as well, courtesy of the recently unlocked prison armory.

The captain's beeped just as they assumed position in front of the main airlock. Taking their place as the prison's welcoming committee.

"Archer."

"Carstairs here, sir. Got a visual on that ship now—it's exactly like the ones that attacked *Enterprise*."

"How many on board?"

"Fourteen, I think, but I can't be a hundred percent certain. These sensors aren't precise enough. Gastornis tried to weasel a number out of their commander—a Lieutenant Covay—but backed off fast when the lieutenant started asking questions."

Dammit. Archer rubbed his brow. He'd warned the colonel to avoid saying anything at all that might raise suspicions aboard the incoming vessel. And now . . .

"He didn't give it away, did he? Gastornis?"

"No, sir. I don't think so."

"All right." The captain was silent a moment. He hated being in this position, having to depend on someone like Gastornis for anything at all, much less something as important as this. Not that he had much choice in the matter.

It wasn't only Gastornis he was worried about. Being honest with himself, Archer had to admit he disliked having to depend on junior officers. In situations like this, he preferred senior staff—Trip and T'Pol, Travis and Hoshi. And above all, Malcolm—Lieutenant Reed, his armory officer/security chief—who lived for and excelled in these moments.

The lieutenant, though, was among the missing.

Reed had been spirited away at the same time as T'Pol. But unlike the Vulcan, whom they'd found in solitary confinement, Malcolm hadn't turned up anywhere on Rava. And no one—not Colonel Gastornis, not the com officer, not even the guards who had escorted Reed to the military vessel that had borne him away—knew where the security chief had been taken. Archer had teams searching through the base's records for clues to Malcolm's whereabouts—so far, though, they'd had no success in finding any. No clues as to where Travis or Hess and Ryan from engineering had been taken either.

First Trip and Hoshi, who had vanished during the attack on *Enterprise* two weeks ago. And now Reed and Travis. Four of his senior staff missing.

Archer was going to have to make do with what—and who—he had.

"They're docking now, sir," Carstairs said over the communicator. "No indication of weapons activity."

"All right. You know what to do. On my signal—"

"Yes, sir."

Archer put the communicator in his pocket, leaving the channel open so Carstairs could hear his cue.

"Stay sharp, everyone," the captain said. "Here we go."

The airlock door was ten meters away. A light above it flashed, and then the door slid open.

Two Denari soldiers—dressed exactly like Archer and his team, in black uniforms with gold piping—stepped through, weapons drawn.

Archer didn't think that was standard procedure. Something Gastornis had said put the ship on alert.

The soldiers pointed their weapons directly at the four men before them.

"Stay where you are. Hands over your heads."

Archer had the only UT among them. He raised his arms. The others followed suit.

"What's the problem?" he asked.

The soldiers didn't respond. Didn't move a muscle.

A moment later, two more Denari stepped through the airlock. One of them had rank insignia.

Archer straightened. "Sir."

The officer stepped forward. "Where is Colonel Gastornis?"

"Trapped in the com center, sir."

"Trapped?" The man—Lieutenant Covay, the captain assumed—frowned. "Who are you?"

"Chief Archer. Block D. These are my guards." The captain gestured toward the three standing alongside him.

Covay nodded. "Well, Chief Archer, what—exactly—is the emergency?"

"Computer system is failing, sir. Repeated malfunctions."

Archer enunciated the last words as clearly as he could. Carstairs had a UT too, but the captain wasn't taking any chances.

"Computer malfunctions?" Covay shook his head. "That hardly seems worthy of an SOS. Or our presence. I'll have a repair ship—"

The airlock door slid suddenly shut with a loud clang.

Covay spun around. "What—"

"It's our computer again." Archer tried to look annoyed. "Same thing happened to the colonel. We've been on high alert for the last twelve hours. If the cell block doors malfunction . . ."

"I see." Covay nodded. "Well. As long as we're here, I suppose we may as well try and help. Mister Lake?"

One of the soldiers knelt down next to the airlock and examined it. A few seconds later, he looked up.

"Definitely a software glitch, sir," he said to the lieutenant. "It could spill over, systemwide, depending on exactly what the problem is."

"What do you recommend doing?"

"Well . . . system reset would be the obvious answer."

"First thing we tried, too," Archer lied.

Covay frowned.

Something beeped. His communicator. The lieutenant answered it.

"Kedlee here, sir. Is everything all right?"

"Everything is not all right, Kedlee," Covay said. "The computer system here is failing. It's locked us out of the ship."

"What should we do, Lieutenant?"

"Stand by." Covay looked down at the soldier by the airlock. "Try the manual release."

The soldier nodded. A few seconds passed.

"Something wrong with it," the man said, shaking his head.

Archer knew that for a fact. They'd disabled it half an hour ago.

The captain caught O'Neill's eye. *Be ready.*

Next to him, Scott tensed. He'd caught the signal as well. The change in his body language was obvious. Luckily, Covay's soldiers didn't notice.

"Mister Lake, we can take you to the computer center," Archer offered. "You might be able to figure out what's happening."

Lake looked to his commander. "Sir?"

Covay hesitated only a second. "Go."

Archer nodded to O'Bannon. He stepped forward. "I'll show you the way." Lake followed him across the cargo hold and out through a nearby door.

One down, Archer thought. Three to go.

Covay took out his communicator again. "Kedlee."

"Here, sir."

"Lake has gone to Rava's computer center. We're going to talk to Gastornis. Contact you again shortly. Out." He closed his communicator and turned to Archer. "Take me to the colonel."

The captain nodded. "Right this way."

Covay took two steps—and stopped.

Archer followed his eyes. He was looking at Crewman Scott, who still looked ill at ease. Nervous.

Covay's hand moved to his belt again.

"I have another idea," he said calmly. "Kedlee may be able to—"

35

He knows, Archer realized. *Somehow, he knows.*

The captain went for his weapon.

Covay got to his first, and fired.

The blast caught Archer square in the chest, knocking him backwards. He was vaguely aware of the ground slamming into him, the air leaving his chest in a whoosh.

He lay on his back a moment, stunned. He heard voices—shouts. The sound of another laser blast.

I drew first, the captain thought. *I had him dead to rights. What happened?*

His vision swam. O'Neill came into view above him.

"Sir? You all right? Sir?"

Archer sat up.

O'Bannon had the drop on the other two Denari. Covay lay on the ground, motionless.

"Let me help you," O'Neill said. Archer waved her off.

"I'm fine," he said, feeling anything but. Getting punched by a laser pistol felt exactly like getting punched in a fight—left you feeling weak, woozy, and vaguely nauseous.

The captain gathered himself and got to his feet.

"What happened?" he asked, nodding at Lieutenant Covay, who lay on the ground two meters away, hand still holding his weapon.

"When he got you, I got him," O'Neill said. "He's just stunned."

The captain nodded. He turned to the other two Denari.

"Sorry about this," he said. "Don't worry, though. Your lieutenant's fine. So is Crewman Lake. We don't intend you any harm."

"So you say," one of them spit out. "Why should we believe you?"

"Believe what you want," Archer said. "All we want is our ship back. To get it, unfortunately"—he managed a smile at the two men—"we need yours."

He stepped forward and relieved the two soldiers of their weapons and communicators. Waving them away from the airlock, he opened a channel.

"Mister Carstairs, restore power to the airlock override."

"Aye, sir."

A door at the far end of the bay opened. Scott stepped through, trailed by half a dozen other crewmen, still dressed in their prison fatigues.

They all formed up next to the airlock.

"Ready?" the captain asked, his finger on the override. Nods all around.

"Then let's move," he said. "On three. One. Two—"

He punched the door open as he spoke, and the assault team flew past him.

Normally, the captain led his crew into battle. This time . . .

He decided discretion was the better part of valor. Considering the way his head was still spinning.

Archer brought up the rear.

The airlock opened into the crew compartment of the small ship. By the time Archer stepped inside, it was full of Denari soldiers, lying stunned on the deck.

He passed from that compartment into a forward cabin, the ship's control center. There were four seats there, arranged in a horseshoe shape in front of a viewscreen. A woman sat in one of them, glaring up at O'Bannon, who held his weapon on her.

"Crewman?" Archer asked.

"Sorry, sir. She got off an alert signal." O'Bannon looked appropriately chagrined. And no wonder.

They'd lost the element of surprise. Sadir's ships would be on the lookout for them now. Some were no doubt racing in this direction, even as they stood there.

Archer couldn't help thinking that Malcolm would never have made a mistake like that.

"What's done is done. Forget it," he told O'Bannon. "The most important thing is that we have the ship."

O'Bannon nodded, though Archer could see his words hadn't had much of an effect on the young man's mood.

Good. He won't make that mistake next time. Assuming there was a next time.

As Covay's crew began recovering, Archer ordered them moved to an unused cell block. The captain followed the last of the Denari soldiers out of their ship into the cargo bay, leaving Scott and Ensign Kramer from engineering on board to begin prepping the ship for their use.

When he emerged from the airlock, he was surprised to find T'Pol waiting for him.

He saw instantly that something was wrong. In the two years they'd served together, he had never—not once—seen a look on her face like the one she wore now. Vulcans were masters at keeping their emotions in check, in showing nothing to the world save an impassive, neutral countenance.

Right now, T'Pol looked as if she'd just discovered the world was flat.

"What is it?" the captain asked. "What's the matter?"

She gathered herself. "I've completed my observations, sir."

"Already?" Archer frowned. "I thought you needed eight hours."

"No, sir. What I've found . . ." She shook her head. "We need to talk, Captain. Immediately."

Four

NOTHING.

Nothing from the PDC, the DEF, the Kresh, New Irla, Charest, Colonna, Halo-1, Halo-2, or Halo-3. Nothing from Dirsch, Elson, Egil, Makandros, or any other members of the Council.

Nothing from anywhere in the Denari system or beyond about *Enterprise* or its crew. It was as if they'd vanished completely.

Trip leaned back from the console and rubbed his eyes. At a guess, he'd just read through over a thousand intercepts—messages the Guild had downloaded and deciphered from traffic across the Denari system, messages between and among the various ships and outposts of Sadir's government—without finding a thing. It was tedious, mind-numbing, eye-straining work, normally the kind of task he'd set a computer to do and then forget about. But there was no way to program in the search parameters he needed: Would the Denari refer to his ship as *Enterprise* in their messages? Would they call it the "alien vessel"? The "humans' ship"? Had they given it a

40

code name in the weeks before the Guild had broken their coding algorithms? There were dozens of possibilities. Dozens of potential ways they could refer to *Enterprise*'s crew as well. That meant that after the computer eliminated intercepts that clearly had nothing to do with ship or personnel movements—and percentagewise, there weren't all that many of those, since most of the com traffic they had access to was regarding the newly intensified conflict with the Guild—Trip had to eyeball each message personally. Not easy work in the best of circumstances, which these most definitely were not.

Behind him in the launch bay—in the half that had been converted into a command center for the Guild's ongoing war effort—he could hear Kairn and one of his officers talking.

". . . and no sign of further troop movements. It may be that whatever conflict was brewing has passed."

"Or it may be about to start. We have no way of knowing." Kairn's voice had an edge to it. This last week had been a trying one for the marshal. The failure of Brodesser's cloak, which had held out such promise. The launching of a major offensive against the Guild's ships, in and around the asteroid belt the rebel forces called home, had racked up losses the Guild could ill afford.

Two days ago saw the destruction of *Shadow*—one of only three large warships the Guild had remaining—by Sadir's elite Planetary Defense Command, the PDC. Three hundred people had perished, including one of the Guild's leaders, Vice Marshal Ela'jaren.

And now . . .

From what Trip had overheard during the last few hours, it seemed as if the Guild's worst fears were coming true.

Members of the planet's ruling council—Sadir's most trusted subordinates, generals and leaders of substantial military forces in their own right—were preparing to go to war, to fight for the chance to rule their system. A consequence of the Guild's failed attempt to kidnap General Sadir, which had resulted in the man's suicide and left Denari without a leader.

He shook his head. What was his mom always saying—misery loves company?

There was sure more than enough misery to go around on *Eclipse* right now.

A shadow loomed over him.

"Find anything?"

Trip looked up and saw Lieutenant Royce, *Eclipse*'s first officer, leaning over him.

"Plenty." He shook his head and nodded at the screen, which was filled with line after line of text, a list of the forty or fifty most recent intercepts he'd gone through. "None of it about *Enterprise,* though."

"I'm sorry to hear that," Royce said, sounding anything but. The lieutenant was a tall, thin man who rarely smiled. He rarely showed emotion of any kind, in Trip's experience—Royce had been on both missions Trip had undertaken for the Guild, Brodesser's rescue and the aborted kidnap attempt—the farmer with the pitchfork in the Grant Wood painting.

"Fane and her team"—Royce nodded behind him, toward the crowded area where Kairn still stood among a group of computer stations—"have just finished going through another batch of intercepts. I'll have her relay those to your station."

Trip sighed. "Thanks. Just what I need, more messages."

"Take a break."

"Can't. You know that." He met Royce's gaze. "Though if you want to give me some help, this'd go a lot quicker."

The first few days combing through these messages, Trip had that help—two crewmen whom Kairn had assigned to assist him—but after the attack on *Shadow*, the marshal had pulled them away, pleading, a scarcity of resources. He wanted every available body and machine involved in the effort to keep tabs on the hostiles tracking them.

Royce shook his head.

"Sorry, Tucker. I wish we could, but . . ."

Trip nodded grimly. "I understand."

"But speaking of help," Royce went on, "Professor Brodesser feels his work on the cloaking device would also go a lot quicker if he had some. From you, specifically."

Trip took a second before responding to get the surge of anger he felt under control.

It hadn't been more than three hours, tops, since he'd told Brodesser he'd think about the man's request. And the professor was already complaining?

"He told you about that, did he?"

"After I asked what progress he was making."

"Did he tell you I said I'd consider it?"

"He did. And now I'm asking. Have you considered it?"

"Hoshi and I need that cloaking device."

"Not until you find *Enterprise*. In the meantime . . ."

"Like I said, I'm considering it."

"Why not let Brodesser at it now, let him find out exactly how it works, then—"

"Because"—Trip got to his feet—"I'm not confident he can put it back together again if he takes it apart."

"You're the one who told us he was a genius. You've changed your mind?"

"The man I knew was a genius. This Brodesser, in case you've forgotten, is not—"

The man I knew, Trip was going to say.

Pain—a crippling, cramping pain—shot up the back of his right leg.

He drew in a breath involuntarily and sat back down.

"Tucker? You all right?"

He managed a nod. "Give me a minute."

He massaged the back of his calf, trying to ease the pain, aware of Royce standing over him the whole time.

"Should I call Doctor Trant?"

"No. Not necessary." Trip knew the pain would stop soon enough. He looked up at Royce again.

"What I was saying—I don't know this Brodesser, and I don't trust him to pull the cloak apart. Period. You take that back to Kairn, and tell him I said so."

Royce's eyes glittered for a second.

"I'll do that," he said slowly. "And you do this, Tucker. Remember that Kairn and I haven't forced you to do anything against your will from the day we rescued you. If you don't want Brodesser to look at the cloak, he won't." He nodded toward the workstation. "Good luck finding your ship," he said, then spun on his heel and was gone.

Trip almost called out after him, but by the time he'd thought of something to say, the lieutenant was out of earshot.

Terrific, he thought. *First Brodesser, now Royce . . . I'm making friends everywhere I go today.*

His workstation beeped. He turned and saw that a fresh batch of intercepts had arrived at his terminal. Six hundred and twelve of them, to be precise.

All at once, he didn't feel up to sifting through them. Maybe Royce was right: maybe he did need a break.

And operating on the misery loves company theory . . .

He decided to visit the one person aboard *Eclipse* who was possibly even more unhappy than he was at the moment.

Trip entered the decontamination chamber and pulled the door shut behind him.

He stripped down to his skivvies, then dropped his uniform and gloves into a nearby receptacle and switched on the UV ray. Filtered light washed over him, eradicating every potential contaminant, germ, and speck of dirt. He put on a clean coverall and opened the inner door.

Hoshi glanced up at his entrance.

She did not look well.

Worse than she had last night, when Trant had drawn blood from her and run a series of tests. Much worse. Her skin had taken on a slightly pale, transparent look that Trip had seen only on the very, very old—or the very, very ill. She looked brittle, as if she might crack at any second. All the weight she'd lost—more than Trip, he guessed, and she had much less to spare to start out with—didn't help.

Behind her, Trip could see the workstation Kairn's men had moved in was still dark. It had probably sat all day, unused. Just as Hoshi had—still and silent, in this dimly lit room.

He'd begged the marshal to let him take some of the intercepts from the bay back here, so that Hoshi could help in looking them over. So that she would have something to do. Kairn had turned him down. Prohibitively inefficient to make hard copies, he'd said, and too much effort to run the necessary conduit all the way from the bay to here. And here was where Hoshi had to stay.

Because while Trip could walk freely through the ship—assuming he took a modicum of care to avoid crowded areas like the mess hall and the upper decks—Hoshi's sensitivities were so acute that even a minute trace of the protein compounds they were allergic to would be enough to send her into anaphylactic shock. She'd almost died once before from such a reaction: she had slipped into a coma that had lasted two full days.

This room was the only place on *Eclipse* truly safe for her. *Eclipse*'s crew had converted these quarters into a hermetically sealed environment, with atmosphere and plumbing supplied through specially designed filtration systems. It was a nice room, twice as big as the isolation room in *Eclipse*'s medical ward.

And for all that, still a prison. Something Trip was

conscious of every time he came here. And even more acutely aware of when he left.

"Commander," she said, looking up. "Any news?"

"Nothing yet. But I've got a few hundred more of the day's intercepts to go through still. We'll find her, Hoshi."

She nodded. "I wish I could help."

There was nothing for Trip to do but nod. "I know. I wish you could too. In the meantime, how about something to eat?"

"I'm not hungry."

"I don't believe that for a second. Come on. Let's see what we've got."

"Commander . . ."

Trip ignored her. Not just as her commanding officer, but her friend, the only one she had on board *Eclipse*, he felt responsible for making sure that Hoshi kept up her strength . . . as much as possible.

He walked to the area of the room that had been designated a kitchen and opened the refrigerator. "Look at this. A veritable feast. What do you feel like?" he called over his shoulder. "Burgers? Sushi? Fried chicken?"

There was no response.

He turned. Hoshi had a smile—a very faint smile, but a smile nonetheless—on her face.

"Ha, ha," she said. "Very funny, sir."

"None of those to your taste?" Trip looked inside the refrigerator again. "How about pizza? I know you like pizza."

"Sure. That'd be fine."

"Pizza it is, then." He pulled a container out of the refrigerator and set it down on the counter. Took down two plates, filled them, and brought them over to the table. Set one down in front of Hoshi, the other at the place opposite hers, and sat.

She looked down at the plate, then back up at him.

"It doesn't look like pizza."

"Use your imagination."

"My imagination is not that vivid."

Trip glanced down at his plate.

His imagination wasn't that vivid either.

She sighed. "I just wish there was something else. Anything else."

"Can't argue with you there, but . . . consider the alternatives. What if there wasn't anything at all we could eat?"

She nodded. "I suppose we should be thankful."

And then she smiled.

"What?"

"Turo. That's what he said. Always remember to be thankful."

"Who's Turo?"

"A man I knew, back on Earth."

"Turo?" Trip frowned. "What kind of name is that?"

"He was Huantamos. Their chief, in fact."

"I hate to sound stupid, but . . . Huantamos?"

Hoshi nodded. "An Indian tribe, down in the Amazon basin. I met him while I was working for a private foundation down there, helping catalog the languages of some of the more remote peoples."

"Really? I didn't know about that." Which wasn't that surprising—there was a lot he didn't know about Hoshi.

"I spent six months with them." She picked up her spoon and stared into the polished surface for a moment before continuing. "The Huantamos live in the densest part of the rain forest. They live off the land in the same way they've been doing the last thousand years. They want no contact with the outside world—at all."

"So how could you learn their language?"

She smiled again. "Believe me, it wasn't easy. Just getting to them, I had to walk kilometers with nothing but the clothes on my back. Even then, it took a long time to convince them to let me stay. Convince them that all I wanted was to learn their language, and then leave."

Trip nodded. Walking into the middle of the rain forest with nothing but the clothes she wore—that took some guts. Some survival skills as well, no doubt. Maybe he'd been underestimating Hoshi just a little bit these past couple years.

"They took you in, though?"

"Eventually. That was a whole . . ." She shook her head. ". . . mess, is what it was. The *brujeira*—tribe's witch doctor is the closest approximation to his title—didn't want me there. He thought my learning the language and taking it away was like stealing. Turo had to . . . convince him otherwise."

The stress she put on the word "convince" gave Trip the feeling that argument had progressed beyond talking into a confrontation a shade more . . . primitive, for lack of a better word.

"Anyway," Hoshi said, suddenly setting down her spoon, "my point is, we always ate meals—the dinner meal, at least—together. Some nights there wouldn't be much more than this for everyone." She nodded to the *pisarko*. "Before every meal, though,

Turo always offered a prayer. Reminded us to be thankful for what we had."

"The Huantamos version of 'grace.' "

"Exactly," she nodded.

"My sister and I used to say grace, too." The memory made him smile.

"That's funny?"

"The way we did it, yeah."

Hoshi leaned forward expectantly. "Which was . . . ?"

Trip cleared his throat. "Good food, good meat. Good God, let's eat."

For a second, the expression on her face didn't change.

And then Hoshi giggled.

"Oh. That is funny," she said, and giggled again. "Good meat."

The way she said those last two words—

Trip snorted and burst into full-out laughter. Hoshi joined in at once, covering her mouth for a second to try and stop herself before giving in wholeheartedly.

It had to be a good ten seconds before they stopped.

"Oh." Hoshi said, smiling and shaking her head. "Commander, I—"

"Yeah." He smiled too. "It feels good to do that."

"Yes." She nodded.

Trip chuckled. "Oh yes." He looked her in the eye. "Good God, yes."

The "yes" came out as more of an exhalation than anything else, because Trip had already started laughing again.

Hoshi was laughing even harder. She grabbed her stomach and bent over, her shoulders shaking.

Even after Trip composed himself, her shoulders were still shaking.

Trip didn't know exactly how long it took for him to realize that at some point, her laughter had turned into tears.

"Hey. Hoshi, come on." She didn't react. He leaned forward and put a hand on her arm. "It's all right. We're gonna be—"

She sat up so suddenly Trip started.

"No!" she said, her voice harsh. "It's not all right, sir. It's not all right at all. I'm sick of this. Sick of feeling tired all the time. Sick of being stuck in this room. I'm sick of feeling useless, and more than anything else I am sick to death of this god-damn food!"

She shoved the bowl of *pisarko* away from her. It flew off the table and smacked into the floor, shattering into a hundred pieces.

Hoshi looked at the mess—shards of the plate, clumps of *pisarko* all mixed together—and suddenly stopped crying. Her eyes widened in horror.

"I didn't mean to do that," she said softly.

"Yeah. I know."

She sighed. "I'm sorry, sir."

"Hoshi." He looked her in the eye. "Like I said, it's all right. Or it will be, anyway. We'll find *Enterprise.*"

"Yes, sir." She smiled ruefully. "Good thing it was just a plate."

"Good thing." He nodded.

She sighed, wiped away another tear, and bent to begin picking up the shards.

Trip bent down to help her, mentally adding another item to the "things he didn't know about

Hoshi" list: under the right conditions, she had a powerful temper.

The door to the decontamination chamber opened again.

Doctor Trant stepped through. Neesa.

Trip looked at her and smiled.

She wore the same green-and-orange Guild uniform as Trip and Hoshi. Her gaze traveled from Trip to Hoshi to the mess on the floor and then back to him.

"Everything all right?" she asked, in such a way that Trip knew she had to have heard something of their previous conversation—Hoshi's rant, most likely.

"Everything's fine," Trip said. "Just an accident."

"My fault," Hoshi said, kneeling down on the floor. She reached for the shattered pieces of the plate. "I'll take care of it."

"Don't," Trant interrupted forcefully. "Leave those."

Hoshi looked up.

"Sharp edges. Last thing we need right now is for you to cut yourself, Hoshi," Trant said in a very reasonable tone. "I'll clean it up."

"I'm not a child," Hoshi snapped. "I'll be careful."

"It's not a question of being careful. Accidents happen."

"Doctor—"

"No," Trant said in a tone that brooked no argument.

Hoshi didn't argue.

But she didn't stop what she was doing either.

Piece by piece, scrap by scrap, she picked up the plate and the *pisarko* and threw them in the trash. Trant fumed.

Hoshi stood next to the bin defiantly when she'd finished.

"That was very foolish," Trant said.

"Maybe."

"No maybes about it." She turned to Trip. "You said 'early afternoon.' It's dinnertime."

He smacked himself on the forehead. The medical ward.

"I'm sorry. I forgot completely."

"What's the matter?" Hoshi asked.

"Commander Tucker was going to come by so I could run a few more tests."

"But we just did tests. Last night."

"The results were . . . at odds with what I expected to find. On both of you." Trant frowned. "In fact, as long as I'm here, I'd like to take a little more blood from you, Hoshi. Just to have a point of comparison."

Hoshi sighed, and seemed to deflate. All at once, she looked completely done in.

"Doctor," Trip said gently, "why don't you start with me now, and do Hoshi later? How would that be?"

Please, he added silently.

Trant caught the message in his eyes. "I suppose. But you're not interchangeable. So first thing after dinner, I'll be back. All right, Hoshi?"

"That's fine. Thank you, Doctor," Hoshi replied. Her eyes thanked Trip as well.

"Not a problem." He got to his feet. "Come on, Doc. Let's get this over with."

"Trip . . ."

Trant shook her head and pointed to the plateful of *pisarko* he'd left on the table.

"Oh, for God's sake," he mumbled, and sat back down.

Trant got out another plate and filled it for Hoshi. She pulled out a chair and joined them.

"Well, what are you waiting for?"

Trip smiled.

Hoshi smiled.

They burst out laughing again.

"At least someone around here's in a good mood."

Trant had waited until they'd passed through the decontamination chamber before speaking.

"Not exactly a good mood," Trip replied. "More like a desperate one." He ran down Hoshi's litany of complaints for the doctor. "The one about feeling useless, that's the big one, I think. At least before, when we thought that contacting Starfleet might make a difference, she had something to do. Now . . ."

Neesa nodded thoughtfully. "You'll have to find something else to keep her occupied."

"Something meaningful," Trip said.

"That she can do alone, in her cabin, without extended periods of contact with any of the crew."

"Needlepoint, maybe." He smiled and shook his head. His momma had done needlepoint almost every night after supper.

Trant looked puzzled.

"It's a hobby. Like making . . ." He thought, ". . . art."

"Is Hoshi an artist?"

He shook his head. "Not that I know of."

"I'm sure you'll think of something," Neesa said.

"I'm drawing a blank right now."

They walked on.

"These tests you want to run again," Trip said. "What are they?"

"Body chemistry studies."

"You weren't happy with the last round?"

"No."

"Why? What did they say?"

"Nothing that made sense," she told him. "That's why I want to run them again."

"Come on, Neesa. What did they say?"

She paused a moment before answering.

"The tests indicated that the rate of mineral depletion . . . is occurring faster than I had originally predicted. Much faster."

"Which means—"

"The trace minerals that your body needs to function optimally are at very low levels in your system. Somehow, they're being—well, for lack of a better word, leeched out."

Leeched. Trip shuddered involuntarily at the images the word brought up.

"It may be," Trant continued, "that there are compounds in the *pisarko* responsible for this process. That's one of the reasons I want to run the tests again—to see exactly what's happening. Also to make sure that the results I got last time were correct."

Trip frowned. "Same basic results in me and Hoshi, though?"

"That's right."

"So what are the odds that both sets of tests are wrong?"

He saw the answer to that in her eyes before she spoke.

"Not high, but still . . . it's worth eliminating that possibility. Before we have to do more expansive testing."

Trip sighed. He was getting almost as sick as Hoshi of being a guinea pig.

Trant put a hand on his shoulder.

"Trip, these tests won't take long, I promise. And we need to do them—there may be some things we can do to head off the symptoms."

"Symptoms like what?"

"Dizziness, fainting, unexplained cramping, feelings of weakness—"

He nodded. "Something I should have told you about before, I suppose," he said hesitantly, and then filled her in on the pains he'd experienced the previous night.

Trant was quiet after he'd finished.

"Well. It seems that those results may have been correct after all. Though another round of tests still might—"

"No." Trip stopped walking. "I don't think we really need another round. Do you?"

She sighed, and nodded reluctantly. "No, I suppose not. There's no news about your ship, I take it?"

"No."

"There's time," she said, and started walking again. "Even with this, there's time. I'll let Kairn know. He may be able to shift more personnel to the decoding stations. Your ship is out there, it's just a matter of—"

"Neesa." Trip hadn't moved a muscle, was still standing in the exact same spot where he'd stopped. She hadn't noticed.

She turned now to face him.

"How much time?" he asked. "How much time do Hoshi and I have?"

"That's hard to say. There are a lot of factors involved."

"When we first found out about all this, you said months."

"I know."

"We're not talking about months anymore though, are we?"

She shook her head. "No. Certainly not for Hoshi. For you . . . if these test results are right . . . if the rate of depletion continues to accelerate . . . if—"

"Neesa."

She looked up at him.

"Just tell me."

She shut her eyes a second, and shook her head.

"Six weeks," she said, sighing again. "That's the high end. A month, on the other side, if—"

Trip held up a hand. He didn't want to hear the rest.

"Okay," he said, nodding. "A month."

Thirty days, more or less. Long before then, of course, he'd be bedridden. Incapable of getting to *Enterprise* even if they found it. And what was true for him would no doubt be true for the rest of the crew. In a month, they'd all be dead.

"Trip"—Trant took one of his hands and squeezed it between hers—"we're going to find your ship. I know it."

But suddenly, despite his own words of encouragement to Hoshi earlier, he wasn't so sure. All this time, all those intercepts sorted through, and they still didn't have a clue. And now, for all intents and purposes, the amount of time they had left could be measured in days.

They had to do something.

And all at once, it was crystal clear to him exactly what that something was.

"Hoshi and I have to go."

"What do you mean?"

"I mean we have to go. Get in the cell-ship, and find *Enterprise* ourselves."

Trant blinked.

"You're kidding."

"No, I'm not."

"Go where? You don't have a clue where to start looking. And those aches you're feeling now, those cramps? They're only going to get worse. Exponentially worse."

"I believe you," he said.

She shook her head. "You can't fly in that kind of pain."

"That's why there's an autopilot."

"Trip, be serious. What if you get sick? What if Hoshi gets sicker? How can you expect to take care of her if you're incapacitated?"

"We'll find a way. We'll have to."

"How?"

"I don't know. You're the doctor—help us."

"I want to help. Assisted suicide is not my idea of help."

"I seem to recall you passing out poison pills not too long ago."

She frowned. "That was different."

"No, that was exactly the same. You wanted me to have those pills in case I got caught by Sadir's people, so I'd have a chance to die on my own terms." He put his hands on her shoulders and looked her straight in the eye. "That's all I plan on doing. Giving myself that same chance."

She shook her head. "But you don't have to make that choice just yet. There are still things—"

"Neesa," he cut her off, "that's wrong. I have to make the choice now. While I still can."

"What about Hoshi? You're going to make that decision for her too?"

"No. I'll give her the choice." He nodded down the corridor, back the way they'd come. "But I think I know what she'll say."

Neesa stared into his eyes a moment without responding.

A Guild crewman wandered past. He looked at them curiously before continuing on his way. Trip would normally have pulled his hands away from her shoulders, made it look like they were just friends talking, but right at the moment he didn't care about all that.

"I'll tell Kairn you're too sick to go. That you're irrational. That—"

"He wouldn't believe it. And even if he would . . ." Trip shook his head. "You'd never do that."

She lowered her gaze.

"No, I wouldn't. Trip . . ."

"Neesa." He touched her cheek gently and tilted her head toward his. "Try and understand."

"I do understand. I'm just not happy, that's all."

"Yeah, well . . . neither am I." Not about leaving her, anyway. He was just the opposite, in fact. Miserable.

All at once, that old saying popped into his head again, and he smiled.

"What?"

He told her.

She sighed. "I suppose that's true. I could certainly use some company now."

"That sounds like an invitation."

She nodded.

"As long as we're not going to the ward," Trip said, "I'm your man."

"For one more night," she said, managing a smile.

Trip nodded. "One more night."

They joined hands and headed off down the corridor.

Five

"THEREFORE," T'POL SAID, sitting back in her chair, "this is the only logical conclusion."

Stunned silence greeted her pronouncement.

Phlox was the first to find his voice. "Astounding. Unsettling. Sub-Commander, forgive me, but . . . could you go through your reasoning one more time? I want to understand—exactly—how you arrived at this conclusion."

T'Pol looked to the captain. He gave her a quick go-ahead nod. Truth be told, Archer could use the time to fully absorb the implications of her discovery.

The three of them were gathered around a small table in what had once served as a canteen for Rava One's guards, a room right off the main cargo bay, where the Denari vessel they'd just commandeered was being prepared for their use.

No sooner had they finished clearing the ship of soldiers than T'Pol had appeared with what she'd deemed urgent news. She'd asked Archer to have Doctor Phlox join them in the nearest available room to hear it.

Urgent, he decided now, was an understatement.

"As you wish, Doctor," T'Pol said. "To repeat. When I was first brought to Colonel Gastornis, he told me his superiors wanted as much information on Vulcan activities within the neighboring star systems as possible. I offered to identify the nearest Vulcan outposts to him, as a way of avoiding his . . . wrath."

Which was one of the blandest euphemisms for torture the captain had ever heard. Torture, T'Pol hadn't entirely avoided, as evidenced by the green welts along both her arms.

"Of course, I had no intention of doing any such thing. My plan was to use the prison's sensors not to find the outposts, but to signal them with our whereabouts, in the hope they would mount a rescue. However, in the course of attempting to locate those garrisons, I ran into some unexpected difficulties."

"Involving those . . . T'ronn Equations you were talking about," the captain supplied.

"T'ronna Equations," T'Pol corrected. "Yes. Those equations set forth a series of unchanging physical constants, which form the basis of much Vulcan astrophysical science. S'ral's Theorem, the Shi'Kahr Principles—"

"Hold on a minute, T'Pol," the captain said. "As long as you're going over this again—this is where I lost you last time."

T'Pol frowned. "Perhaps if I eliminate the references to Vulcan scientific theory, and speak in terms of human traditions?"

"Couldn't hurt," Archer said.

The Vulcan nodded. "Very well, then. Are you familiar with the Hubble Constant?"

"Sure," the captain said. Phlox, he saw, was frowning.

"Named after a twentieth-century astronomer, I believe," Archer continued. "Sets forth the rate of the universe's expansion."

"Exactly," T'Pol replied.

"Ah." The Denobulan smiled. "Parnikee's Theorem."

Both of them looked at him.

"Parnikee. You've never heard of Parnikee?" Phlox shook his head in amazement. "Most peculiar. I would think he warranted mention in any survey of the galaxy's great scientists. Not only did he invent the matter/antimatter engine on our world, but he led the first Denobulan exploratory vessel—"

Archer held up a hand. "We get the point, Doctor. T'Pol?"

"Yes. To continue, the Hubble Constant, for all intents and purposes, is the same as T'Ronna's third equation. As Parnikee's Theorem, Doctor."

"As I said," Phlox responded.

"That number is useful in a multitude of applications. In this case, I used it to help calculate the location of the nearest Vulcan outpost. Rather, I should say I tried to use it. To make a long story short, I failed."

She looked around the table.

"I tried again. And failed again. I repeated this process so many times that the colonel grew frustrated with me, and . . ."

Archer nodded. She didn't need to fill in that particular blank.

"Naturally, I was puzzled at this turn of events. So

much so that I felt it necessary to speed my return to duty in order to check my calculations. Which I have just done. This time, however, I took nothing for granted, not even the Hubble Constant. I decided to measure that myself." She looked around the table. "As I said before, the number I came up with for the constant differs by .02 kilometers per second per megaparsec from the accepted value."

"That's significant?" Archer asked.

She looked at him as though he'd just grown two heads.

"There is a reason it is called a constant, sir. The number does not change. Under any circumstances."

"And yet this number is different," Phlox said.

The Vulcan nodded. "I measured it two dozen times over the last half hour, and in each instance, arrived at the same number. It is still a constant. However, it is a different constant."

She looked around the table.

"A different constant. A different rate of expansion. Therefore, a different universe."

A different universe. Her logic was impeccable, as always. And yet . . .

"This begs the question: if we are in a different universe, how—and when—did we get here?" Phlox asked.

It came to Archer all at once.

"The anomaly," he said. His eyes met T'Pol's.

She nodded.

"It is within the realm of possibility," she said. "Black holes have been proposed as potential gateways into parallel worlds. Preliminary studies of the anomaly revealed similar characteristics."

"When that mine crippled us, we were close enough to the anomaly to get caught in its gravitational field," Archer said. "To be drawn inside. To cross over. But assuming we're right, and this is a different universe—it's an awful lot like the one we came from."

"Which Parnikee predicted," Phlox said. "The existence of parallel universes. Worlds virtually identical to ours, with minor differences that could account for the variable in this constant you're speaking of." The doctor frowned. "Which could also account for the unexplained weakness you've been feeling, Captain"—he nodded to Archer—"as well as the crew's reactions—the illnesses I've been treating."

"Precisely what I suspected, Doctor. That is why I wanted you to hear this as well. There may indeed be a biochemical difference in molecular compounds between continuums."

Phlox nodded. "At the least, this information suggests a new avenue for my research."

"It also suggests that we need to return to our own universe as soon as possible. That brings us back to the search for *Enterprise.*"

About time, too, Archer thought. Not that it had been wasted time, but they'd spent ten minutes in this room they didn't have. They still didn't know what message Covay's com officer had gotten off. More hostiles could be headed their way at this minute.

"T'Pol." Archer turned to his science officer. "You said you hurried your return to duty. How do you feel now?"

"Sustained physical exertion would be unwise, but otherwise . . . I am quite capable of performing my duties."

"Then I'll want you with me on the Denari ship."

"Yes, sir."

That, left him with the question of whom to leave in charge here at the prison. Lee? O'Bannon? O'Neill? None of them had any real experience in these kinds of situations. Again, he wished for Malcolm. Or Trip. Or someone with just a tad more seasoning whom he could leave in charge.

But they weren't here. And there was no telling when they would be back.

He decided on O'Neill. She'd had command experience and had done a commendable job managing the incident with the Jantaleyse ambassador. Archer left her fairly general instructions—no heroics, defend the prison as best they could, but if any substantial force showed up, surrender.

"We'll be back with *Enterprise* to get you out of here, one way or another," he promised.

While D.O. began organizing the prison's defenses, Archer stopped at a hastily arranged interrogation chamber, where Chief Lee had taken the newly captured Denari. The captain walked in to find Lieutenant Covay answering—or rather, not answering—Lee's questions.

Both looked up. The Denari officer sneered.

"You're a dead man, Chief Archer. Makandros will track you down and eat you for breakfast."

"Makandros," the captain said. "Who's he?"

"Their commander," Lee supplied.

"Makandros?" Archer frowned. "I thought this Sadir person—the general—was in charge."

"Sadir is dead. Assassinated, apparently," Lee supplied.

"Surrender now, Chief," Covay said. "The general will go easy on you—move you to a more secure facility after a minimal punishment. That's if you haven't damaged the ship yet. Those Stingers are his pride and joy."

Stinger. Archer took note of the name, which indicated the ship's class, he supposed.

"That's Captain Archer, Lieutenant. And no, I haven't damaged your vessel, nor do I intend to. All I'm interested in is getting my ship back. *Enterprise.*"

Covay met his gaze head-on.

"As I told your man here, I know nothing about that."

Archer nodding, not breaking eye contact.

"Crewmen of mine were taken from here—Lieutenant Malcolm Reed, Mayweather, Hess, and Ryan. I'm wondering if you know anything about that."

"Never heard those names before. We're a military ship, Captain." Covay put a sneer into that word as well. "Not a prison transport."

Still the man didn't blink. He was either a very good liar, or . . .

"I hope for your sake you're telling the truth right now, Lieutenant Covay," the captain said. "Because if not . . ." He leaned forward till his face was inches from Covay's. "I'll have you for breakfast. Do we understand each other?"

"Perfectly." Covay said.

"Good."

Archer stood. He motioned Lee to join him outside the interrogation chamber, which the man did, shutting the door behind him.

"You find out anything useful?" the captain asked.

"Not a thing. Believe it or not, that lieutenant's the most talkative one of the bunch." Lee shook his head. "It's a hard group, sir. Name, rank, and serial number. They won't crack unless we . . . do something drastic."

Archer frowned.

"If you're suggesting torture, Chief . . ."

"No, sir. Just telling you the facts."

"Understood."

His communicator beeped.

"Archer."

"This is Sub-Commander T'Pol, sir. Denari vessel is prepped and ready for launch. We await your arrival."

"Be there in five minutes," the captain said. "Out."

He turned to Lee.

"Keep at it. Relay any information you find through Lieutenant O'Neill."

"I will, sir."

"Good man." The captain clapped him on the shoulder.

Lee was a good man. Reed had trained him well. *I have a hell of a crew,* the captain thought.

He didn't like to think about leaving the vast majority of them here, where there was a good chance they would be overwhelmed by whatever force came in response to the signal Covay's crew had gotten out.

But it wasn't as if he had much choice in the matter.

T'Pol had proposed starting their search in the area near the anomaly where they had been attacked. Archer doubted his ship would still be there, or even anywhere nearby, but it might be possible to pick up *Enterprise*'s trail . . .

Well, he couldn't counter with anything better, as he passed through the airlock into the Denari vessel proper, Archer continued to "illogically hope" the search would be a short one.

He joined T'Pol in the cockpit, where she was hunched over one of the forward stations, fingers flying across the sensor panel in front of her.

Archer settled into the chair to her right—the pilot's seat—and studied the controls.

"A fairly standard configuration," T'Pol said as she worked. "You should have no trouble flying this vessel."

The captain nodded. Standard was right; the layout mimicked, to an uncanny degree, the instrument set on the early fleet courier vessels. Archer had cut his teeth on those.

"Looks straightforward enough," he said. "Any signs of other ships approaching?"

"Nothing. However, Rava is in the heart of this system's asteroid belt, many of which are large enough to hide enemy fighters, particularly if they are as small as this ship."

The captain nodded. "We'll travel on alert, then. Can you open a channel to Rava?"

T'Pol nodded. The captain saw she was wearing a com earpiece identical to Hoshi's.

Archer had to wonder if he was ever going to see the ensign again.

More than anyone else in the crew, he felt responsible for Hoshi. She would never have come into space if he hadn't twisted her arm. And though he'd worried about her ability to cope on occasion, over the last few months she'd really settled in as a member of the crew. But to think of her all alone out there . . .

No, not alone. Not necessarily. Trip could still be with her. The thought gave him some comfort.

"Channel open, Captain," T'Pol said.

Archer nodded. "Lieutenant O'Neill."

"Here, sir."

"We're about to launch," Archer said. "Maintain com silence unless absolutely necessary. We don't have a secure channel to talk on."

"Aye, aye, Captain."

"Good. Archer out."

T'Pol had already plotted their course. Archer took a moment to study it before they launched. He saw she hadn't been kidding about Rava being in the heart of the asteroid belt; there were literally hundreds of rocks of all shapes and sizes whizzing past the prison satellite.

It turned out to be a very good thing that flying the ship came so easily to him. Otherwise, they wouldn't have made it very far at all.

An hour into the journey, they were finally past the most crowded portion of the Belt, and the captain felt sure enough of their course to switch on the autopilot and stretch his legs. He went back into the main compartment of the vessel.

Weapons stations—two on either side of the ship, one at the rear, all with access to fixed gun emplacements on the hull—took up most of the interior. They'd brought along enough crew to man all of them. He'd put Yamani and Rodriguez, two of his best armory officers, according to Reed, in charge of organizing the weapons detail.

"Captain," Yamani said, nodding his head in acknowledgment as Archer came to stand by his shoulder.

"What's the word?" Archer asked. "You have a handle on these yet?"

"Yes, sir. A lot of the same kind of stuff we used to train on back in the Academy."

"And lots of it," Rodriguez put in from the station behind them. "These ships are built for one thing only, Captain. War."

Archer frowned. "Suppose we were on *Enterprise*, and came up against a half-dozen of these. How would we do?"

"Oh." Yamani shook his head and smiled. The captain saw him exchange a glance with Rodriguez.

"This is nice stuff, sir," the ensign said. "But old."

"That's right," Rodriguez added. "Shielding is nowhere. *Enterprise* could blow a dozen of these out of the water. No problem."

"That's good to hear. Let's hope it doesn't come to that," Archer said.

"Captain?"

That was T'Pol, calling him from the front of the ship.

Archer strode back into the cockpit.

"Something coming in from Rava," T'Pol said, touching her earpiece. "It's Lieutenant O'Neill."

The captain shook his head, irritated. He'd as much as told her to maintain com silence.

"Put it up," Archer said.

Stinger's small viewscreen filled with static. A second later, D.O. came on. She looked worried.

"Captain, sorry to—"

Her voice crackled. The image wavered.

"T'Pol . . ."

"Trying, sir. A lot of interference." She punched buttons quickly and calmly. "I have audio. No visual."

The captain nodded.

". . . say again. We boosted sensors and picked up—"

The signal died.

An alert sounded.

T'Pol shifted her attention to the sensor panel in front of her. Archer took a quick look over her shoulder as he settled back into his seat.

A lot of ships. Closing fast.

"Hostiles," she said. "Identical to our vessel."

"Stingers," the captain said. "Too many to fight. Send the data to me. I'll plot us a course out."

"A moment." She paused. "Eight ships now. No, ten. Closing in formation."

"I see them," Archer said. He disengaged the autopilot as the information came in to his station. Ten Stingers, identical to his vessel, moving at high impulse, in a perfectly regimented formation. No, not quite perfect.

"The two above the ecliptic," the captain said. "Their spacing's off. That's our way out. Hang on. This is going to get a little rough."

He braced himself and punched thrusters.

Nothing happened.

"The autopilot still has control," T'Pol said.

"Thank you, Sub-Commander. I can see that." The captain frowned. *What's the matter with this thing?*

He tried to disengage again—and again, he failed.

"The autopilot is dropping our speed," T'Pol said. "Point three impulse. Point two—"

Archer was close enough to her station that he could see the other ships closing in.

"T'Pol," he said, "can you manually reroute control?"

"Trying." Her hands flew over the sensor panel for a moment.

Then she sat back and shook her head. "No, sir. Control of primary flight functions has been disrupted."

"By who?"

"I cannot say. Most likely, an external guidance system. I will attempt to disrupt its transmissions." She swiveled slightly in her chair and accessed a different set of controls. Almost immediately, she sat back.

"Communications are inoperative as well."

"Weapons?" Archer shouted, standing and looking back through the open cockpit door.

Yamani and Rodriguez were absorbed in working their respective consoles. Both men looked utterly frustrated.

"Weapons as well are off-line," T'Pol said.

Archer sat back in his seat, stunned.

"What can we do? How can we regain control of the ship?"

"Short of shutting down everything, including life support . . ." She shook her head. "I cannot say."

The ship slowed even further.

"Something else headed our way," T'Pol said,

studying her sensor screen. "A much bigger vessel. About the size of *Enterprise.*"

Archer nodded. This ship he could see coming, first as a small silver glint in the upper right-hand corner of the viewscreen, then as a long, slim, dangerous-looking vessel. Without a doubt, a warship.

It filled the viewscreen as it drew close.

"Intensive signal traffic between that vessel and ours, Captain. It would seem that . . ."

Her voice trailed off.

The warship loomed over them. On the underside of its hull, Archer could see a small hatch sliding open.

They were being drawn inside the larger vessel.

". . . a preprogrammed docking sequence is being initiated," T'Pol finished.

The captain shook his head, watching the big ship draw closer. Docking wasn't the way he would have described what was happening. It was more like they were being swallowed whole.

Eaten for breakfast.

Archer sighed.

He had a funny feeling he knew exactly who their host was going to turn out to be.

Six

"Could use your help here a second, sir," Hoshi said.

Trip pushed back from the pilot's station and stood as best he could inside the cramped interior of the cell-ship. Hoshi was hooking up the last of the new relays to the cell-ship's power grid. He held the unit in place while she finished.

"Thanks," she said, taking a seat. She powered up the console in front of her. "I'll just run a few tests, and then . . ."

Trip nodded. "And then we're ready." He'd already done a systems check—as far as he could check systems on a ship whose operation remained largely a mystery to him—and stocked the overhead compartments with an emergency repair kit and enough *pisarko*—this time, in the form of ration bars—to last them a week.

Beyond that, they'd have to plan on returning to *Eclipse*, or finding another Guild ship, or some other place to resupply—though Trip didn't really think they'd have much longer than a week, being honest with himself. Hoshi was certainly in a much better mood this morning, but even the smile on her face couldn't mask her worsening condition or her physical weakness. Even though the com relays weighed barely as much as a good-sized stack of laundry, she'd been unable to hold them in place herself and had to ask Trip to reattach them for her. He'd found them surprisingly heavy as well. Not a good sign.

No, a week was about what they had. And Trip didn't plan on returning to *Eclipse*. If they didn't find *Enterprise*, his plan was to push the cell-ship to the outer limits of its warp capabilities and head back toward Earth, looking for a Starfleet or Vulcan outpost. His bet was that a more advanced civilization might be able to help them. Accent on the "might." And if their condition worsened even faster than expected, if they didn't have the time to make that kind of journey . . .

Maybe, he'd been thinking, they should take a chance on flying through the anomaly themselves. Though that was probably more of a suicide mission than anything else, given the gravitational forces swirling around that phenomenon. Still, Trip would do that—go out fighting—rather than face the possibility of wasting away to nothing on a bed in *Eclipse*'s medical ward, tubes and equipment hooked up to every orifice in his body. He was not going to die that way, no matter what.

Of course, he hadn't said a word of that to Neesa last night. He'd told her he'd be back if they didn't find *Enterprise* or its crew. A little bit of a white lie, but he didn't want a confrontation with her. Saying good-bye had been hard enough. Trip was glad they'd done it last night, rather than waiting until this morning. It let him focus on the task at hand. Royce and Fane had passed on a list of Denari military bases where *Enterprise* wasn't, information gathered from Guild patrols over the last few days. Now it was simply a matter of checking out other outposts, though of course Royce couldn't guarantee that they knew the location of every single—

"Commander?"

Trip blinked.

"Sorry, Hoshi." He looked up and smiled at her. "Thinking about something else there for a second. What do you need?"

"Nothing I need, sir." She gestured through the window of the cell-ship to the launch-bay outside.

Victor Brodesser stood there.

He pointed at Trip, motioning for him to come out and talk.

"I understand you're leaving."

Trip had barely come through the hatch before Brodesser began speaking. He took a second to gather his thoughts.

Truth was, he'd been avoiding the man all morning, as he'd avoided him last night, ever since reaching the decision to depart. It made their confrontation over the cloaking device yesterday academic, as far as he was concerned. He'd hoped to avoid any further discussion of the issue.

But if the anger evident on the man's face was any indication, that was a vain hope.

"That's right." Trip had brought one of the diagnostic sensors out with him. He ran it along the exterior of the cell-ship, doing a last check for signs of stress and/or minute cracks in the hull as he talked. "We're not making any progress finding *Enterprise* through the intercepts, so Hoshi and I—"

"Trip, I know what's going on."

He turned to meet the professor's gaze.

"Kairn told me about the test results—what Doctor Trant found."

"He did?" Trip hadn't exactly asked the marshal to keep the news quiet, after he'd told Kairn last night why he and Hoshi had to leave immediately, but still . . .

"That's right, he did. What I want to know is, why didn't you?"

"What?"

"Why didn't you tell me?"

Trip looked into Brodesser's eyes and saw something else there now besides the anger.

Hurt.

It made him stumble over his words.

"I was going to, but—"

"Before or after you'd left?" Brodesser shook his head. "Were you even going to say good-bye?"

"Of course I was going to say good-bye," he replied instantly, though in truth there was no "of course" about it. His only desire had been to avoid an argument, and he would have dodged Brodesser entirely if he could have. "Listen, I'm sorry I didn't come talk to you yesterday about the cloak, but—"

"Trip." Brodesser stepped forward and looked him in the eye. "I don't care about the cloak."

"What?"

"Well." The professor managed a thin smile. "I suppose that is a bit of an exaggeration. I do care, of course—I'd like to help the Guild. I'd like to see Sadir's government—what's left of it, at least—fall. I have a certain degree of intellectual curiosity about why the device I constructed is now failing. But I care more about what happens to you."

Trip didn't know what to say to that.

"I don't know why we haven't been able to find common ground these last few days. I do know that since you came back from the Kresh"—he frowned— "you've treated me like a total stranger."

"But . . ." No sense mincing words here, Trip realized. "We are strangers, sir."

"Strangers? You and I? No." Brodesser shook his head. "I know you as well as I know anyone."

"That's just not true."

"Isn't it?" Brodesser smiled again. "Isn't it true that you spent more time in high school hanging around the old Cape Canaveral base than the classroom?"

Trip frowned.

"Yes, but—"

"And the year you worked on *Daedalus*, you were in the middle of a relationship—a long-distance relationship—with a woman named Natalie who—"

"Right," Trip said quickly, recalling one particularly risqué transmission Natalie had sent him that had somehow gotten broadcast, to his undying embarrassment, everywhere in the *Daedalus* complex. "But—"

"And this," Brodesser said, rolling up his sleeve to display a thin, barely visible scar along the inside of his arm. "Do you remember this?"

A chill ran down Trip's spine. He did indeed remember that scar. How could he not?

Brodesser had gotten it saving Trip's life.

It happened the first time they'd tested the El Cid—Cascading Ion Drive—prototype—a near-tragedy that the *Daedalus* disaster had pushed to the back of his mind. It all came rushing back in an instant.

He and Chief Cooney had been in *Daedalus*'s engine room. Cooney had spent the day working with a team of engineers, connecting the prototype engine to the ship's systems. It was late by the time they'd finished. Two days behind schedule, with another full day of testing to go.

The delay made Trip anxious. Brodesser was under a lot of pressure from Starfleet to produce results; he knew that. So Trip had pushed Cooney to continue testing through the night. He'd offered his own services to assist. The two men were in the middle of verifying conduit integrity when the professor walked in on them.

He'd been furious. Understandably so, Trip realized in retrospect. Brodesser had yelled at them for ignoring safety protocols, for not having someone at the main control station to monitor their work. He'd been particularly upset with Cooney, who he'd declared "should have known better." Trip remembered wondering what that said about him.

He was still wondering, he supposed, as he began to disconnect the testing equipment. And whether it was because of that wondering, the lateness of the hour, some combination of the two or just plain carelessness, he could never be entirely sure.

What happened was that he accidentally brushed the testing leads against charged conduit.

In an instant, blue fire arced up from the conduit

surface and sparked through the air to touch the testing probe in Trip's hand.

He didn't know how many volts he took, but it was more than enough to freeze him where he stood, for his muscles to lock in place, including his hand around the probe.

The ions within the conduit began to swirl about, flowing toward the probe as well. The energy flow grew in intensity. Trip knew it was all happening in milliseconds, and yet it seemed to be taking place in slow motion.

I'm going to die, he realized in that instant.

And in that instant, Brodesser, moving with a speed that belied his years, thrust his own arm into the middle of that blue fire coming off the conduit, breaking the connection.

Two things happened: the professor screamed in agony, and Trip flew backwards as though shot out of a cannon.

He slammed against the nearest wall and slumped to the ground. He remembered being vaguely aware of Cooney moving as well then, remembered the engineer reaching and punching the emergency cut-off switch.

They'd been unreasonably lucky. The engine prototype, the testing equipment, even Trip himself—all had been entirely undamaged. The only physical evidence that anything untoward had happened was the scar on Brodesser's arm.

The same scar that this universe's Brodesser was now showing to him.

Trip sighed.

The man was right. They weren't strangers, and yet

he wouldn't—couldn't—treat this universe's Brodesser the same way he'd treated the professor who'd died aboard *Daedalus*.

Maybe that's part of the problem, he thought.

Maybe he was angry at this man for having lived when his Brodesser had died.

And thinking that, he realized something else as well.

Maybe he was angry at himself. For not stopping the *Daedalus* launch when he could have, the night before that first flight, when Brodesser had called him into his quarters and they'd talked about damping down the cascade reaction.

Maybe every time he'd been looking at and listening to this man, he'd been unconsciously feeling his own guilt.

That's a lot of maybes, Trip thought. He didn't have time to sort them all out right now. But one thing was for certain.

No matter their relationship, he could treat this man now standing in front of him with a little more courtesy.

"I do owe you an apology," he said.

The professor smiled. "Accepted."

"And I do wish I could stick around even a little longer—let you take a closer look at the cloaking device. But Hoshi and I . . ."

"You have to go. I understand." He nodded. "There is something you could do to help us, though. With regard to the cloak. When you launch, can you engage it immediately? We've set up a sensor grid to measure those initial energy states and look at how they interact with an engaged warp field."

Trip nodded. That sounded easy enough to do. He opened his mouth to tell the professor as much—

And saw, all at once, that Brodesser was no longer looking at him. Rather, the professor's gaze was focused at a point somewhere over his right shoulder.

Trip turned and saw why.

Across the launch bay, in the makeshift command center the Guild had set up, a crowd was gathering.

"Something's happening," Brodesser said.

Trip nodded.

"Let's go find out what."

They crossed the bay at a clip somewhere between a walk and a jog, heading toward Lieutenant Fane's com station, where fully half a dozen of *Eclipse's* top-ranking personnel—including Marshall Kairn and Lieutenant Royce—had gathered.

Royce acknowledged them with a nod, raising a finger to his lips just as Trip was about to ask him what was going on.

"Got him again, sir," Fane said just then, turning to Kairn. "Channel is open."

The marshal nodded grimly, reached over her, and pressed a button.

"This is *Eclipse*. Go ahead, Lieutenant."

At the far end of the bay, the viewscreen—filled with a map of the Denari star system that showed the position of the Guild ships and their opponents— went dark for a second, then came to life again. The map was gone, though. In its place was the image of a young man, a Guild soldier barely out of his teens, who looked scared and quite out of his depth. The soldier stood in front of a scene of utter devastation.

"Thermonuclear explosions," he said. "Two of them, at least. Centered around the base near Charest. Hit the power plants as well—half the continent is without electricity."

"Deaths?"

The young man shook his head. "No word yet, sir. Depending on the bombs' yield, we could be looking at a million casualties."

Kairn sighed heavily and closed his eyes.

Trip could only imagine what he was feeling now. The plot to kidnap Sadir—and prod the Guild to assume all the risks that went along with it—had been undertaken at his urging. The plot had failed, and now it seemed their worst fears had come true.

War had broken out on Denari, and Trip had no doubt Kairn felt entirely responsible for it.

The viewscreen split. The young lieutenant's image shrank to fit one side. The other filled with the image of Guildsman Lind, an older man who was the longtime leader of the Guild. Though as Trip had gotten closely involved with the organization, he recognized that real power was split between Lind and its military commanders, of whom Kairn seemed the most powerful.

"I would lay odds they used clean bombs, Marshal," Lind said. "We can be grateful for that much, at least."

"I think you're right, sir," Kairn said. "General Elson has no desire to rule a wasteland."

"We have proof it was Elson?" Lind asked.

"Lieutenant?" Kairn asked.

The young man shook his head. "No. Nothing definitive."

Elson. Trip recognized the name. One of Sadir's

most powerful lieutenants as well as a member of the planet's ruling council.

"Marshal?" the young man said hesitantly.

"Go on."

"There's something else, sir. A short time ago, I heard a rumor—just informal, not from the news services. This rumor has it that the Guild was responsible for the attacks on Charest. If that rumor spreads . . ."

Next to Trip, Royce tensed.

"Bastards," he said, loud enough that both the young lieutenant and Lind looked up.

"It's to be expected, I'm afraid," the Guildsman said. "Blame this atrocity on us, it will give Elson— give anyone—the excuse to come after us in full force. Finish us off for good."

"So is Elson operating alone? Or with the other members of the Council?" Kairn asked.

"We don't know."

"Try and find out, Lieutenant. Keep us informed."

"Aye, sir. Guildsman. Out."

His half of the screen went dark. The Guildsman's picture expanded to fill it.

"We need to know if Dirsch is still alive," Lind asked.

"The EMP will make that hard to determine. The lieutenant will be our best source on that." Kairn frowned. "I'm more concerned about Makandros. His troops will follow him without question."

"Agreed. If he decides to believe those rumors, and comes after us . . ."

"We need to be prepared for the worst," Kairn said.

"Plans need to be made." Lind sighed heavily. "I'll

need to break this news to my crew first, Marshal. Then we should talk again. Lind out."

He nodded, and the screen went dark for a second before filling with the map of the Denari system again.

Kairn sighed heavily and straightened. He saw Trip and shook his head.

"As you can see, Commander Tucker. What we most feared appears to have come to pass."

"I'm sorry, Marshal."

"So am I. We had been talking to General Dirsch about a ceasefire, a truce between the Guild and his forces. Burkhelt was never as virulently anti-Guild as New Irla. I had hoped that he could convince the Council to bring an end to this war. But now . . ." He shook his head. "Dirsch appears to be gone."

"So what's your next move?"

"As you heard. Prepare for the worst. And wait. Elson has control of the Kresh and now, with this attack, he appears to have control of the entire planet as well."

"That's not good," Royce said.

"No. Elson will never make peace with the Guild."

"And what about this Makandros?" Brodesser asked. "How do you think he's likely to react?"

"That's what we don't know—yet. He holds a seat on the Council as well. More importantly, he commands half the fleet—the entire Denari Expeditionary Force. The DEF control all space beyond the Belt. And his troops are all personally loyal to him. Makandros has earned that by fighting alongside them for years."

"As we well know," Royce said wryly.

"Yes. The general has been responsible for inflicting a great many defeats on the Guild, though we've had our share of victories as well. At least we did, once upon a time." Kairn frowned. "Still, I would rather deal with him than a bootlicker like Elson."

"Or a corrupt swine like Dirsch," Royce put in.

Trip looked from one of them to the other. Despite the seriousness of the situation, he couldn't help but smile.

"I don't envy your position," Trip said. "It sounds complicated."

"It is. I don't envy you yours either, Commander." He nodded in the direction of the cell-ship. "I assume you're ready to go?"

"We are."

Kairn held out his hand. "Then I wish you luck. And I thank you for everything you've done for us."

"Thank you, sir. For rescuing Hoshi and me in the first place. For taking such good care of us."

The two men shook hands.

"You should be thanking Doctor Trant for that." Kairn frowned and looked around the bay briefly. "I would expect to see her here, to see you off."

"We've already said our good-byes," Trip replied quickly.

"I see." Kairn looked at him strangely a moment, and Trip wondered suddenly if the marshal knew about his relationship with Neesa. *No*, he decided. *Impossible*. And yet . . .

In so many ways, Kairn reminded him of Captain Archer. And he couldn't see the captain letting something like that escape his notice.

"If you do find your starship, remember what we talked about," the marshal said.

Trip did. If they found *Enterprise*, Kairn had told him earlier this morning, he would send *Eclipse* to help recapture it. Trip had agreed to contact them for assistance, if it was at all possible.

But he had no intention of doing so. He was not going to let *Eclipse* get anywhere near the much more powerful Starfleet vessel. *Enterprise* would see the Guild ship coming a hundred kilometers away and blow it—and the hundreds of people aboard—out of the sky. *Enterprise*'s weapons, even in the hands of relatively untrained Denari personnel, were . . .

He frowned.

"Commander?" Kairn asked. "Everything all right?"

Trip didn't respond.

A little bell was going off in his head. They'd talked about this before. The weapons were what Sadir—and now, whoever had control of the starship—wanted from his vessel. Weapons to appropriate, to duplicate, just as they'd duplicated *Daedalus*'s technology ten years ago. A massive undertaking that had required the construction of a huge, highly specialized facility.

He smiled.

"What is it?" Brodesser asked.

"*Enterprise*," Trip said. "I think I know where she is."

Seven

TRIP WENT straight to the decoding station that had been his home for the last week. It was unoccupied, its link to the main power conduit severed.

He hooked it back up.

"What are you doing?" Kairn asked, coming back to stand over his shoulder.

"You'll see in a minute. Fane?" Trip called out. "You still have the intercepts on-line?"

"We do."

"Can you send them to this station?"

"Done."

"Thanks." Trip sat down then, flexed his fingers, and keyed in his query. Kairn read the words out loud as he typed.

"Kota Base?"

Trip nodded, his eyes focused on the screen.

Kota was located in a neighboring star system of the same name. It was the place where, fifteen years ago, Sadir had taken *Daedalus* after capturing it. Where he'd ripped that ship apart, and with the aid of its captain, Monique Duvall, replicated its weapons and warp technology. It made only sense to send *Enterprise* there now, for exactly the same reasons.

He explained his reasoning to Kairn as the computer ran his query. Just as he finished, the display screen flashed.

SEARCH COMPLETED

The screen went to black for a split second, and then began filling with a list of results: the first few lines of each message that had mentioned Kota.

"Most of these are from cargo transports on their way to the base. Most of them in the last week," Kairn said, reading off the screen. "They're bringing in supplies—a lot of them."

"Which could mean they're building something," Trip said. "Weapons."

"Could be."

All at once, Trip sensed someone leaning over his other shoulder. The professor.

"It's not just equipment they're bringing in," Brodesser said. "Look."

Brodesser pointed to a message toward the bottom of the screen. Trip read the first few lines and blinked.

"What is it?" Kairn asked, leaning closer so he could see.

"Vox Four," Trip replied, and brought the full text of the message up on-screen.

**ISHENQ COMMANDER DEF CRUISER
JAQUANDRA
TO KOTA BASE SECURITY**

SPECIAL TRANSPORT
VOX 4 PICK-UP
SECURE DOCKING BERTH REQUIRED
SECURE QUARTERS REQUIRED

Vox 4 was the prison they'd rescued Brodesser from. The prison where they'd expected to find the remainder of *Daedalus*'s crew, but instead had come upon only empty cells.

Now, Trip suspected, *I know why.*

"Vox Four pick-up complete?" Kairn said. "You think they brought them back to Kota? The *Daedalus* crew?"

He nodded. "Look at the dates. Right before we tried to break them out . . ."

"They were ferried aboard *Jaquandra*. To fly your ship?"

"I think so," Trip said. And not just to fly it, of course. To run every critical system aboard the vessel. He should have seen it before. Who better to work a Starfleet vessel than a Starfleet crew? Especially a crew that you'd already beaten the resistance out of.

"DEF," Kairn said. "That's Makandros. He's got *Enterprise.*"

"Not necessarily." Royce spoke for the first time, making his presence known. "Special transport— that could be any of the generals, requesting those prisoners."

"But whoever has them—my shipmates—they're all at Kota," Brodesser said quietly.

"Without a doubt," Trip said.

Brodesser turned to face him.

"You have to take me with you."

Trip shook his head.

"Can't do it, sir," he said. "This is a combat mission. You're not trained."

"Those are my people, Trip," Brodesser replied. "I have an obligation to rescue them—the same way you have an obligation to rescue your crew."

"I understand you feel that way, and believe me, I'll do everything in my power—"

"Tell me you couldn't use an extra hand piloting the ship," Brodesser went on. "Tell me that if you go into a combat situation, Hoshi could do a better job on sensors—on your cloak—than I could."

His gaze bore into Trip's.

"I know those systems now, Trip. Almost as well as you, I warrant. I know Kota too, in case you've forgotten. I can help you."

Trip sighed. The man was right, in everything he was saying. And yet . . .

"I don't know. Three in that cell-ship—it's going to be kind of tight, sir."

Brodesser managed a smile.

"You forget where I spent the last seven years, Trip. The cell-ship is actually somewhat . . . palatial, by comparison."

"Palatial."

Brodesser nodded.

"Besides, it'll give me a chance to see the ship's ion drive in action."

He smiled then, as Trip's mouth dropped open in surprise.

"Or did you think I'd missed that as well?"

Trip's silence was the only answer the man needed.

"I'll collect a few things," Brodesser said, clapping him on the shoulder. "Give me twenty minutes."

The professor was as good as his word. His gear—and sufficient supplies to last him for a week—was stacked in a pile next to the cell-ship less than half an hour later. In another pile were three EVA suits Kairn had pressed on them, suits Trip had gratefully accepted after learning that the main weapons fabrication facility at Kota was located on an orbital platform above the base itself.

All the above items, however, weren't going anywhere just yet. Certainly not aboard the cell-ship—not until they were checked over thoroughly, not until it was certain that they contained no trace of the proteins that Hoshi and he were so allergic to. A check that only Doctor Trant—with the scanner Trip had given her from one of *Enterprise*'s medkits—could perform.

Trip and the professor had been standing next to the new gear, making small talk, for perhaps five minutes when the door to the launch bay opened and the doctor stepped through.

A second later, Ferik followed.

As always, seeing Neesa's husband—especially in her presence—made Trip uncomfortable. He managed a smile, which Ferik returned. Then Trip turned to the doctor.

She, however, was all business.

"Commander. Professor." Trant took out her scanner and motioned Brodesser to stand apart from Trip. "This will only take a minute."

She calibrated the scanner and studied its readout, stepping around Brodesser slowly and carefully.

Ferik clamped a hand on Trip's shoulder.

"You didn't come to say good-bye," he said. "I wanted to say good-bye."

"Sorry." Trip managed a smile. "It's been hectic."

"You come back here, Tucker?"

"No." Trip shook his head. "I don't think so."

Neesa's back was to him, but he thought he saw her flinch ever so slightly.

"Okay." Ferik stepped between him and the doctor, and held out his hand. "Good-bye, Tucker. Yes?"

"Yes," Trip said, taking the man's hand and shaking it. "Good-bye, Ferik."

The man nodded and let go. He stood there a moment, a blank expression on his face, temporarily at a loss.

"Say good-bye to Hoshi, Ferik," Trant said without looking up from her scanner.

"Hoshi." Ferik nodded, and turned to face the cellship. He waved to Hoshi through the viewscreen. She waved back.

"You're all clear, Professor," Neesa said, looking up from her scanner. "You can board."

"Thank you." Brodesser nodded to her and then Ferik. "Good-bye. Trip, I'll see you aboard."

"Just as soon as we get these other things checked out."

"Won't take a minute," Trant said, and began to scan the new gear. She pushed one of the EVA suits to the side, and then spoke again.

"Ferik," she said quietly. "I wonder if you could go down to the ward now, just in case anyone shows up."

"Be on duty?"

"Yes. Be on duty."

"Okay." He nodded, then turned back to Trip again. "Good-bye again, Tucker."

Trip said good-bye again as well, and watched the man leave through the door he'd entered.

And then he and Neesa were all alone, standing in the shadow of the cell-ship, the command center behind them blocked from view.

"This is all clear," she said, stepping back from the gear.

"Thanks," Trip said, taking a step forward. "Neesa—"

"And I have something else for you," she said hurriedly, reaching into her pocket and pulling out a metal box the size and shape of a communicator. After a few seconds of fiddling with it, Trip found the release and opened the lid.

There were pills inside—big pills, looked almost like horse tranquilizers. A couple dozen in all.

He looked up questioningly.

"Pain-killers. I made them up this morning for you and Hoshi. Derived from the same compounds as the *pisarko*, so you shouldn't have any reactions."

"Thanks."

"They're strong, Trip. One a day—only."

"I understand."

"I was going to send Ferik up with them, but then Kairn called and said Brodesser was going with you, and all his gear needed to be checked out, so—"

"Neesa."

He moved forward, as if to kiss her.

"Don't." She blinked away tears. "This is why I didn't want to come. I didn't want to go through this all over again."

"I understand. Last night was good-bye."

"Yes," she said. "Last night was good-bye."

Trip cleared his throat, intending to say something poetic. He'd thought about it for the last half hour, ever since realizing that he would see her one more time—something about there being another Trip out there in this universe, another *Enterprise*, and that maybe one day, that ship would come to Denari, and she and that Trip would meet, and . . .

The words wouldn't come, though. They suddenly seemed infinitely false to him—false comfort, false dreams, false hopes.

They were never going to see each other again. That was the hard truth.

"Good-bye, Trip." She touched a finger to her lips, and then his.

Before he could respond, she turned and walked away.

Trip watched her go.

Then he loaded up the cell-ship, climbed inside, and sealed the hatch.

Brodesser, he saw, had taken the station directly behind his and was even now hard at work analyzing the ship's code.

By the time we reach Kota, he'll know the systems better than I do. The thought made Trip smile.

But for some reason, his eyes were moist.

"Sir?" Hoshi asked. "Everything all right?"

"Not yet," Trip said, turning away from her. "But it will be—once we find *Enterprise.*"

The bay doors opened then, and they were away.

Eight

SOMEONE LAUGHED.

Archer, who'd been pacing back and forth in the cell from the moment they'd been put in it—a good hour ago, at a guess—frowned. He turned to seek out the guilty party.

His gaze swept along the back wall of the cell and came to rest on Rodriguez. The young man was sitting on the floor, shaking his head, a trace of a smile still on his face. Yamani, sitting next to him, was smiling too.

Archer walked over to them. Their conversation died out.

"You find something funny about our current situation, gentlemen?" the captain asked.

Both men suddenly straightened.

"No, sir. Sorry, sir." Rodriguez wiped the grin off his face. Yamani did the same.

"Then what were you smiling about?" Archer sounded Queeg-ish to his own ears, and tried to damp it down. But he was frustrated, and he was angry. To have spent two weeks planning an escape from one prison, only to be trapped in another . . .

"My fault, captain," Yamani put in.

"Go on."

Yamani looked at Rodriguez. "I said, any minute we'd be drawing straws. To see who got to play Dwight's part."

Archer shook his head then, and managed a small smile himself.

"You've got the part, Crewman," he said to Yamani. "I'll let you know when you go on."

"Thanks, Captain," Yamani answered.

Archer resumed his pacing.

Eighteen strides before he had to turn around and head in the other direction—which made the cell roughly twenty meters wide. He figured it for half again as deep. "Cell" was maybe the wrong word, though, since the back wall was the only permanent thing about it. The other three sides were composed of a force field, a sheet of floor-to-ceiling pale yellow light that gave a nasty shock when touched.

Holding pen, Archer thought. A temporary one, probably, yet for all that it was less solid than Rava, it felt far more escape-proof. That feeling came from this ship's crew—no Tomons or Gastornises here. The men and women who had held weapons on them as they'd marched off the Stinger had been completely silent—and utterly professional. A dozen soldiers, none of whom had spoken a word or let their concentration lapse for even a nanosecond.

They'd simply marched Archer and his crew into the cell one at a time, stripping them of weapons, communicators, and anything that might be used to fashion an escape.

And despite Archer's protests, they'd stripped him of the UT module as well—which he found the most disturbing thing of all.

"Not a good sign," he told T'Pol once they were all inside the cell. "That they don't intend to talk to us."

"Perhaps they simply intend to return us to Rava."

Archer nodded. Covay had suggested that would be the case.

On the other hand . . .

There was another, far more sinister implication to what had occurred.

"Captain." T'Pol must have caught the look on his face. "If you're suggesting that they intend to kill us out of hand, I must point out that they have had ample opportunity to do so at any point since we lost control of the ship."

"They didn't want to damage their vessel before."

"They wouldn't have needed to. They could have opened all the airlocks."

"They could have . . ." Archer shook his head. He hadn't thought of that.

"So they want us alive."

"Perhaps."

"But they don't plan on talking to us."

"So it would seem."

"So what do you think they intend to do?"

"Without further information, I have no way of knowing."

Archer frowned.

And at that point, he'd started pacing. Thinking about a way out of this. But what? Another escape didn't seem likely—not for a long, long time. After Rava, the Denari were going to be very focused on Archer and his crew. He doubted there would be many opportunities for them to gather en masse, unsupervised. There was always a way out of any prison, of course, given enough time, but Archer wasn't sure how much time they had.

Rodriguez and Yamani might have been kidding about who got to play Dwight's part, but the truth of the matter was they were all going to end up looking like the young ensign in a little while.

Again, the captain wondered how his captors had done it—seized control of their ship. Those last few minutes before the voice had come over the ship's intercom, ordering them out of the vessel, T'Pol had spent in fruitless study of the ship's underlying software protocols, ultimately coming to the conclusion that it was a part of the vessels' control system, not a jury-rigged thing.

Across the room, a door opened, and a man and a woman entered. More soldiers, though these two were older, instantly recognizable as officers, the man Archer's height, dark hair, dark skin, the woman a few centimeters taller, blond and fair.

"T'Pol," the captain said as they approached the force shield.

He turned to see his science officer already on her feet and walking toward him.

They stood together as the other two approached.

Archer got a better look at them now. The man was older than he'd first thought—crows feet in the corners of his eyes, his hair a uniform shade of jet black that suggested it had been dyed—and the woman younger. They were talking animatedly as they approached. Arguing, Archer guessed, though of course he couldn't understand a word they were saying, since they spoke in Denari.

The woman was in the middle of saying something when the man looked up at the captain, and their eyes met.

The man held up a hand, and the woman fell instantly silent.

"I think," Archer said out of the corner of his mouth, "this is General Makandros."

T'Pol nodded, and opened her mouth to speak.

The man beat her to it.

"Yes. I am General Makandros," he said. "And you are Captain Archer. And you, Sub-Commander T'Pol. Won't you come with us, please?"

Archer's eyes widened in surprise.

Not only did Makandros know who they were, but he'd just spoken in perfect, unaccented English.

How?

The question burned in Archer's mind as he and T'Pol followed the general and his aide out of the holding cell and into a corridor every bit as squeaky clean as the interior of the Stinger. That impressed the captain; whatever else was true about Makandros, he obviously ran a tight ship. A tight fleet.

But tight ship or not, how could he know their language? It had been only three weeks since *Enterprise* was attacked; even Hoshi would have had trouble picking up a completely new tongue in that span of time. No Earth vessel had been out this far before. Archer supposed it was barely possible that a human being had come this way aboard an alien ship, but even if that were true . . . unless the general was a fanatical student of language, why would he bother to learn English?

There were ways that the general could have known who T'Pol and Archer were. He could have gotten that information from Rava, for one thing. But the language . . .

That was a mystery only Makandros could provide the solution for. And right now, the general was talking not English, but Denari, having resumed his conversation with the woman almost the instant Archer and T'Pol had stepped out of the holding cell. Again, the captain had the sense it was an argument, and watching their body language now, he had the sense that whatever reasoning the woman was using, it was failing to convince Makandros of anything.

Still, the captain couldn't help but regard it as a good sign that Makandros was willing to listen to such vigorous debate.

Archer was going to have to do some vigorous debating of his own to not only convince the general to let them go, but help in the search for *Enterprise*.

The corridor curved, revealing a door on their left.

"Through here," Makandros said, again in perfect English, and opened the door. The woman walked through first, Archer and T'Pol a step behind. The general followed, shutting the door behind him.

They were in a conference room—a round metal table, half a dozen chairs, a viewscreen along the far wall. Two soldiers, ostentatiously armed, flanked that screen, indistinguishable from the two who had followed them down the corridor—who had no doubt assumed positions outside the conference room door.

Makandros sat. The woman did as well, on his immediate right. Archer and T'Pol took seats across the table from them.

The general leaned forward and spoke.

"Captain Archer. Sub-Commander T'Pol. Welcome aboard the *Hule*. I apologize for keeping you waiting, but Colonel Briatt"—he nodded to the woman next to him—"and I had urgent matters to discuss. I hope you'll forgive me—I don't normally treat flag officers in this fashion. Even if they have just stolen one of my ships."

Archer had intended to draw Makandros out in conversation gradually—to find out why the general had brought them here, what he intended to do with them, what, above all, he wanted. But the trace of a smile on the man's face irked him—and his complaint about stealing another man's ship only made it worse.

"That's funny," the captain said. "You being concerned about a stolen vessel. Since my ship is the one that was attacked and taken away in the first place."

"Yes, *Enterprise.*" Makandros nodded. "I was operating under long-standing orders when your ship appeared. I had no choice in the matter."

"Wait a minute." Archer looked at Makandros, long and hard, and felt the anger rising up inside him. "Are you saying you're the one who attacked my ship?"

Makandros nodded. "Yes. The DEF boarded your vessel at my command."

Archer saw red.

"We were crippled. We declared ourselves non-hostile, and yet you fired—"

"Please, Captain. As I said, I had no choice. Then. Things are different now. Allow me to explain."

The captain got control of himself.

"Before you do that, General, I must admit to being curious. How is it that you speak English?"

Makandros smiled. "Years of practice."

Archer frowned.

"I don't understand," he said.

"The other Starfleet vessel." Makandros looked from T'Pol to the captain, and his smile slowly faded. "You don't know about it?"

"No." The captain shook his head, even more puzzled than before. "Other Starfleet vessel? That can't be—we're the first ship out this far."

"*Daedalus,*" Makandros interrupted. "That was the name of the ship."

Archer blinked.

"*Daedalus?* No." He shook his head. "It can't be. *Daedalus* was . . ."

Destroyed, he'd been about to say. But what if . . .

He looked at T'Pol.

"*Daedalus.* Starfleet's attempt to build a cascading ion drive. Almost fifteen years ago."

"I am familiar with the project," T'Pol said.

"In our universe, it blew up. Here . . ."

"It may be," she said. "It seems a logical explanation."

"For a lot of things," the captain suddenly realized. The laser pistols that seemed remarkably similar to old Starfleet issue. The familiarity of the Stinger's control layout, and the Denari communicators.

"Our universe?" It was Makandros's turn to look puzzled. "What do you mean, our universe?"

Archer exhaled—a long, slow breath.

"General," he said. "We've got some explaining to do as well."

T'Pol did most of the talking; having gone through this particular explanation twice before, she had it down to a science. Archer glanced around the table as she talked, noting that Briatt and Makandros both seemed to be following her well enough. Though the colonel looked skeptical—she kept adjusting the UT module in her ear, which had been brought to her at T'Pol's suggestion, as if she didn't think it was working properly. Archer could understand why. Not an easy thing to swallow, the idea that he and T'Pol—and the rest of *Enterprise*—were from another reality altogether.

For his part, Archer was still having trouble digesting the news Makandros had given him about *Daedalus*. In particular, the part about Captain Duvall turning traitor.

He'd met her on several occasions, usually in the company of her younger sister, who was in the NX program with him. Monique was several years older, already a captain in Starfleet, who'd commanded several of the early warp-1 vessels. A deep-space veteran. She'd have to be a very different person in this continuum to have done the things Makandros had described. Possible, he supposed, but he had a hard time believing it.

Part of that, Archer had to acknowledge, was the fact that he'd been, quite frankly, infatuated with

Duvall. There had even been a time when he thought the two of them—

"This is the most ridiculous story I've ever heard in my life, General," Briatt said, interrupting his train of thought. "A parallel universe."

"You may be right, Colonel," Makandros said.

"Any of your staff will be able to duplicate my calculations, General," T'Pol said.

He smiled. "Of course. Although we have only your word about the value of this constant in your universe, is that not so?"

T'Pol nodded. "For the moment. The data is, of course, available in *Enterprise*'s computers."

Which brought them right around to where Archer wanted to be.

"Where is my ship now, General? What have you done with *Enterprise?*"

Makandros leaned back in his chair, and spread his hands in puzzlement. "I'm afraid I don't know the answer to that question."

Archer frowned. "But you said—"

"I helped capture your ship, that is true. But the last I heard, *Enterprise* had been taken to Denari for repairs. I've since learned those repairs were completed, and the ship was taken elsewhere. Where"— he shrugged again—"I cannot say."

"What about my crewmen—Tucker, Reed, Hoshi . . ." He ran down the list of everyone who was missing.

Makandros frowned and shook his head. "I don't know any of those names."

"Tucker was the engineer, General," Briatt said. "The one who—"

"Yes, that's right. Thank you, Colonel." Makandros nodded. "I remember now. One of our soldiers identified him. He escaped during the initial attack. Aboard a small craft that seemed to have the capability to . . . disappear."

Archer exchanged a glance with T'Pol. The Suliban cell-ship.

So Trip had gotten away. Odds were Hoshi had gone with him—though that didn't answer the question of where the two were now, or how the captain could go about finding them. Still—

"I'd be interested in hearing about that technology, Captain," Makandros continued. "How you go about making a ship invisible."

"It's alien technology, General. Not ours."

Makandros smiled. "Really?"

"Yes."

Briatt snorted. "More lies."

Archer shot her a glance. "Again, this information is all in our computers. Get us our ship back, we'll be happy to show it to you."

Makandros nodded. "We'll be interested in seeing that information. However, all this—your tales of parallel universes and alien technologies—is beside the point. There is a reason I have had you brought here, and not simply returned to Rava."

"I had wondered about that," Archer said.

Makandros nodded. "Things have changed, as I said before. Most importantly, General Sadir is dead."

"We know."

"You may not be entirely aware of the implications, however. Sadir came to power in a crucial period in our planet's history. We were weak—internal strife, political bickering, crisis after economic crisis. He made us strong. The council he installed in power—the council he ruled—enabled us to achieve great things."

Archer kept the frown he felt inside off his face. Those weaknesses Makandros described—they didn't sound like weaknesses to him at all. In fact, they sounded like the normal growing pains any representative government went through. Earth had certainly experienced enough of that kind of strife in its history before achieving a unity of purpose. That unity could be maintained only if it grew organically, in his opinion—not if it was imposed.

He didn't think now was the right time for a discussion of political theory, however.

"Unfortunately," Makandros continued, "Sadir's death has led some of those on the Council to attempt to seize control of its power for themselves."

Archer nodded. That too, sounded like a familiar story. When a dictator fell . . .

Chaos often followed.

"One of those men is General Elson, Sadir's chief of staff. A man who I once trusted. No longer."

Makandros nodded to Briatt, who touched a control pad embedded in the table's surface. The viewscreen on the far wall came to life.

The screen showed a scene of devastation unlike any Archer had ever seen.

A black swath of space littered with broken, charred ship hulls. Too many to count. Some of them looked familiar to the captain.

Stingers, he realized all at once. Makandros's ships.

"The vessels you see before you are all that remains of the DEF's First Battalion. Two days ago, on Elson's word, I ordered those ships to rendezvous with others under his command. The general swore he had intelligence that would lead us to the Council's sole remaining enemy, a group of miners who—"

"The Guild," Archer interrupted.

Makandros eyed him curiously. "Yes. The Guild. How do you know about them?"

The captain smiled. "Have you ever been in prison, General?"

"I can't say I have had the pleasure, no."

"Well, trust me. There's not a lot to do in prison except talk. That's where I learned about the Guild," Archer said. "I take it they weren't there, though— where Elson told you they would be."

"No. The entire exercise was a trap. Elson's own forces came out of the Belt and attacked my ships. Did this." He gestured to the screen. "I cannot conceive what lies he told his troops to get them to fire on us. And then"—Makandros's voice shook with rage, and he leaned forward across the table—"he had the effrontery to contact me and accuse the Guild of perpetrating this atrocity."

"He wants you to retaliate," Archer said.

"Which we would now be doing, had not one of my ships escaped the massacre and brought me word of who was truly responsible. He has to be stopped. I think you would agree with that, Captain."

Archer nodded. He realized they'd arrived at the reason why Makandros had brought them here— what the general wanted.

He also realized something else.

Sadir—and by extension, Elson—had seized control of Denari using Starfleet technology. His technology—and Archer couldn't help but feel responsible for that. Even though, logically, since he wasn't part of this universe . . .

No. Something told him he had to think with his heart, not his head now. Logic aside, he was Starfleet here and now. He had to help put this right.

But first . . .

"I agree with you, General," Archer said. "But I have the feeling you want more than my agreement."

"You're right." Makandros leaned forward. "I want you to carry a message for me, Captain."

"To . . ."

"There is a convoy of Guild warships nearby. What I would like you to do, Captain Archer, is carry a message to them for me. A proposal for a truce."

"Why don't you just communicate with them directly?"

"We have been attempting to, for some time now. With no response." Makandros shrugged. "They have ample reason to distrust us, I'm afraid. Almost fifteen years of war—numerous betrayals of ceasefires on both sides. There is no love lost here."

Archer shook his head. "I don't understand, then. Even if it comes through me, why are they any more likely to believe what you say?"

"Because I am going to give you something besides a message."

Next to him, Briatt exploded.

"General, I've held my tongue this long, but—"

"We've had this argument, Colonel. I've made my decision."

"Sir, this is a bad idea. None of them can be trusted."

"We'll find out, won't we?"

"Some of us will," Briatt snapped. "Others won't be around to enjoy that discovery, however."

"I'm well aware we're taking a risk, Colonel. Again, I don't see as we have any choice."

"Sir—"

"That's enough," Makandros said firmly.

Briatt sat back in her chair, frowning. She glared at Archer.

The captain got the feeling that if he and T'Pol hadn't been present, the colonel would still be arguing her point.

"Now," Makandros said, leaning forward. "What I propose to give you, Captain, is information. Critical strategic information regarding the disposition of the DEF within the Belt."

Archer nodded, impressed. Nothing like showing your underbelly to an opponent to convince him of your good intentions.

"We take the ship we came in on, I assume?"

"That's correct."

"And just fly right up to these warships, and—"

"Not any warship. You are to insist on delivering this information to Marshal Kairn, aboard the *Eclipse.*"

"And if they accept your truce . . ."

"We'll give you a secure com frequency to transmit their agreement. And then we—Kairn and I—will begin talking directly."

"Sounds straightforward enough." Archer frowned. "Unless, of course, this Kairn decides to blast us out of the sky."

"There is that danger," the general agreed. "Which is why it's imperative you approach with defensive systems down, and do not charge your weapons. Give them no reason to suspect you intend harm."

"Like a lamb to the slaughter."

Makandros frowned. "Excuse me?"

"Sorry. An Earth reference. All it means is, you're asking an awful lot of us."

"I realize that."

"You're taking a chance as well."

"Oh?" Makandros frowned. "How so?"

"How do you know that instead of delivering your information, we won't just fly off and . . ."

Go find Enterprise *ourselves,* Archer had been about to say.

Then he saw a smile tugging at the corners of the general's mouth. Why . . .

All at once, he got it.

"My people on Rava."

Makandros nodded. "They are safe. Don't worry."

"But you have control of the prison again."

"Of course."

"Of course." Archer couldn't keep the anger out of his voice. The general held all the cards here, and Archer didn't like it one bit.

"I'm sorry, Captain. But you may recall there were other prisoners among your people—they at least needed to be secured. And I'm told, by the way, there were no injuries incurred on either side during the operation."

Archer nodded. No heroics, he'd told O'Neill, and apparently she'd listened. That, at least, was good news.

"So you'll hold my crew hostage to make sure we deliver your message?"

"That is essentially correct."

"Sir."

Archer turned to T'Pol.

"With the crew back in custody, the general should be made aware of Doctor Phlox's theories, I believe."

Archer nodded. She was right, of course.

He filled Makandros in as quickly as he could.

"We'll send medical personnel to the prison then. At once." The general frowned, and looked from the captain to T'Pol. "Are you two suffering from this as well?"

"To some extent," Archer said, suddenly aware of how tired he was. He must have been running on adrenaline these past few hours—which he'd have to do just a while longer.

Because Makandros and he hadn't quite finished cementing their bargain yet.

"Supposing we do this for you, what then?"

"I help you find your ship."

"How about if you start looking now?" Archer said.

"We have been doing just that, for the last several days, in fact." At the captain's questioning look, Makandros continued. "*Enterprise* is a very powerful weapon, as I'm sure you're aware. It would be foolish of me not to try and locate it, especially since it may be used against me in battle."

"You're assuming someone hostile to you has it?"

"I am. In fact, I believe General Elson has control of your vessel."

"You know this for a fact?"

"No. It is only supposition on my part. But Elson controls the machinery of Sadir's government, the Kresh. It makes sense he would be controlling your ship's movements."

Archer saw where this was headed. Makandros wouldn't be able to look for *Enterprise* until Elson was defeated. He didn't like that either.

"No offense, General, but if I risk my neck for you, I'd like something a little more substantive in return. Something other than promises."

"What did you have in mind?"

"Ships." At Makandros's questioning look, the captain continued. "Stingers. Enough to carry my entire crew—so we can all search for *Enterprise*."

"We'll have to see," Makandros said. "As you can tell, we are at war. I cannot promise anything."

"You're asking a lot," Archer said.

"I realize that." The general sat back in his chair. "It's the best I can do for now. If you won't agree to help us on those terms, I'll find another way to get that message to the Guild."

The captain frowned. His gut was telling him that Makandros was on the level, but still . . . his head wanted a concrete show of the general's good faith before committing to any course of action.

"How about my missing crewmen? Will you begin a search for them now?"

Makandros nodded. "We can try."

"All of them besides Tucker and Hoshi were at Rava for a few days."

Makandros nodded. "There may be a record of where they were taken. We can look."

"Good."

"And your other crewmen were . . ."

Archer gave him the whole list.

"Anyone else?"

No, the captain was about to say.

And suddenly realized that in all the rush and excitement of today's events—today's discoveries—he'd forgotten that there was someone else missing. Someone else close to him who he had last seen aboard *Enterprise,* and hadn't heard a word about since.

"Yes, there was someone. Actually, not someone. My dog."

"Dog?" Makandros said the word as if he'd never heard it before. "What is that?"

"An animal—a companion. My companion." Archer described Porthos.

Briatt rolled her eyes. *"That* animal."

"Now, Colonel," Makandros said. "Just because you don't like—"

"Wait a minute," Archer said. "You know where he is?"

"Of course." Makandros turned to one of the guards and spoke in Denari. The guard nodded and left the room. "A very clever creature, your—dog, was it?"

"Dog. Yes."

"And its name is Porthos. A shame."

"Why?"

"I had gotten used to calling it something else."

"You had—"

The door opened, admitting the guard who'd just left the room . . .

And a small, brown creature who barked once and jumped into the captain's lap.

"Porthos!"

Archer broke into the first honest-to-goodness smile he'd worn in weeks.

"Hey, boy. Hey."

The captain scratched behind the dog's ears. Porthos wagged his tail and licked Archer's face. Normally, the captain didn't like that. Didn't let him do it without a stern warning.

Not now.

"He's happy to see you," Makandros said.

"Yes," Archer nodded, suddenly at a loss for words.

The dog barked once more, and then jumped out of Archer's lap and strode, head high, around the table to where Makandros sat, hand outstretched with something in it. A biscuit. Archer recognized it as being from the stash he kept aboard *Enterprise* for Porthos.

At least he's not going to get sick anytime soon, the captain reflected.

Porthos took the biscuit and started munching happily.

Makandros started scratching behind the dog's ears.

"He's happy to see you, too," Archer said.

"That's right."

The general looked up. The two men shared a smile.

"I've found," Makandros said, continuing to scratch, "your dog tends to be an excellent judge of character, Captain."

Archer nodded. "Funny. That's just what I was going to say."

Nine

"O'CONNELL?" Brodesser's voice was pitched soft and low, so as not to wake Hoshi. "No. O'Connell was in that first group of five."

"The first ones Sadir shot," Trip said. He shifted position in his seat, but didn't open his eyes. The burst of energy that had carried him through the day was gone. He was running on fumes now, resting while he could. If he hoped to make it through the next twenty-four hours, he'd need to husband every last bit of his strength.

"That's right." Brodesser's voice came from his left, where the professor sat, technically on watch—though there was little for him to do, with the cloak engaged and the autopilot on.

Behind Trip and to his right, Hoshi slept on, oblivious. Trip listened to her breathing a moment, and then nodded, satisfied. Whatever fumes she'd been running on had dissipated just after they'd emerged from the Belt, and she'd virtually collapsed in her seat, falling right asleep. Her breathing then had been shallow, and somewhat rapid. Trip had hoped it would even out on its own, which it seemed to have done. For the moment, at least. She was sleeping like a baby.

Despite his exhaustion, Trip hadn't been able to follow suit. For one thing, he was too keyed up. His intuition was right, he knew it—they were going to find *Enterprise* at Kota. That was one reason. There was also a nagging ache in his right leg—not the calf, where he'd been getting all the cramps, but in the upper thigh. Stiffness, he decided. He'd been unable to get comfortable. He debated taking one of Trant's painkillers but decided he would save them for when he was really hurting.

"Makin was killed then too," the professor continued. "Her, Dubrow, Ferrara . . ."

"So who's left?" he asked. "If we're right about all this—if the *Daedalus* crew is aboard *Enterprise*— who's running engineering? Who's piloting the ship?"

"Piloting? Westerberg. Engineering—there's Fitzgerald. Al-Bashir. Yee." Brodesser paused a moment, then ran off a half-dozen more names.

All at once, Trip realized there was one very prominent one missing from his list.

"What about Cooney?"

"Cooney. I don't know." He could almost hear the frown in the professor's voice. "He worked at Kota for a while, then they moved him. An incident with one of the guards." Brodesser paused. "He was not the most . . . tractable of workers."

Trip had no trouble imagining that. This universe's Cooney, from what the professor had told him already, had a lot in common with the engineer he remembered from his own. A man who marched to his own drummer, and anyone who got in the way had best step aside or get hurt.

If Cooney was on board *Enterprise* . . . well, Trip couldn't help but think that would be a good thing.

He and the professor had been talking over what they planned to do at Kota for the past half hour. Now, Trip tried to picture the base in his mind as Brodesser had described it to him.

Kota had started as a small research facility—the Denari people's first tentative steps into the galaxy beyond their solar system, two years before *Daedalus*'s arrival—built on a small, lifeless moon, which circled a gas giant the size of Saturn. When Sadir had captured the Starfleet vessel and her technology, he'd turned the research station into a factory, where he churned out the weapons and ships that enabled him to seize power.

Over the years, Kota had grown even bigger, grown to encompass mining facilities, living quarters, and weapons research labs. Above the base, in geostationary orbit, Sadir had built a mammoth orbital platform, constructed in the shape of a cross, with massive hangars—ship-building facilities, each one big enough to hold a half-dozen *Enterprises*— dangling from each arm.

Trip's gut told him they'd find *Enterprise* inside one of those hangars, but whether they found it there or in orbit, their strategy was basically the same: bring the cloaked cell-ship alongside a hangar, use the EVA suits Kairn had given them to board through a side airlock. Go right for the engineering deck.

That was where the *Daedalus* crew was supposed to come in. And yet . . .

Despite the professor's reassuring words ("They've been prisoners for fifteen years, Trip—they'll jump at the chance to escape"), Trip frankly was worried about how those people would react. So much time spent cowering in a cell . . . it tended to beat the fight out of you. What if they refused to help? Even worse, what if they turned him and Brodesser over to the Denari?

Trip was working out a plan B in his head to cover that eventuality when the console beeped.

"Dropping out of warp," Brodesser said. "Coming up on Kota Base."

Trip opened his eyes. He'd dimmed ship's lights to let Hoshi sleep. Now he leaned forward over his console to bring them back up.

Then Brodesser's console beeped again, several times in succession.

Trip turned to the professor, who was frowning.

"What is it?" he asked.

"I'm not sure I'm reading this right," Brodesser replied. "Could you—"

A brilliant white light flared in front of them.

The cell-ship shuddered, and dropped like a stone.

Trip's stomach heaved. He barely managed to stay in his seat. He heard a thump behind him and realized Hoshi hadn't.

"Commander!" she yelled. "What—?"

Trip hit the cabin lights.

"Some kind of pulse weapon hit directly above us," Brodesser said, reading his console. "No structural damage. Some disruption of higher-level computer functions—"

"I can see that," Trip said. "The autopilot's out."

"Warp drive as well," Brodesser said.

Trip switched over to manual control and tried to steady the ship.

"Professor, tell me who's out there. Who's shooting at us?"

"No one is shooting at us, Trip. I remind you we're cloaked. We appear to have wandered into the middle of someone else's fight. I count two dozen small ships—a few larger ones—all coming under attack from emplacements on the moon's surface and the orbital platform—"

Light exploded near them again. Again, the cellship shook.

"I suggest we wander back out again," Brodesser finished.

"That's what I'm tryin' to do," Trip said. He was having a hell of a time getting control of the ship, though. They were wobbling like a wounded duck.

They stabilized.

"Is *Enterprise* out there?" Hoshi asked.

"Not picking it up, no." The professor frowned. "Hmmm."

"What is it?" Trip prompted.

Brodesser shook his head. "That blast that almost hit us—it must have been a wildly errant shot. I can trace the energy signature for it back to the orbital platform, but the ships who might have been its target . . . there are none near us."

"Bad aim, I guess," Trip said, as he started to plot a course around the main battle. "See if you can pick up any com chatter out there, Hoshi. Find out what this is about."

"I can tell you what it's about," Brodesser said.

"The war. They're fighting for control of the weapons facilities here."

"Maybe over *Enterprise*, too," Trip added.

Brodesser nodded. "Yes. That would make sense."

It would also make their task much more difficult, Trip realized. The ship, if it wasn't involved in active fighting, was going to be heavily guarded.

From the look on Brodesser's face, he realized the same thing.

"We might need a new plan," the professor said.

Trip nodded. The cell-ship shuddered under his control again—stopped almost dead, then started forward once more.

"Commander?" Hoshi asked from behind him. "What was that?"

"Not sure."

"Let me check," Brodesser said.

Out of the corner of his eye, Trip saw the professor's hands flying across the Suliban-built console.

"I think I've found our problem," he said a few seconds later. "The cloak."

"What about the cloak?"

"It's failing."

"What?"

Trip brought up a diagnostic screen on his own console, and saw immediately the professor was right. The cloak was damaged; the field projector itself was down to ten percent of nominal output. It must have been hit during that first blast.

"It's stealing power from other ship's systems to maintain function," Brodesser continued. "That's why the engines are failing—"

The lights flickered.

"—and so on," the professor finished.

The console beeped.

"Two of the smaller ships have just spotted us, and locked on weapons," Brodesser said.

"And we're being hailed," Hoshi said. "Don't think they know for certain we're here, but . . ."

Trip tried to punch the cloak back in again. The display indicator flickered, then held.

Weapons exploded on either side of them.

Trip's console beeped.

He looked down and saw that the oxygen content of the ship's atmosphere was dropping. The cloak was stealing power from life support, too.

"How far off is that orbital platform?"

Brodesser shook his head. "At the rate we're losing power now, we won't make it."

"Commander?" Hoshi asked. "What should we do?"

Trip looked down at the console.

Out the viewscreen at the ships tracking them.

Back at the console.

"I'm thinking," he said.

Ten

T'POL CONFIRMED what the Stinger's computer was telling them now. What Makandros had told them earlier. The Guild ships were hiding in the middle of one of the densest portions of the asteroid belt—scattered among rocks containing large concentrations of the heavier minerals. Enemy vessels picking up their readings would be inclined to dismiss them as sensor ghosts—echoes of the rocks around them. Anyone not knowing what to look for, that is.

Archer had a complete set of readings at his disposal to match sensor data against—spectrograms and other telemetry from previous Guild/DEF encounters. Makandros had also given them a list of the Guild fleet's most likely hiding places this morning, right before the Stinger launched.

They'd struck gold the first time, to use mining terminology.

The Stinger had approached the hidden fleet at half impulse for the last hour, transmitting messages of friendship and truce. There was no response yet, but—

"I can isolate sensor signatures now, sir," T'Pol said.

"Go ahead."

"On the viewscreen." She punched a button on her console, and the screen in front of them filled with a map of the Belt. She punched another control, and the image zoomed in. Individual asteroids came into focus—a concentrated field of them, white dots on the black screen.

"Our position is at the zero axis," T'Pol said. Archer noted the grid lines superimposed over the image, and nodded. That put them just shy of a grouping of a dozen or so of the white dots. Half of those were blinking.

"The flashing markers indicate ship locations. We are most interested in this one here, the one now blinking red."

She touched another button on her console, and the dot furthest to Archer's left—the largest of them, the captain noted—changed color.

"Telemetry from that location indicates it is most probably *Eclipse.*"

"Can we have a look at it?"

"Yes, sir. One minute."

It took closer to thirty seconds, if the captain was any judge of time, before T'Pol straightened again.

"On-screen now," she said.

The map of space disappeared, and the screen went to black for a second.

Then it came alive again, filled with the image of what was one of the oldest spaceships Archer had ever seen.

He couldn't help the snort of distaste that escaped his lips.

"My God. It's a bucket of bolts."

"Sir?"

"A piece of junk." Archer shook his head. "It looks like it could fall apart any second."

T'Pol frowned. "May I remind you, Captain, this is a computer-generated image, based on the telemetry we are receiving. It is not a hundred percent accurate depiction of the Guild ship."

"It's close enough, though. Unbelievable." Why on Earth would Makandros want to join forces with the crew of this ship?

From what he'd seen of the general's forces, they were light-years ahead of the Guild in terms of technology. Admittedly, much of that advantage derived from the Starfleet technology they'd stolen, but what they'd done with it . . .

The little trick that had allowed them to seize control of the Stinger while Archer was at its helm was a perfect example. A trick that Makandros had finally explained last night to the captain, after Archer had seen all of his crew settled into more comfortable, but still guarded, quarters.

"That," Makandros had said, smiling. He and Archer were walking through the one corridor of the ship the captain had seen. Porthos, wagging his tail, followed behind. Without being obvious about it, the general was keeping the vast majority of his ship and crew hidden, and thus limiting Archer's knowledge about both. The captain had noticed. He thought he knew why as well: if his mission to the

Guild failed, Makandros wanted to limit the damage Archer could do.

It didn't make Archer feel any better, but no doubt he would have done the same in the general's position.

"Yes, that," the captain replied. "How did you do it?"

"The initial idea came from Kota—it's one of our weapons facilities, not a person," Makandros said, at Archer's questioning look. "I can't claim credit for it."

"But—"

"But . . ." Makandros smiled. "Kota suggested we implement software revisions to allow the computer on one ship to control another. Should harm come to its occupants, we could at least salvage the vessel. From there, it seemed to me a short step to linking an entire attack group together, to one central computer. Coordinate ship movement at a level of precision no man could hope to achieve."

"I see."

"That's how we took control of your Stinger. Simple, really." Makandros shrugged. "We've never actually used the system to its fullest capabilities. Though when we first picked up your ship—*Enterprise*—on our scanners, I thought we might need to. We even planned our approach with that eventuality in mind, though it proved unnecessary, as you know."

Archer smiled thinly. "I expect that if *Enterprise* hadn't been crippled, we might have been able to see how man matched up against machine."

"Well, I suppose we'll never know, will we?"

Makandros smiled as well.

* * *

"Captain?"

Archer snapped back to the here and now.

"Weapons are targeting us, sir." That was Yamani, from the weapons control station Briatt had configured for him in the cockpit. He was on Archer's left, while T'Pol's station was to the captain's right.

Archer looked at his sensor display. What he saw there gave him pause.

Eclipse might be a bucket of bolts, but according to the data coming in, she did have pulse weapons fully capable of blasting them halfway across the Belt.

"Are they responding to our hails yet?"

T'Pol shook her head. "No."

"Weapons locked, Captain."

"Transmit surrender," Archer said to T'Pol.

"Yes, sir." She listened a moment, then shook her head. "No response."

He sat back in his chair and shook his head.

"They're not just going to blow us out of the sky, are they?"

"The possibility exists. They are at war, Captain. With the persons whose ship we are in."

Archer knew the possibility existed, of course, but he'd assumed that approaching with shields down, weapons unarmed, would at least convince the Guild to listen to them.

"A second ship has locked weapons on us, sir. Recommend evasive action—now," Yamani said.

The captain shook his head. "No." Any action they took at this point other than remaining on course would give the Guild an excuse to fire.

"T'Pol."

"Sir?"

"Are you picking up any com traffic between the Guild ships?"

"One minute." She bent over the console, listening intently to the traffic coming in over her earpiece.

"I am picking up considerable activity on several frequencies," she said. "Some of it is between the Guild vessels, but I cannot be certain if the transmissions are simply relaying telemetry between vessels or if actual communication is taking place."

"You can determine the frequencies, though?"

"Yes."

"Let's cut in."

"Sir?"

"Broadcast a transmission over the frequencies they're using."

"Their computers may be programmed to ignore unauthorized transmissions as noise."

"Let's just try it, Sub-Commander."

"Very well." She worked for a moment, adjusting the controls at her station. "Ready, Captain."

Archer nodded.

"Attention, Guild ships. This is Captain Jonathan Archer of *Enterprise*, flying under a flag of truce on behalf of General Makandros. Please respond on this channel. Over."

They waited.

"T'Pol?"

"No response."

"Let's try another one of those frequencies."

"Yes, sir." Again, she made adjustments at her station. "Go ahead."

Archer repeated his message, and waited.

"Still nothing."

"We're too close, Captain," Yamani said. "Sir, traveling at this speed, we will be unable to evade fire."

"Damn it." Archer frowned. One last try.

"T'Pol, give me back standard hailing frequencies. Let's try and target one of the smaller ships with our message."

"Not *Eclipse*?"

"Not *Eclipse*. The smaller vessels are less likely to have command staff on board and may—"

The screen came to life.

A man—his upright, military bearing instantly reminding the captain of Makandros—was staring at them, a look somewhere between confusion and anger on his face.

"You're Archer? Of the *Enterprise*?"

"That's right."

"A moment, please."

The screen went dark again.

"Well, we seem to have made contact," Archer said, letting out a breath he hadn't even known he was holding.

"They've still got weapons locked on us, sir," Yamani said.

"That's all right." Archer slowed the Stinger's velocity so that they held the same position relative to the Guild fleet.

Just as he looked up from his station, the screen lit up.

The same man stared down at him, only now, a strikingly beautiful woman stood behind him at his shoulder. She looked at Archer and nodded.

"You're right, sir," she said. "Same uniform."

Same uniform? Archer frowned.

Before he could ask what the woman meant by that, the man spoke.

"Thank you, Doctor." He cleared his throat. "Captain Archer, I'm Marshal Kairn, commander of the Guild *Warship Eclipse*. And I must ask you what you mean by flying on behalf of the DEF."

"Exactly what I said. I'm here on behalf of General Makandros to propose terms of a truce." Archer frowned. "Now I have to ask you: What did you two mean, 'same uniform'?"

"Exactly what I said." Kairn smiled. "Same uniform as Trip and Hoshi."

Archer's heart leapt into his throat.

"Commander Tucker?" Archer couldn't keep the surprise out of his voice—or off his face. "Ensign Sato. You've seen them?"

Kairn nodded. "They've spent most of the last two weeks with us, Captain."

"Let me talk to them, please."

"I'm afraid they're gone," Kairn said.

"What? Where?" the captain asked. "Can you get a signal—"

"Save your questions, Captain," Kairn said. "Why don't you come aboard, and we'll talk."

Eleven

"SIR?" Hoshi prompted again.

Trip sat in the pilot's seat aboard the just barely cloaked cell-ship, hands poised over the controls, thinking. He had to decide what to do before they were blown to bits.

As if on cue, space in front of them flashed white again.

He couldn't help but whistle admiringly.

"That is one big gun."

"Not a very accurate one, though," Brodesser said. "That blast missed its target by a considerable distance as well."

Trip nodded. He was reading the same sensor console as Brodesser. Whoever was firing that weapon—a fixed gun emplacement on the orbital platform above Kota—needed a little more practice. Either that, or glasses.

Trip frowned. Something about the energy readings from that weapon suddenly looked very familiar. For the life of him, though, he couldn't place it.

"I've identified the DEF ships. Makandros's

forces," Brodesser said. "I recommend we make for their positions and surrender."

That seemed to be about their only option. They could not escape on impulse, and it would be suicide to stay where they were. Trip only wondered why the professor had suggested surrendering to Makandros, rather than the forces defending Kota, then realized that he had the answer to that himself.

A solar system away from here, the civil war was raging on the Denari homeworld as well. And there, Elson had dropped at least two nuclear warheads. On his own people.

Giving up to a man capable of doing that didn't seem like a good idea to Trip either.

On the other hand, he didn't like the idea of giving up at all.

"I've isolated their hailing frequencies," Hoshi put in. "All transmissions are scrambled, but I can get us through to them. Say the word."

That word being surrender.

That word, when said, would put their fate back into the hands of others.

Trip had had quite enough of that over the last few weeks.

"Nah," he said.

Brodesser turned to him, surprised. "Trip?"

"Sorry, sir," Trip said. "But Hoshi and I—we're just about out of time. I don't think we want to spend the next few days trying to explain ourselves all over again."

"But—"

"You really want to see the inside of a prison

again? Not me. And I've just been breaking people out. You've been on the other side of those bars."

Brodesser hesitated. "What do you propose we do instead?"

Trip frowned. That was the question, wasn't it? The display showed him the cloak had about thirty seconds worth of life left in it, and then they would be visible for one and all to see.

Shortly after that, if they didn't surrender, they would be space dust.

What to do? Kamikaze run? No point in that. He'd just ruled out surrender—the cell-ship's weapons wouldn't do much for them, and there was nothing else aboard the little ship that—

Trip's eyes fell on the storage compartments above them, and he smiled.

"I have an idea about that."

"Shutting down sensors," Brodesser said.

"Roger," Trip replied.

"Disabling the UT module," Hoshi said.

"Copy that as well." Trip looked down at his console. Those were the last systems to go; they had already cut power to everything except the cloak and the maneuvering thrusters. Shields, weapons, communications—all were off-line to enable them to keep the cloak functioning, to stay hidden, for as long as possible.

Check that. The last systems to go save one.

Trip took a deep breath.

"Disabling life support," he said, reaching for the console.

At the last second, before punching the buttons

that would shut off the flow of oxygen to the cabin, he turned to Brodesser.

"All set?"

The professor nodded.

Trip turned around to Hoshi. She too, nodded her readiness.

He punched the button.

A light began blinking red on the console. Trip watched the diagnostic for a moment longer, as the status indicators for the ship's circulation systems fell below the nominal line . . .

And kept falling.

He opened the com circuit on his EVA suit.

"Everyone all right?"

"Fine."

"Yes, sir. So far, so good."

"Glad to hear it." They were all in the Denari EVA suits now. They had only a half hour's worth of oxygen, but that half hour should be more than enough to get them inside one of the orbital platform's hangars—specifically, the one farthest from the main battle theater, which sensors had shown them was empty—and from there, into a contained atmosphere.

Assuming, that is, the cloak could hold out that long.

Trip activated thrusters and set his sights on the platform. He was flying without instruments, by what he saw in front of him. The fighting was more sporadic now. Makandros's ships seemed to have regrouped just out of range of the platform's weapons, though every few minutes one of them would buzz in close and draw fire.

Good. The lull enabled him to take them straight

into the platform, rather than having to curve around weapons fire that might accidentally disable them.

It also gave him an opportunity to study the massive platform up close—which was easily the size of the Warp Five complex, and then some. Not that much of a surprise, considering how many ships Trip knew of that had come out of this facility. Though it had obviously seen better days: the platform arm closest to them was pitted and scarred all across its surface. Repair crews in EVA suits of their own scurried in and out of an area near a large gun emplacement that was particularly badly marked. The gun emplacement, Trip realized, where all that errant fire had come from.

As they banked toward the hangar, he got a head-on look at the weapon, and blinked.

"Hoshi."

"Yes, sir, I see it too." She was leaning over his shoulder, peering through the forward glass.

"Tell me that's not a phase cannon," Trip said.

"That's what it looks like to me."

Trip smiled. He supposed the Denari's inability to shoot straight with the weapon could be forgiven. After all, they couldn't have had it for more than a week or so.

"*Enterprise*," Hoshi said, unable to keep the excitement out of her voice. "She's here."

"Could be. Let's not get our hopes up," Trip said. They hadn't picked the ship up on any of their scans, after all—though who was to say this was the only part of the Kota system where fighting was taking place? *Enterprise* could be in the middle of a battle on the other side of the moon, or the gas giant, and they would have no way of knowing. And as far as the phase cannon was concerned, yes, the most likely scenario was that the ship had been here and the cannon constructed by copying the one on board *Enterprise*. Trip realized with a start that cannibalized parts from *Enterprise*, along with sufficiently gifted engineers—*Daedalus's* engineers, for example—could have built it from scratch, using plans. Another possibility was that *Enterprise* had been here and gone. No way of telling for certain right now.

The cell-ship passed into the vast, empty hangar. Trip maneuvered it close to one of the hangar walls and used mooring clamps to secure it in place.

He powered down the thrusters. Then he shut down the cloak.

They waited in silence.

"Nothing unusual. No increase in message traffic," Hoshi announced a minute later, listening to the reactivated com. "They don't know we're here."

"Good." Trip nodded. "Then I'll get going."

He reached for the airlock hatch.

"Trip." Brodesser's voice stopped him. "You're sure about this? Why don't we see if Hoshi can—"

"Professor, with all due respect," Trip said, "we've talked this through. You work on the ship. Let me see what I can find out from their computers." He nodded out the forward window port, in the direction of the orbital platform. "I won't take any risks, believe me."

"Please don't. Remember, you lack a cloaking device of your own."

Trip smiled. "Yes, sir. I know. Maybe you could build me one."

Through the EVA helmet, Brodesser returned his grin. "After I fix this, I'll see what I can come up with."

"Fair enough." He turned to Hoshi. "I'm taking one of the communicators. You hear anything that I ought to know, contact me."

"Aye, sir. Good luck."

"Thanks." He also fit one of their phase pistols to the suit—just in case. Then, having vented the ship's atmosphere earlier, he opened the hatch. With a final thumbs-up to both of them, he pushed himself free of the cell-ship.

Trip hadn't been EVA in a long time in a suit other than the high-tech ones *Enterprise* carried. The Denari one lacked the kind of precise controls those had. His gentle push out of the hatch took him thirty meters straight toward the open end of the hangar before he could get turned back around, headed toward one of the airlocks that dotted the vast interior walls.

On his way, he floated past the forward window port of the cell-ship, and waved.

Inside, he saw Brodesser and Hoshi shucking their EVA suits. They'd already repressurized the vessel and reactivated the systems they'd need in order to work. That made them vulnerable in there; it was kind of like turning on a night light in the middle of a vast empty room and hoping no one noticed. A stray sensor beam, a ship happening to drift by the hangar and peer in . . .

They were sitting ducks in there. It wasn't just Trip who had to hurry, it was all of them.

He pushed off then, headed toward the nearest airlock.

A minute later, he was through it and inside the hangar proper, in a high-ceilinged chamber the size of a small church. It was a staging area where the workers gathered before heading out into the hangars to their jobs. EVA suits, tools of all kinds, airsleds and other small utility vehicles lined the walls. There was nothing that looked like a com terminal or a data station anywhere in sight.

Trip shucked his own EVA suit and left it in the airlock he'd come through.

He passed through the chamber to a door at the far end and opened it.

A long corridor, gun-metal gray, dimly lit, stretched out before him. Off in the distance, it bent sharply to the left and disappeared. If memory served him correctly about the station's structure, it led toward the central platform.

He paused a moment and listened. Nothing.

He started down the corridor. At the bend, he paused again. Still nothing.

He frowned. Perhaps fifty meters ahead, the dim lighting suddenly brightened. That part of the station was clearly active—and he doubted that in the middle of an all-out attack like the one they were currently experiencing, it was deserted.

He took a step back the way he'd come and flipped open his communicator.

"Hoshi?"

"Right here."

"Anything on the com?"

"Nothing about *Enterprise*. But the professor was

right—the ships attacking are Makandros's. They're demanding that Kota surrender."

"And—"

"Kota's telling them to go to hell. How about you, sir? Any luck?"

"Nothing yet. I—"

A noise sounded behind him—machinery, starting up. Trip turned and saw a bulkhead lowering from the ceiling.

When it hit the floor, it was going to cut off his escape route.

Operating on instinct alone, he dove to the floor and rolled up underneath the bulkhead. He came up on his knees . . .

And saw a second bulkhead coming down ten meters ahead of him. This section of the corridor was being sealed off.

Instinct, again, told him he did not want to be inside it.

He rolled back underneath the bulkhead as it slammed down to the floor, making an airtight seal.

He was cut off from the cell-ship.

"Sir?" Hoshi said over the communicator. "You all right?"

"Fine." His eyes scanned the wall, looking for some sort of control panel, something that might let him raise the wall in front of him. Nothing. "Listen, I'll call you when I can. Out."

He flipped the communicator shut just as a red light above the bulkhead began flashing. The corridor lights came on full.

This was not good.

The bulkhead had a clear panel set in it at eye

level. Trip pressed his face up against it and peered through.

Inside the newly formed chamber, a hatch was swinging open.

Somebody—whether it was Makandros's forces, the troops defending the platform, or someone else entirely—was about to join him on this part of the base.

Trip suddenly realized that someone would not be at all welcoming. Not just because he'd sneaked aboard, but because—as he was all too aware of now, looking down at his clothes—he'd made a terrible mistake.

He was wearing a Guild uniform.

Either side was likely to see him and shoot first, probably with no questions for later.

A leg stepped through the hatch.

Trip turned around and ran.

The lights came up around him as he went, almost as if they were chasing him down the corridor. He glanced left and right, looking for a place to stop and hide, even an alcove of some sort that he could duck into. But there was nothing.

He came to a T and halted.

Off in the distance behind him, he heard voices. Footsteps as well—several people, from the sound of it, had entered the platform behind him and were following at a brisk pace. No, following was the wrong word. They didn't know he was here. Unfortunately, that didn't make a bit of difference. He had to run anyway.

Trip went left. Another T, and he went left again. And then again, a third time, making the way back as easy to remember as possible. The corridor took on a curve, as if he was looping out away from the central platform.

And then all at once, it ended. Trip came up short.

He was looking out on the stars.

His view was courtesy of a long, curving, clear panel that dominated the front of the room the hall emptied into. A crescent-shaped room twice the size of *Enterprise*'s bridge. There were dozens of computer consoles laid out in curving rows that matched the shape of the room. In the back, a glassed-in control booth, and at the front, three much larger stations, one of which was instantly familiar. It was a weapons control station, exactly like the one back in *Enterprise*'s armory—the one they used to operate their phase cannons.

This station, however, was nonfunctional, like the rest of the room, which was in a state of disarray. Conduit and optic cable lay loose everywhere.

Trip's heart sank just a little. He'd thought for a minute he'd stumbled across exactly what he'd been looking for—a computer station he could tie in to Kota's central system and use to find out about *Enterprise*. But as he walked through the room, every station was dark.

His eyes fell upon the glassed-in booth at the back of the room. In the darkness within it, a light glowed.

Trip walked to the booth and stepped inside.

He flipped open the communicator.

"Hoshi?"

"Right here."

"Put the professor on, will you? I might have something."

"Hold on."

"Trip?" Brodesser's voice came back. "You found one?"

"Yes, sir." He looked down at the computer. Trip's UT couldn't help him navigate this machine. He needed to use the Denari language itself, which he didn't know, but luckily, Brodesser did. "If you could guide me through this, maybe we can find what we're—"

He heard voices, then footsteps coming at a fast walk.

He barely had time to shut the communicator and duck down behind the station before the footsteps were in the room with him.

"—we'll find out if you've been telling us the truth, Lieutenant."

That was a woman's voice.

"He's lying, Major. He's been lying all along."

A man.

"We'll see," the woman—the major, Trip assumed—responded. "Down here."

More footsteps, and then a clatter of equipment. Something—someone—falling to the floor. A grunt, an exclamation of pain. From a third voice, Trip thought.

"Get up." The man again. "Before you make me angry."

A mutter in response. Definitely a third voice. Another man, but that was all Trip could tell from this far away.

Trip drew his phase pistol. Three against one. He didn't love those odds, but they were doable. Better than he'd expected, in some ways. And he had a hunch that this lieutenant—the third voice—

just might welcome Trip's intervention. So two against one.

"Remove the targeting mechanism, please." The woman again.

"It's not—"

Another thump—the sound of someone being struck. Trip cocked his head, tried to move closer.

That third voice—in the split-second it spoke clearly, it had suddenly sounded familiar.

"You heard her," the first man said. "Remove the targeting device."

There was a long silence. Then the sound of someone getting to his feet. More noise—equipment being moved. The targeting device being taken out, he assumed. Why?

"You see!" That was the man again. "There. The device is incorrectly calibrated, just as the others were."

"I do see," the woman said. "You've sabotaged our equipment, Lieutenant. Why?" Though her voice was calm, her tone even, Trip heard the menace in her words and shuddered involuntarily. This lieutenant was in a lot of trouble.

"You think we're idiots?" the woman asked. "Did you think we wouldn't realize something was wrong?"

"No. I knew you'd find out—sooner or later." The third voice came clear again. "The thing is, you're bloody thieves. Murderers as well. And I'm quite happy to have bollixed up your little plans."

Trip's eyes widened. That voice . . .

He risked a peek out from behind the console he was crouched under.

Three people stood near the main weapons console. Facing Trip, a short, thick woman, medium-length brown hair. The major, no doubt. Beside her, hand on a phase pistol, a much younger man, his features contorted with rage.

And between them, the lieutenant they'd both been yelling at. Who still held the phase cannon's targeting module in his hand. Who, even though he had his back to Trip, was instantly recognizable.

And who would most definitely welcome Trip's intervention.

Tucker stood and raised his weapon.

"Don't move," he said, his pistol targeted on the younger man.

He paid Trip no mind, and started to swing his weapon around to fire.

You are an idiot, Trip thought, and shot him.

The blast caught the man square in the chest. He flew backwards through the air, slammed into the glass panel, and slid to the floor, unconscious.

Trip turned back and saw the major reaching for her weapon. She was fast.

But the lieutenant was faster.

He drew back a fist and clocked her on the jaw.

Her eyes rolled back in her head and she too fell to the ground, out like a light.

Trip holstered his weapon and stepped forward.

"Thank you," the lieutenant said. "I was in a bit of a spot there."

"I could see." Trip smiled. The lieutenant didn't know who he was. Understandable, he supposed. The beard, the uniform, all the weight he'd lost . . .

"Still, hitting a woman. What would the captain say?"

The man frowned. "The captain?"

"Archer. You remember Captain Archer, don't you?"

The lieutenant stared at him a second longer . . .

And then Malcolm Reed's jaw dropped.

"Bloody hell." He blinked, shook his head, and smiled. "Trip."

Twelve

THE STINGER DREW up alongside *Eclipse* and docked. Leaving Yamani in charge, Archer and T'Pol proceeded to the airlock.

When it opened, the woman he'd seen on the viewscreen was standing in front of them.

"Captain, I'm Doctor Trant. Please, put these on." She handed Archer and T'Pol what looked like old-fashioned gas masks.

"These are for . . ."

"Your protection. I hate to be the bearer of bad news, but . . ."

She explained the reason for the masks: the discoveries she had made—stereoisomers, the basic protein incompatibility Trip and Hoshi had displayed—and Trip's own realization that *Enterprise* had traveled into a parallel universe.

Then it was Trant's turn to listen. Archer let his first officer do the talking, as the doctor led them through the corridors of the Guild vessel.

As they walked, Archer couldn't help but contrast what he was seeing now—*Eclipse*'s crowded, dirty, interior, with people living practically on top of one another—with the pristine shine of Makandros's ship, inside and out. If the condition of this vessel was anything to go by, the Guild was losing this war—had been losing it for some time now. Every face he passed looked worn and tired—on the edge of defeat.

Just ahead of them, a steel door connected to a two-meter-long tunnel of thick gray-black fabric stuck out into the corridor. The tunnel's other end, Archer saw, ran up against a door frame on the corridor's interior wall.

"Homemade decontamination chamber," Trant said, opening the steel door. "Hoshi's quarters the last week she was here. She was extremely sensitive to the proteins I was telling you about."

They followed her into the chamber. She shut the door behind them, and then squeezed past to the other end of the tunnel and opened the door there. They emerged into a room about half again as big as Archer's quarters aboard *Enterprise*.

As they entered, a man rose from a table set in the middle of the room. Marshal Kairn.

He and Archer shook hands.

"Captain. Thank you for coming aboard."

"Thank you for holding your fire," Archer replied, his voice distorted by the mask.

"You can remove those now," Trant said. "This room is sterile."

Archer and T'Pol both took off the masks.

"Marshal, this is Sub-Commander T'Pol, my science officer."

Kairn nodded. "Sub-Commander, Captain, you'll

forgive me if I skip the usual pleasantries and get right to the heart of the matter. You said you had a proposal of truce from General Makandros."

"I do. The general wishes to call off hostilities between you, to focus on the enemy you now have in common."

"And who might that be?"

"I believe he's referring to a General Elson."

"General Elson?" Kairn shook his head. "Does he take me for a fool? Captain," Kairn looked Archer square in the eye. "Commander Tucker told me more than once that you were an intelligent man. Makandros and Elson are members of the governing council. They share a history of broken promises and surprise attacks. It is beyond belief that—"

"Sir," Archer interrupted. "Forgive me. But the general thought you might suspect something like that. Which is why he gave me this." The captain held up a memory chip in his hand.

"What is that?"

"Current battle positions of the Expeditionary Force in the Belt."

Kairn did a double take. "What?"

"These are the current battle positions of his forces." He held out the chip to Kairn. "Go on—take it."

The marshal frowned. "Is he serious?"

Archer shrugged. "Why not see for yourself?"

Kairn's eyes went from Archer to the chip, then back again. He looked uncertain, as if he thought the module might explode if he touched it.

"Very well," he said finally, and removed it from Archer's grasp.

"Doctor Trant," Kairn said. "Will you give this chip to Lieutenant Royce and have him correlate the information on it with our own intelligence?"

"Of course." Trant took the chip and turned to go.

She was halfway to the door when Kairn frowned and raised his hand.

"Wait, please."

Trant stopped in her tracks.

Kairn leaned forward in his chair. "I should have asked this earlier. Captain, why are you here? Why are you acting as Makandros's ambassador?"

"It wasn't my idea, frankly." Archer explained the circumstances of their capture, and Makandros's promise to help them find *Enterprise*.

Kairn nodded thoughtfully when he'd finished.

"Which means you are nothing to him. A game piece to be sacrificed. Excuse me a moment." He crossed to a com panel on the wall.

Archer exchanged a quick glance with T'Pol.

He had the sense that nothing Makandros could do or say was going to convince Kairn of his good intentions. Must be quite a history between the two of them—maybe even something personal, he decided.

He wondered briefly if they were a pawn in some larger game here between the two men. The two sides. But the general had been so convincing . . .

"Kairn to Royce."

"Right here, sir."

"Doctor Trant is bringing you something. A memory chip that supposedly contains some very critical information."

"I understand."

"Royce, I want you to be very careful with this

chip. Have it tested—rigorously—before it interfaces with our systems."

"Yes, sir."

"It may contain a computer virus. It may be programmed to transmit a signal with our location on being scanned. It may be an explosive. Anything and everything you or the others can think of—check it. All ships stay on full alert for the time being as well. Understood?"

"Understood."

"Good. Trant will be along shortly. Out."

With a nod, he sent the doctor on her way.

Kairn sat back down at the table.

"I'd offer you something to eat or drink, but—"

"Doctor Trant explained it to us already. Thank you, though. Marshal, while we wait, you said Trip and Hoshi had been here."

"That's correct," Kairn said, and then went on to fill Archer in on what his two crew members had been doing for the last few weeks. Trying to find *Enterprise*. Trying to find the captain and their shipmates. Helping out the Guild, within certain limits. In short, doing pretty much what Archer himself would have done in their shoes.

After what happened with the cogenitor, and the Xyrillians, the captain would have thought Trip would be a little more . . . cautious about inserting himself into alien affairs. He could tell T'Pol was thinking the same thing, from the way she'd straightened in her chair when Kairn told them how Trip had piloted the Suliban cell-ship for their failed kidnap mission.

That was in the past, as far as Archer was concerned. He wouldn't concern himself with it.

"But they're gone now, you said? In search of *Enterprise?*"

"That's right. They left yesterday."

Archer sighed in frustration. To have missed them by less than twenty-four hours . . .

"Headed where?"

"The next star system over. Kota."

The com buzzed. "Marshal?"

"Royce. You have news for me?"

"It checks out, sir. We sent ships to verify several of the positions encoded in the chip. Makandros's ships are there."

"Thank you, Lieutenant." He closed the channel.

Archer leaned forward in his chair. "Seems like he was telling the truth, doesn't it?"

Kairn took a long time to respond. "I suppose," he said finally. "We'll have to find out. You said Makandros gave you a channel to transmit on?"

The captain nodded.

Kairn stood. "Well then. If you'll accompany me to the command deck, we'll see what the general has to say."

Archer and T'Pol flanked Kairn at his command chair.

Makandros's image filled the viewscreen.

"It's been a long time, Marshal. You're looking well."

Archer could tell by the way Kairn reacted to Makandros that he'd been right—the two men did know each other.

A fact that Kairn clearly didn't care to dwell on.

"General. Say what you have to say."

Makandros smiled. "Never one for the social niceties, were you, Kairn? All right. What I have to say is simple. I propose an alliance between our forces. An end to the war between us."

"After ten years of hounding our ships, killing our people, destroying our bases . . . I have to say I find your change of heart puzzling. Difficult to believe, in fact."

"You've seen the information I sent?"

"Yes."

"It checked out, I presume."

"It did. Which is the only reason I'm speaking with you."

"I have some more information for you, Marshal."

And then Makandros told Kairn about the trap Elson had set for him, the ships and the men he'd lost.

Kairn was silent for a moment after he'd finished.

"I see," the marshal finally said. "Your change of heart is not without cause, then."

"No. And I believe you have reason to distrust General Elson as well, Marshal. The rumors about Charest I've been hearing blame the Guild for those explosions. That strikes me as . . . uncharacteristic of your actions over the last decade, to say the least. As much as we have been at odds, you have never attacked civilian targets."

Archer frowned. Most of what Makandros had just said made little sense to him—the reference to recent actions, the war gone past. . . . The captain knew he was not going to catch up on fifteen years of history all at once. The general's words had an effect on Kairn, however.

For the first time since the conversation between the two men had started, the marshal was—be it ever so slightly—smiling.

"Much as it pains me to admit it, General, you're entirely correct. We had nothing to do with Charest. But I certainly never expected you to believe that."

"Times have changed," Makandros said.

"I can see that. So what, exactly, do you propose?"

"We meet. Face to face. I want Lind there, as well."

Kairn laughed out loud. "The Guildsman will shoot you on sight."

"Tell him if he still wants to, he can shoot me after the meeting."

"It might be easier to arrange if I knew what you were offering."

"Besides your lives, you mean?"

"We started this war for a reason," Kairn said. "To overthrow a dictator. To restore the presidium."

"Noble goals. Impossible goals, for the moment."

"Then we have nothing to talk about, General."

"I think we do," Makandros said. "Hear me out. I said those were impossible goals for the moment. You cannot deny that truth, Marshal. The Council—the military—will not accept a complete dismissal from power. They've grown too accustomed to it."

"You should know."

"I do. All the more reason why you should believe what I'm telling you. Democracy in a number of years, yes. Democracy now, no. They will never accept it."

"Why not let the Council decide that?"

Makandros shook his head. "I misspoke. What I should have said was, Elson will be able to convince

155

them not to accept democracy. They will fight for him. To the bitter end."

Kairn was silent a moment. "And your plan? Assuming we agree to a truce?"

"We join forces," Makandros said. "We back Sadir's son for leadership of the Council. He takes command in his father's name and, in turn, gives Lind a seat."

Kairn shook his head. "The Guildsman will never agree to this. Be a figurehead? No."

"Not a figurehead," Makandros said. "With Lind, myself, and the boy, we will be able to fashion a majority. Submit a plan for a gradual transition back to democracy."

"And Elson? What does he do during all this? Sit back and watch his power being snatched away?"

"He'll have no choice. Move against the general's son?" Makandros shook his head. "His own troops would turn against him."

"You have a lot of faith in Sadir's child."

"I know him," Makandros said. "He will listen to me."

Kairn nodded slowly. "Where is the boy now?"

"With his mother. Where that is, we don't know for certain. We know they are no longer in the Kresh. Our best guess is that they have taken refuge in one of the new satellite colonies."

"Between the Belt and Denari."

"Exactly."

"Elson's forces control that portion of space. You'll have to go through them to get at the boy. How do you propose to do that?"

Makandros smiled. "The general has made a common amateur's mistake. He has spread his forces too thin, on too many fronts. He has removed the Planetary Defense Battalion from their positions around Denari and sent them scurrying all around the system—to attack my forces, seek out your ships, secure the outer colonies. Only a minimal force remains on defensive duty. Within the past twenty-four hours, I have sent the bulk of my forces to attack the weapons facilities at Kota, which will further pressure him—"

"Kota?" Archer and Kairn spoke at the same time. They glanced at each other. The captain nodded for Kairn to continue.

"Two of Archer's crew members have gone there, in search of his vessel. We had recently intercepted intelligence stating that it was there."

Makandros shook his head. "I'm sorry to disappoint you, gentlemen, but *Enterprise* is not at Kota. I can tell you that for certain. I would have received news."

Archer's heart sank. Not only had Trip and Hoshi gone off on a wild-goose chase, but they were flying into the middle of an all-out war.

"That is unfortunate news," Kairn said. "We can only hope for their safe return here."

"Indeed," Makandros said. "But to return to the matter at hand, do we have an agreement, Marshal? Can we meet to discuss this further?"

"An agreement." Kairn nodded slowly. "Yes. At least the beginnings of one. I will contact the Guildsman, and we will talk further."

Makandros smiled. Kairn, albeit grudgingly, did the same.

Archer couldn't help but feel the tiniest bit of satisfaction at his own small role in bringing about the truce. But that satisfaction was tempered by the question now burning in his brain: If his ship wasn't at Kota, where was it?

Thirteen

THE DOOR to the mess slid open, and the two Denari soldiers threw him inside.

Travis—Ensign Travis Mayweather of Starfleet, helmsman aboard *Enterprise*, now a prisoner aboard his own ship—landed facedown on the deck, his hands somehow managing to splay out in time to avoid actually landing face-first.

He heard footsteps coming toward him.

His legs shuddered involuntarily, the movement courtesy of the electric shocks Colonel Peranda had been applying to him in the hope of forcing a confession. Since Travis had nothing to confess, though, this session—their second in as many days—was mostly a matter of Peranda applying the shock rod until Travis was unable to speak.

A shadow fell over him.

Travis managed to turn his head.

Chief Cooney stood over him, hands on hips.

"You all right, kid?"

"Been better," Travis said.

Cooney knelt down next to him and slowly

helped Travis onto his hands and knees. The ensign rested there a minute, trying to get himself under control.

"All right," he said finally.

The chief eased him up on his feet and held his arm while he got his balance.

The others—the rest of the humans who were helping run *Enterprise* for Peranda—had come forward as well: Hess and Ryan from his ship, Al-Bashir and Yee from *Daedalus*. Someone was missing, Travis realized. Right. Westerberg—he was piloting the ship. He was the only other qualified helmsman besides Travis aboard. They could use the autopilot for limited amounts of time, of course, but while they were on impulse—in normal space—Peranda needed a capable hand at the helm.

And since the warp engines had failed yesterday morning, impulse was the only method of propulsion available to them right now. "Failed" was the wrong word, actually.

The warp engines had been sabotaged—a neat bit of damage done to the intermix circuitry, which would take them days to fix. Peranda was convinced one of the humans was responsible, and he was determined to find the guilty party. So far, his torture sessions had failed to force a confession.

That only seemed to be making him madder. And his sessions more intense.

Hess stepped forward and took Travis's other arm. "Here. Let's sit you down."

She and Cooney guided him to a nearby table and pulled out a chair for him.

"You want something to eat?" the lieutenant asked.

Travis shook his head. "In a minute."

"That bastard," Cooney said, "Peranda. Don't know what he thinks this is going to get him, except a crew too sick to work."

"I'll be all right," Travis said, though he didn't know for sure that he could take many more sessions. But no matter, Travis couldn't confess to something he didn't do.

Though he did have a sneaking suspicion who the guilty party was.

A few days earlier, Lieutenant Reed had been brought on board. He'd been largely confined to the armory—the Denari, it seemed, were intent on building a phase cannon or two of their own. Reed had been plucked out of the prison where the captain and the rest of the crew were being held to help them do just that.

"I'll help build them their cannons, all right," he'd said to Travis, the first time the two of them were alone in the mess hall. "Not that they're ever going to get to use them."

Travis had frowned.

"Sir?"

"There's a war going on, Ensign," Reed had told him. "These people who attacked us, and someone else. I don't know who they're fighting, or why, and I don't care. All I know is, I'm not going to let them use our weapons to kill other people. The captain wouldn't want that."

"No, he wouldn't," Travis agreed. "But how can you stop them?"

Reed had smiled cagily. "I've got a few tricks up my sleeve, don't worry. But here's the question for you," he leaned in closer. "How can we stop them from using *Enterprise* to do the same?"

"Sir?"

"They're going to take our ship into battle, Ensign. We can't let them do that—no matter what."

"Are you suggesting we destroy *Enterprise?*"

Travis had spoken louder than he'd intended. Luckily, the only other people in the mess were Yee and Ryan, at a table in the far corner.

"Keep your voice down," Reed said. "No, that's not what I'm suggesting. But . . . there are other ways of incapacitating her."

He nodded. "Go on."

Reed had opened his mouth to speak—

At which point Cooney sat down at their table, and the lieutenant clammed up like a shell. Travis had no opportunity to talk to him in private after that, but he saw Reed one more time, just before the lieutenant left the ship. He'd come to the bridge to show something in the firing control circuits to a Denari officer, and on his way out, glanced over at the helm and at Travis. A satisfied glance. An everything-is-taken-care-of kind of glance.

Travis was now pretty certain it meant that the problem of sabotaging *Enterprise* had been taken care of.

The door to the mess opened, and Peranda strode in, four soldiers a step behind. He looked angrier than Travis had ever seen him.

The colonel put his hands on his hips and glared daggers around the room.

"I'm deciding," he said between gritted teeth, "which one of you to kill."

Cooney snorted. "If you haven't figured it out already, Colonel, none of us knows a thing about the warp drive. Maybe it was one of your own idiots who are always poking around down there."

Peranda drew a phase pistol and took a quick step toward their table.

He put the barrel of his weapon right up against Cooney's head.

"It sounds to me as if you're volunteering to sacrifice yourself, Cooney. Is that the case?"

Cooney didn't flinch. "I'm just offering a little advice, Colonel. I hate to see you wasting so much of your time chasing after answers you're not likely to get."

Peranda smiled. "I'm not talking about the warp drive now. We have another problem—another case of sabotage, I fear."

Travis exchanged a quick glance with Hess. *What problem?* She shook her head. It was clearly the first she was hearing of it as well.

"Go on," Cooney said.

"This problem is with our impulse engines. We're losing power. And none of my engineers can figure out why."

"Your engineers can't figure it out?" Cooney smiled. "Gee, that's a surprise."

Trip could see Peranda visibly control himself. Cooney hadn't been on *Enterprise* more than a week, but the man already knew the systems inside and out. As well as Hess, if not better. The colonel knew that, no doubt—which was why he didn't do what he so clearly wanted to: squeeze the trigger and blast the man across the room.

"All of you," Peranda said, looking around the room, "have an interest in seeing this problem fixed. In giving me answers, if you have them. I won't continue to be as patient as I've been, I can promise you that."

Lieutenant Reed, Travis thought. It had to be him—again. Of course, disabling the warp drive would only stop them from reaching the war quickly. To make sure they didn't get there at all . . .

He'd have to do something like this.

"Mayweather."

Travis looked up to find Peranda's eyes fixed on him.

"Is there something you want to tell me?"

Travis blinked. Some of what he'd been thinking must have shown on his face, and the colonel had picked it up. Not good.

"No, sir. There isn't."

Peranda smiled. "I think perhaps there is. I think, perhaps, another session is in order."

Travis's hand shook involuntarily.

Cooney stood up, so suddenly that Peranda had to step away. The soldiers, who had remained behind the colonel while he was talking, had their weapons trained on the engineer in a heartbeat.

"Easy, fellas," Cooney held up both hands. "Let me take a look at this problem, Colonel. Give Travis a break."

Peranda was a good-sized man; he had Archer's build, if not the captain's character. He looked like he could handle himself in a fight.

Cooney made him look like a little boy.

The engineer was one of the biggest men Travis

had ever seen—definitely the biggest he'd ever encountered aboard a starship. Sometimes, he had no doubt, that size got in the way: when trying to track down a wiring fault, crawl through an access tube, or work in a space designed for the average-sized man.

Not now, though. Now the size was an advantage.

Peranda, despite the fact that he held a weapon, gave ground.

"I'm not interested in your opinion, Cooney. I think Ensign Mayweather here knows—"

"Colonel, just let me have a look. If I can't find what the problem is, you're free to talk to Mayweather."

"I'm free to talk to Mayweather anytime I want," Peranda said. He looked from Cooney to Travis then, and nodded. "Very well, Cooney. There's no sense in our being at odds over this—if it truly is a mechanical fault. Come with us, and see what you can find out."

Cooney nodded and then, with a quick glance back at Travis, followed Peranda and his soldiers out of the mess.

The door slid shut behind them.

Travis sat back in his chair and exhaled a sigh of relief.

"I owe him one," he said. "I couldn't have gone through another one of those sessions right now."

Hess nodded. "He's a good man, Cooney."

She was looking at Travis with a strange expression on her face. "Ensign? Is there something you want to tell me?"

Travis suddenly realized that whatever Peranda had seen on his face before, Hess had noticed it too.

Should he tell her what he suspected about Lieutenant Reed? She was his superior officer, after all.

And it wasn't as if she was going to run down to Peranda and tell him.

And yet . . .

He hesitated. All he had were suspicions. What if he shared those, and they turned out to be wrong? Worse, what if he shared those, and Peranda forced Hess to talk? Lieutenant Reed would suffer then, for no good reason. And if his suspicions were correct, and Peranda found out . . .

Not only would Reed suffer, but the Denari would have an invaluable clue as to exactly what had been done to the warp drive. It would be easy to trace Reed's movements around the ship, and figure out when and where he could have accessed the intermix circuits.

"Ensign," Hess repeated, "did you hear what I said?"

Travis nodded slowly. "I did. And you're right. There is something." He smiled. "I think I am hungry, after all. Excuse me a minute."

He got to his feet and headed for the kitchen. He sensed Hess's eyes on him the whole way.

He wasn't happy about lying to her, but the alternative, he decided, was worse.

In the kitchen, he found Ensign Ryan sitting at a long, low counter, cutting vegetables with a tablespoon. Yee was standing over him.

"Travis," Ryan said, smiling. "I'm making stir-fry. You hungry?"

"I am, but—not for that, thanks." Travis was starving, in fact, and it was going to take Ryan far too long to put together his meal. The Denari had gone through the kitchen and taken out anything that could be used as a weapon, which included, unfortunately, all the knives and forks.

Food, though, was the only good thing about this enforced bit of captivity. Those who'd been left aboard *Enterprise* had the run of the mess—and there was a lot to run through. Hess, Ryan, and he were eating like kings every night. Or captains, anyway. Lobster, steak, ice cream—anything and everything they could want, in whatever quantities they cared to consume. Funny thing was that neither the *Daedalus* crew nor their Denari captors were able to enjoy the ship's bounty along with them. Something about *Enterprise*'s stories made them ill. They had to stick to the supplies the Denari had brought aboard.

That was fine with Travis. Kept them out of the kitchen, and left more for him. Not that there was any shortage—after all, there was food enough for a crew of eighty. A year's worth, if rationed correctly.

Though every time he went into the stores, it did seem to him like they were making a small dent in the vast quantities inside.

Travis put together a quick sandwich and took it back to his table. He sat down and began to eat.

Every so often he looked up to find Hess still watching him, that same skeptical expression on her face.

Fourteen

ARCHER HAD BEEN BACK aboard *Hule* for half a day, after the two fleets—Guild and DEF—had rendezvoused for a series of meetings between their leaders. The captain had even managed, courtesy of an eager Porthos, to squeeze in a moment with Makandros early that morning and make two requests of the general. First, that he bring the *Enterprise* crew from Rava here, so they could all be together. Second, that he give Archer the Stingers he had asked for.

Makandros had readily acceded to the first—the ships from Rava were just now arriving, a half-dozen in all. The captain was waiting in *Hule*'s cavernous launch bay, waiting for his people to begin disembarking. As for the second request . . .

"I'll need some time to consider that," had been the general's answer.

From the look in Makandros's eyes when he said that, though, Archer was not optimistic. It was hard for him to fault Makandros's reasoning, however. With the truce between Guild and DEF forces a seeming *fait accompli* all-out war with Elson would soon follow. It would take six ships to transport his crew, and the captain realized that six ships was far too many for the general to spare under these circumstances.

He should scale down his request and ask for a single vessel, one that he himself would pilot. In fact, rather than wait for Makandros to turn him down flat or, worse yet, send a subordinate to do that—worse because Archer would be unable to bargain with a subordinate; he would have to wait until the general agreed to see him again, and that could be a long time once fighting began—the captain decided he should seek out Makandros now and present his alternative proposal.

T'Pol, Yamani, and the remainder of the crew that had been aboard the Stinger with them were there with Archer, along with Doctor Trant, who had come over from *Eclipse*. They formed a kind of welcoming committee, guiding the crew to the area that had been set aside for them in the bay. Trant moved among them, passing out the masks she'd had made up for them. The rest of them gave out supplies Makandros's people had prepared at her direction.

The captain found Doctor Phlox and introduced the two physicians, and then found Lieutenant Covay, who had commanded the convoy on its way from Rava, and apologized for the treatment he'd given him. He found D.O. and thanked her for watching over the crew. Chief Lee, Carstairs, O'Bannon—he shook hands, it seemed, with every member of his crew.

"Sir?"

Ensign Dwight stood before him, looking much

improved from the last time the captain had laid eyes on him. Archer told him so.

"Feeling better too, sir. Except—" Dwight held up a bowl in front of him at arm's length, an expression of profound disgust on his face. "What is this stuff?"

It was the food Trant had supplied for them— some sort of tasteless mush that was, nonetheless, safe for them to eat. Archer felt the same way about it as Dwight obviously did. One taste, and he'd added another item to his list of reasons to find *Enterprise* as quickly as possible: the mess—or more specifically, the food in it.

"Think of it as medicine, Ensign. Or a bowl full of vitamins."

Dwight grimaced again. "I'd rather not think about it at all."

"You don't have a choice, I'm afraid."

The ensign sighed. "Yes, sir."

Dwight took his bowl and went to sit along the far wall of the bay, where Makandros's soldiers had set up tables and benches for the new arrivals. Archer looked for T'Pol, hoping to discuss his idea for requesting a single ship with her, but she was nowhere to be found. He scanned the bay, looking for Covay or Briatt, hopeful that one of them might be able to get him in to see Makandros—

And his eyes fell on Phlox and Trant, standing in front of a table piled high with the masks *Eclipse*'s physician had been giving out. The two of them were in the middle of what looked to be an argument.

Archer heard a little of it as he strode across the bay toward them.

"—a precaution, more than a necessity," Trant was saying.

"Such precautions, I believe, would be unnecessary if optimum sanitary conditions were maintained aboard your ship, Doctor. Such practices are the building blocks—the foundation, if you will—of any modern medical treatment," Phlox said.

"I understand that, Doctor."

"But—" Phlox looked genuinely puzzled. "By your own admission, your ship is contaminated with the very substances that our crew is allergic to. What is your explanation for that, Doctor?"

"My explanation, Doctor," Trant said, visibly trying to keep control of her temper, "is that *Eclipse*, a ship originally built for a crew of sixty miners, hastily refitted as a warship to carry approximately two hundred soldiers, now carries almost four hundred passengers. It is simply not possible to maintain a pristine—"

"Ah." Phlox smiled. "Not pristine, Doctor. Sanitary."

Trant looked angry enough to spit nails.

Archer cleared his throat. "Doctors, is there a problem?"

"No," Phlox said. "We were simply discussing hygienic practices aboard *Eclipse*."

Trant reared back, ready to respond in a way that Archer sensed would be counterproductive . . . at the very least.

"Let's all take a deep breath," the captain said. "Every one of us has been operating under very, very stressful conditions these last few weeks."

Trant nodded. "You're right, Captain. That's worth keeping in mind."

"Most certainly," Phlox said, smiling at Trant. "In

which regard, I must congratulate you, Doctor, on your successful diagnosis of the problem: the discovery that we were dealing with a problem at the molecular level. Most resourceful. Intuitive. I would have been hard-pressed to perform a similar analysis under the same conditions."

Trant nodded grudgingly. "I'm sure you would have done just fine."

"Perhaps. Irrelevant. What is relevant, however, is the fact that now that I am aware of the problem, I may have a solution."

Trant frowned. "A solution? What do you mean?"

"A way to facilitate digestion of the particular protein we're discussing. Some study will be required, of course—perhaps even a degree of experimentation—"

"Hold it." This time it was Archer's turn to interrupt. "Are you saying you can find a way to keep us from getting sick while we're here?"

"Yes, sir. As long as we maintain a sufficiently hygienic environment."

Trant looked utterly dumbfounded—too surprised, Archer noticed, to realize that Phlox had brought the conversation around full circle to sanitary practices again.

"How?" she asked. "How in the world can you do that?"

"The Negattan aquaflyer," Phlox said. "It secretes stereoisomeric protein compounds through a rather unique digestive process."

"The what?" Trant looked at Archer. He just shook his head.

"The Negattan aquaflyer. A study of the enzymes it uses to facilitate digestion should—to borrow

Commander Tucker's terminology—enable us to reverse-engineer the process."

Archer could only smile.

"Get on it then, Doctor."

"Of course. As soon as we can obtain a Negattan aquaflyer."

Trant frowned. "Where's Negatta?"

Before Archer could respond, someone tapped him on the shoulder.

He turned and saw Colonel Briatt, flanked by two soldiers.

"General Makandros would like to see you," she said.

"Good. I'd like to see him too," Archer said.

Leaving the two doctors to deal with the question of Negatta's whereabouts—if it even existed in this universe, he thought wryly—Archer followed Briatt and the guards to the general's cabin. Makandros was alone, seated behind a desk.

"Captain, please." Makandros indicated a chair.

Archer sat.

"I'm afraid I don't have much time to spare at the moment, so forgive me for speaking bluntly. Those ships you asked for—"

"You can't spare them."

Makandros nodded.

"That's right. I'm sorry, Captain. I'm afraid you and your people are going to have to be with us awhile longer."

"I'll remind you," Archer said. "We had a deal."

"Our deal was I would help you find your starship, which I fully intend to do, once this crisis is past."

"And we're just supposed to sit around here in the meantime, and wait?"

"I'm afraid so."

"You understand that we don't belong here? That my entire crew is sick, on their way to dying if we don't—"

"I understand," Makandros said sympathetically. "Believe me, I do. Try to understand my position, Captain. I am preparing for a war that may decide the future of millions of people. I ask you to be patient. Please."

Archer nodded.

And then asked the question he'd been intending to ask all along.

"What about one ship, General? A single vessel, to search for *Enterprise*."

Makandros frowned.

Archer pressed his point. "The absence of a single vessel, from a fleet this size, General. Could it make that much of a difference?"

The door com sounded again.

Makandros shook his head.

"I'm sorry, Captain. I do not have time for this conversation now. Enter!" Makandros called out.

Briatt stepped in, followed by Marshal Kairn and an older man whom Archer hadn't seen before.

"Gentlemen," Makandros said, stepping out from behind his desk. "Thank you for coming. Time is short. We should pick up immediately where we left off."

"I agree," Kairn said. Nodding to Archer, he took the seat the captain had just vacated. "I have discussed the reconnaissance issue with several of our outlying patrols. As you know, since our ships lack warp drive, our capabilities are limited. I suggest—"

Kairn had stopped talking because the older man had put a hand on his shoulder.

"Who is this?" he said, gesturing to Archer.

"Forgive me for not making introductions," Makandros said. "Guildsman Lind, this is Captain Jonathan Archer, of the *Enterprise*. He was just leaving."

"I thought I recognized the uniform, Captain." Lind extended his hand. The two shook. "Your crew does you honor."

"He means Tucker," Kairn said.

"They all do, Guildsman." Archer nodded. "I'd like to continue our conversation, General."

"When time permits, Captain."

Meaning when hell freezes over. Frustrated, angry, Archer turned to leave the room.

"You were saying, Marshal," Makandros continued smoothly. "About your scout ships."

"Ours and yours," Kairn replied. "Elson's ships appear to be transmitting on frequencies we can no longer intercept. We must obtain intelligence of his movements."

The door was halfway shut behind him when Archer suddenly realized what he was hearing.

"Wait," he said, stopping in his tracks and stopping the door from closing.

Briatt put a hand on his arm. "Captain, please come with me."

"A moment, Colonel." Archer turned and stepped back through the door.

Makandros was staring at him, clearly unhappy.

"Captain?"

"Forgive the interruption," Archer began, "but—"

"Come with me, Captain. Now." Briatt had followed him through the door and taken firm hold of one elbow.

"I said we would speak later," Makandros said.

"I heard you. Then and just now." He looked from the general to Kairn. "Am I wrong, or are you looking for a reconnaissance vessel?"

"You heard correctly," Kairn said. "Why?"

Archer looked at Makandros. "General?"

For a split second, Makandros didn't realize what the captain was asking.

Then his frown turned into a grudging smile.

"Perhaps," Makandros said. "Why don't you close the door, and we'll discuss it?"

Fifteen

TRAVIS CAUGHT a few hours of sleep and went to relieve Westerberg at the helm. It was ship's night—normally, a quiet time on the bridge. A time when stations were manned by a minimal crew complement—helm, sensors, auxiliary control. . . . Even with the ship under Denari command, there were usually only a few additional soldiers on duty.

Tonight was different, though.

He entered the bridge to the sounds of an argument in progress between Cooney and several Denari crowded around the auxiliary engineering station. Peranda was in the captain's chair, still on duty—a shock to Travis, who had never seen the man on this late before—looking every bit as angry as he had down in the crew's mess. All stations—communications, sensors, weapons—were occupied, and the tension on the bridge was so thick that he could have cut it with a knife.

"—not sure what waiting around is going to gain us, Chief Cooney," one of the Denari was saying. "It seems to me we should begin a thorough check—"

"Oh, for God's sake," Cooney interrupted. "Do you know what an intermittent problem is?"

"I know what an intermittent problem is, yes."

"It doesn't happen on a schedule," Cooney continued, as if the man hadn't spoken. "You can't plan for it, you just have to be ready to diagnose it when it happens. And we've just spent the last few hours getting ready." He spread his arms wide to indicate the increased crew presence on the bridge. "The next time the power fluctuates, we'll know what's happening. And why."

"We've waited five hours for that next time to occur, Chief. How much longer are we supposed to wait?"

Cooney laughed. "You're an idiot. Do you know what intermittent means?"

"Enough." Peranda leaned forward in his chair. "We'll wait. One more hour, Chief Cooney. If the problem does not manifest itself again, however, we will begin a full systems check."

"It's your time," Cooney said. "Waste it if you want to."

Travis walked past, as unobstrusively as he could, and stopped next to the helm.

Westerberg looked up at him and rolled his eyes.

"Good luck," he said, standing. "I'll see you in eight hours."

"Anything I need to know?" Travis asked, taking his station.

"Stay alert," the older man said. "That power fluctuation they're talking about? When it happens— bam!" The man slapped his hands together. "Engine speed drops like that. You have to be on it, or the ship starts wobbling like a top."

"Sounds like fun."

"Oh," Westerberg smiled, "believe me, it's all fun."

Travis knew he was referring to more than the engine cut-out.

He settled himself at the helm and ran a quick systems check. They were halfway between Kota and Denari, he saw. That meant that sometime tomorrow, they'd be hitting the Belt. He and Westerberg had talked about it this morning, on the previous shift change. The course Peranda had laid in called for them to go through the asteroid field, rather than around it. That was not going to be fun at all.

In the same way, Travis suspected, that the rest of this shift was not going to be fun either.

"Colonel." Travis turned and saw it was the Denari soldier at the communications console who'd spoken. "General Elson."

Peranda stood up. "In there," he said, nodding to Archer's ready room. He strode quickly across the deck, then paused at its entrance and turned back to the group of engineers.

"Notify me if the fluctuations start again."

Cooney looked up from his console. "Believe me, if they start happening, you'll know."

"Notify me," Peranda snapped, and entered the ready room.

Cooney shook his head and turned back to work. Travis spun around in his chair and did the same.

Time passed. Peranda strode out of the ready room. Travis looked up quickly and, just as quickly, back down.

Peranda was ashen-faced and angry. Whatever this General Elson had said had clearly upset him, and Travis knew Peranda well enough to know that when the colonel was upset, the best thing to do was stay out of his way.

Peranda went to the communications console.

"The general wishes to speak to our passengers," he said.

"I'll set that up, sir," the com officer said.

"Yes. You do that." The colonel spoke slowly, as if afraid that speaking more than one word at a time would cause him to explode.

Travis wondered what "passengers" he was talking about.

He heard Peranda take the center seat—Captain Archer's seat—again. "Nothing on those power fluctuations?"

"Not yet." Even Cooney sounded subdued— seemed like he knew Peranda's moods as well.

"Link is established, sir," the com officer said.

"Good."

All at once, the lights dimmed.

The ship lurched. Travis was on the controls in an instant. He boosted power to the aft thrusters, stabilizing the ship, and at the same instant cut their forward motion in half, to match the reduction in speed.

"There it is!" Cooney shouted triumphantly. "What did I tell you, there it is!"

Travis was too busy to turn around, but he heard the frenzy of activity the fluctuation had started. Every one of the Denari who had been, up until that instant, standing around waiting sounded like they were now in motion.

"Reactor output is at nominal," one called out.

"Power grid stable."

"Conduit integrity verified."

"Got it," Cooney said. "You tricky little bastard."

"What?" Peranda snapped. "What is it?"

"Plasma flow," Cooney said. "We're losing energy through the exhaust manifold." Travis could hear the note of puzzlement in his voice. "Sensors show the manifold is clear, though. I don't—"

The lights came on, full intensity.

"Flow is back to normal," Cooney said. "Huh."

Travis had full power at the helm again. He pushed their speed up to full impulse.

A problem with the plasma exhaust. That sounded familiar to him, for some reason.

"Now that we know what the difficulty is, what do we do about it?" Peranda asked.

"We still have to figure out why it's happening," Cooney said. "Give us a minute to correlate all the data."

"Colonel." It was the communications officer again.

"Yes?"

"General Elson again."

"Very well." Peranda started back toward the ready room.

"Sir," the com officer said, "he says now. Sir."

Peranda sighed. "Very well."

The star field on the main viewscreen cleared. A man took its place.

An older man—early sixties, Travis guessed—dressed in a simple black tunic, with a wave of silver-white hair that fell across his forehead. He looked exactly the way a general was supposed to look, and yet, there was a light in his eyes that struck Travis the wrong way. Calculation? Cruelty?

He couldn't say what, but it filled him with an instant, instinctive dislike for the man.

Peranda moved to the center of the bridge and spoke.

"General Elson."

"Colonel Peranda. Tell me you've solved the problem."

"No, sir, not yet. But as you can see"—Peranda gestured toward the knot of engineers at the back of the bridge—"we're working on it."

"Work toward being here tomorrow morning."

"Yes, sir."

"We'll check back in four hours. If it's necessary to send another ship to fetch them"—Elson smiled—"we'll have time to do that then."

"Yes, sir. I don't think it will be."

"We'll see, won't we?"

The screen went dark.

Peranda sighed again and sat back down in his chair.

Travis tried to make sense of what he'd just heard. Elson was pushing to have "them" there by tomorrow morning. Clearly, it was the reason why Peranda had been so worked up about first the warp engines, and now this problem they were having with the power fluctuating. The "them" the general had referred to was just as clearly—at least as Travis saw it—these passengers Elson had asked to speak with before. Passengers whose identity Travis had no idea of.

But he was certainly going to find out more about them.

The engineers returned, talking quietly among themselves. Peranda continued to sit and fume.

A problem with the plasma exhaust, Travis thought again. And again, that struck a chord with him. Why?

Well, if he couldn't remember, maybe the computer could.

Travis checked space ahead of them—a few rocks, a comet on a very erratic orbit around Kota that had already passed as close to them as it was going to get . . . Nothing large enough to merit concern, or his attention, for that matter. All he had to be worried about was another power fluctuation cropping up.

He'd take the chance it wouldn't in the next few minutes.

He set the helm to autopilot and, working casually, accessed the main computer.

RUN HISTORY PLASMA EXHAUST PROBLEMS

The computer acknowledged his request.

As it worked, Travis wondered, suddenly, if this wasn't Lieutenant Reed's work again—another little piece of sabotage to keep the Denari busy.

The lieutenant's smiling face flashed before Travis's eyes, and he couldn't help but smile too.

"Something funny, Ensign?" Peranda asked.

Travis was all at once aware that the colonel had risen from his seat and was standing over his shoulder, watching.

"No, sir."

"What are you doing? That's not the helm console."

Peranda wasn't as thick as he seemed, Travis realized. He thought quickly.

"Well, we passed a comet a little ways back. In our solar system, they tend to bunch up—travel in groups—Oort clouds, we call them—so I thought it would be worth cross-checking the database to see if—"

Peranda held up a hand. "Enough. Is it a danger to us?"

"Doesn't seem to be, no." Travis made a show of frowning and clearing the console, as if he were dissatisfied with what he saw there.

"Very well." Peranda turned on his heel. "Cooney, how are we doing?"

"We're busy."

"Busy?" Peranda sounded ready to explode. Travis turned in his seat and saw that Cooney looked just as frustrated as the colonel. He was, in fact, glaring right at him, as if daring him to say something else.

One of the Denari engineers saw the same thing, and moved to head off any possible confrontation.

"We do know a few things, Colonel," the engineer said. "Even if we have yet to reach any conclusions."

"Well?" Peranda folded his arms across his chest. "Go ahead."

"The exhaust is not venting properly," the Denari replied. "As the instruments show."

Another Denari spoke. "We need to go EVA and clear the blockage."

"There is no blockage," Cooney said. "The sensors show that as well."

"The sensors must be wrong," the Denari said.

"Then why is all the other data we're picking up from them checking out?"

"I don't know, but—"

"Cooney, would we benefit from physically examining the manifold?" Peranda put in.

"Sure," Cooney said.

"Then I suggest we do just that."

"Fine." Cooney threw up his hands. "Give the order. I'll tell engineering to start preparing to shut down."

"Shut down?"

"To send someone out to examine the manifold, we'll have to turn off the reactor."

"What?" Peranda turned to the Denari engineer who had spoken. "Is this true?"

"Yes, sir."

"Of course it's true," Cooney said. "That exhaust is coming out of there at about a hundred million degrees Kelvin. No one in an EVA suit can get within a mile of it." He smiled. "I don't think your General Elson would be too happy about us stopping dead in space for the six hours it would take for that surface to cool down."

Peranda did not look happy. "Is there no other way to see what's happening in that manifold?"

"No," Cooney said. Then, "Well, give me a minute."

Travis was thinking too. All of this was seeming familiar to him now—a problem with the plasma exhaust, looking for a way to find out what that problem was without going EVA . . .

He sat up straight in his chair.

This exact same thing had happened before. Not more than a couple weeks after they'd started out from Earth. They'd found a ship—a cloaked ship—

hiding in the trail of their plasma exhaust. Using it to recharge their own depleted engines. Causing unexplained power fluctuations aboard *Enterprise*.

A cloaked ship, belonging to a race called the Xyrillians.

His mind raced. Could they be back again? Not likely. Not this far out. And wouldn't they just hail *Enterprise* this time? So not the Xyrillians.

Could it be another cloaked ship? Someone else who knew their trick of siphoning off energy from a starship? Who, then? The Klingons? The Xyrillians had done the same thing to them, after all. Except this was too far out from Klingon space. And the Klingons didn't use cloaked ships.

But the Suliban did. Except they were so far ahead of Starfleet technologically, why would they—

The answer hit him like a ton of bricks.

He suddenly knew, without a doubt, that there was a ship out there. And he knew, just as certainly, who was aboard it.

"I might have an idea," Cooney said slowly. "What if . . ."

All at once, a chill went down Travis's spine. He didn't like the thoughtful tone that had crept into the engineer's voice. It made him wonder if Cooney had reasoned out the problem the same way *Enterprise*'s crew had, those many months ago.

He couldn't take that chance.

Acting on pure instinct, Travis abruptly cut *Enterprise*'s speed in half.

The ship's inertial dampers, try as hard as they might, couldn't compensate entirely.

Everyone on the bridge who hadn't been firmly

seated went flying forward. Travis heard the sound of bodies hitting the deck, grunts of pain, shouts of surprise and anger.

"Mayweather! What the hell!" He heard feet tromping toward him.

He looked up and saw Cooney, face beet-red with anger, leaning over him.

"Why did you do that?"

"I didn't do anything," Travis said, trying to sound as frantic as possible. "It happened again. Look."

He pointed at his console.

Cooney responded even as he was looking down.

"I almost cracked my skull wide open because of that little stunt of yours, so—"

To the man's credit, when he saw the message Travis had put up on his console, he didn't freeze up. His eyes widened only slightly as he took it in—

DO NOTHING

—and then continued talking, as if nothing at all had changed.

"—I'd like an explanation for what you think you're doing."

"And I'm telling you," Travis said, putting an edge on his own voice, and at the same time wiping the message off his screen, "if you look right here, you'll see we had another fluctuation."

Cooney bent over the console, as if studying it.

"We didn't pick up anything back here," one of the Denari engineers said.

Travis sensed someone else coming up behind him—Peranda.

"Well, Cooney?" the colonel asked.

"Seems like something went through the circuit here, all right," Cooney said, straightening. "Seems like Mayweather here overreacted a bit as well, though."

Travis almost smiled, the man sounded so convincing. Instead, he said angrily, "Anytime you want to take the helm, be my guest."

Cooney chuckled in response, and went back to his station.

"Now then, Cooney," Peranda said. "You were going to suggest?"

"Ah." Cooney made a disgusted noise in his throat. "It's not going to work."

"What?"

"What I was going to suggest." He sounded frustrated. "I need a break."

"We do not have time for breaks," Peranda said icily. "We have a schedule to keep."

"I need a break," Cooney repeated. "I'm not doing anyone any good up here."

Travis had turned just enough in his chair to see Cooney nod to one of the other engineers, ignoring the colonel entirely. "Keep working," he said to them. Then he looked up at Peranda.

"Colonel, I'm going to get something to eat, and I'll be back in half an hour."

Then, without waiting for a response, he left the bridge.

Travis, though, was stuck.

He had six more hours to go on his shift, and there was no way he could do anything now until that time was up. And what if he was wrong, anyway? What if he'd just taken considerable risks with his own safety and Cooney's for nothing?

Someone tapped him on the shoulder. He'd been so absorbed in thought he hadn't heard their approach.

He looked up and saw Westerberg.

The man smiled.

"You want to break early?" he asked. "I had too much coffee."

Their eyes locked. Travis felt like he could read the man's mind.

Cooney had sent him.

"Yeah. Sure," Travis said, standing. "Getting hungry anyway."

Westerberg settled into the helm chair. "See you in a few."

Travis turned to go.

Peranda was standing in front of him.

"Mayweather, is there a problem?"

"Not as far as I'm concerned," Travis said. He forced himself to smile. "Westerberg's doing me a favor."

"A shift change. It's early for that, I believe, isn't it?"

"Like I said—he's doing me a favor," Travis said.

"Out of the kindness of his heart?"

"Out of my inability to sleep," Westerberg said. "Not that big a favor. You'll cover the next one for me Travis—right?"

"We'll talk about it," Travis said.

Still, Peranda didn't move. He eyed the two of them—Travis and Westerberg—for a moment longer. Finally, the colonel nodded. "All right. Go."

Travis moved to the turbolift.

Footsteps fell into place beside him. One of the Denari soldiers.

The two stepped inside the turbolift together. Travis's last sight of the bridge was Peranda, spun all the way around in Captain Archer's chair to watch him leave.

He nodded to the soldier next to Travis, who nodded back in return.

Not a good sign, Travis thought. *The colonel suspects something.*

They rode the lift down to E-deck in silence. The soldier followed him out, heading toward the mess. Another bad omen. They had soldiers with them all the time—heck, the ship was crawling with them— but this one was following him, specifically. To see what he did.

Which meant he couldn't go straight to Cooney. Peranda would know something was up then. But he didn't have time to waste. Cooney had told Peranda he'd be back in half an hour, and a big chunk of that time was gone already. And even assuming Travis was right about who was out there, he still didn't know how to go about contacting them, much less trying to get them back aboard *Enterprise*. That would require a miracle of sorts. Or at the very least, a remarkably good sleight-of-hand. A magic trick.

The old saw—Arthur C. Clarke's maxim about any sufficiently advanced technology being indistinguishable from magic—popped into his head.

All at once, Travis had an idea. The beginnings of one, at least.

He refined it as he entered the mess. The soldier stopped at the door, joining the other guards there.

Cooney was seated by himself, at a table near the observation window. Ryan and Yee were the only other ones in the room, seated next to the kitchen entrance.

Travis walked past them and joined *Daedalus*'s engineer.

"You know," Cooney said as Travis pulled out a chair, "that guard is watching you."

"I know. Peranda told him to."

"You know?" Cooney's eyes went wide. "Then why did you sit here? He's going to think we're up to something."

"We are."

"And you don't mind if he tells the colonel about it?"

"Not at all."

"Not at all." Cooney looked at him in disbelief again, then shook his head. "You just put my neck in a noose, you know. Mind telling me what's going on? Why you pulled that little stunt back there, with the engines?"

"To stop you from finding out what's really causing the power fluctuations."

"Why?"

Travis told him.

Cooney frowned. "That's a lot of supposition."

"Maybe. I have a way to test my theory."

"Go on."

"I need your help."

"I gathered that."

"It's going to be risky."

"I've been in Denari prisons before. They don't scare me. Only thing is"—he nodded toward the guard—"how are we going to do anything with him watching us?"

Travis smiled. "We'll bring him along."

"Bring him along?"

"That's right. We don't want to keep the colonel in the dark, do we?"

Cooney shook his head. "You lost me now, kid."

Travis leaned forward. "All right. Here's what I propose we do."

He took a deep breath then, and laid out his plan.

Sixteen

"Sir?"

Archer looked up from his seat. Riley—Ensign Katreen Riley, probably the best pilot on *Enterprise* besides himself and Travis—was standing over him.

"My shift, Captain."

Archer nodded and stood up.

"Charts say smooth going for the next few hours, Ensign. After that . . . well. You wake me if you need to."

"I won't."

Archer almost smiled. Riley was a pit bull. She probably wouldn't wake him if a comet exploded in their path.

"All right," he said, and turned to go.

Rodriguez was on weapons; Kowalski was doing double duty on sensors and communications. They were B shift too. Archer nodded to them as he left the cockpit, and entered the main cabin.

One weapons station on either side of the ship was manned; O'Neill and Lee had drawn the short straws. They were peering intently through the gunnery ports as the captain walked past, as if they might be able to pick up something the sensors had missed. The others were sleeping on bunks that folded out from the back wall.

All except T'Pol. She was nowhere in sight. That meant, of course, there was only one place she could be. The ship's sole passenger cabin.

Archer smiled. He hadn't thought he'd have to fight her for it. He was the captain, after all.

But he just might, if it came down to that.

It had been a long day. Full enough, even before Makandros and Kairn had agreed to his suggestion. Even before they'd spent hours dodging in and out of the Belt, on the trail of one of Elson's patrol squadrons. He'd been happy to have something to report so quickly, and Carstairs had assured him the general sounded happy as well.

Now if only they would stumble on *Enterprise* . . .

He knocked on the door.

"Sub-Commander?"

He waited. No response.

He lifted his hand to knock again—

And the door swung open.

"Captain." T'Pol stood in the doorway. There was a blanket spread out on the deck behind her.

"You're not sleeping," he said.

"No. Meditating."

"I'm sorry. I didn't mean to interrupt." Phlox had told him on more than one occasion that Vulcans used the discipline not only to focus and concentrate their thinking, but to actually heal their bodies. And after her experience at Rava . . .

She certainly needed that healing time.

"That is all right. I was going to come find you anyway."

Archer looked in her eyes and frowned.

"What is it?"

"I have just now become aware of something," she said. "Something very important."

Archer had served with T'Pol long enough to read the subtle differences in her expression.

"This isn't going to be good news, is it?"

"No, I'm afraid not."

She held the door open.

With a sigh, Archer entered the cabin and sat down.

"My meditation began as an attempt to enter a healing trance," T'Pol told him. "And yet my injuries are no longer severe enough to require my full attention. My mind began to wander. I considered our current situation and began to visualize the procedure we would need to use to escape it."

"You mean to return to our own universe."

"Yes, sir."

"You're assuming we're going to find *Enterprise.*"

"Any other assumption seems pointless," she said. "If we do not get the ship back, we die."

Archer couldn't argue with that.

"Go on."

The cabin was a third the size of his quarters on *Enterprise*, with a single bunk and a desk. Archer had sat on the bed. T'Pol pulled up the desk chair now and sat as well, facing him.

"I first had to visualize the exact method by which we crossed over. A simple enough task."

Archer nodded. "The mine crippled us. We drifted through the anomaly."

"Exactly. But there the simplicity ends. Because in order to return to the universe we came from, we need to recreate our journey exactly. The same trajectory, the same speed, the exact same entry point. Any difference, and we will not return to our own world, but go to yet another parallel universe."

"One time through this is quite enough for me, thanks." The captain sighed. "We should be able to go back the way we came. The sensors—"

Archer stopped short.

"The sensors," he said slowly, "were damaged."

"Yes, sir. They were completely off-line, even before we went through the anomaly."

"The mine."

"Indeed. I have spent the majority of my time trying to recall the nature and extent of the data we had amassed before the explosion—on the structure of the anomaly itself, our own course and speed—to see if it is possible to extrapolate the information we need."

"And?"

She shook her head. "The chances of success are unlikely, at best. I'll know more once we're aboard *Enterprise* and can see the sensors firsthand."

"We need a plan B."

"Sir?"

"Another way to get that information." He thought a moment. "Makandros. He said he picked us up the second we came out of the anomaly. Maybe *Hule*'s computers . . ."

T'Pol was shaking her head. "They may have some of the data we need. Perhaps we can calculate our point of entry—our initial speed and trajectory. But in order to completely plot out our journey—"

Archer saw where she was headed. "We need data from our side of the anomaly. From our universe."

"And our course and speed within the anomaly itself."

The captain sat back. This wasn't just bad news, this was catastrophically bad news.

"I'd appreciate it if you didn't mention this to anyone else," Archer said. "Until we know one way or another what we're going to do."

"Yes, sir."

He sat a moment longer, thinking. "T'Pol, this anomaly. Isn't it possible the gravitational forces within it will guide us along the correct trajectory, once we enter?"

"Possible? Yes, I suppose it is possible. In the same way that it is possible Commander Tucker will float by this window port"—she pointed behind her—"in an EVA suit."

Archer frowned. "Is that Vulcan humor?"

"No, sir. Simple logic."

"The odds are infinitesimal, in other words." The captain got to his feet. "We may have to take them anyway. Ending up in another parallel universe might be our only option. We certainly can't stay here."

"Perhaps."

"Perhaps? You heard what Doctor Trant said. It's definite. We can't stay here."

"You misunderstand me, sir. I was not arguing with her conclusion. I simply meant that entering the anomaly is not necessarily a safer course of action."

"We might end up in another universe even more dangerous to us?"

"No, we might enter the anomaly in such a way that the gravitational forces within crush us."

"Ah."

"I would like to return to my meditation, Captain. Perhaps visualizing the problem again may lead me to other possible solutions."

"Let's hope so." Archer stood and rubbed his eyes. A sudden wave of exhaustion hit him.

"Sir?"

"What?"

T'Pol gestured to the mat. "Would you care to try? You may find the technique relaxing as well."

Archer smiled. He'd seen T'Pol's meditation technique. The last time his body had bent that way, he'd been body-surfing off Sydney. And it hadn't been on purpose.

"No, thanks. I think I'll get my rest the old-fashioned way. A few hours of sleep."

"Do you wish to use this bunk?"

"No. You keep thinking. If you come up with anything, let me know."

He hoped she would. *Otherwise,* Archer thought, *I'm going to have a very restless night.*

Seventeen

PERANDA LOOKED from Cooney to Travis and frowned.

Then he looked past them to his own engineers, standing in a knot just behind the two men.

"Is this possible?" the colonel asked.

One of the engineers stepped forward.

"It seems like a workable plan, sir. A way of, at the very least, determining what the problem is."

Peranda sighed. "I'm not asking about the plan. The plan makes perfect sense. I'm asking about this device, the transporter. Is this possible that it does what they say?"

"Ah. Forgive me, sir. Yes, the device is possible in theory. And the circuitry—at least as far as we can tell—appears to match that theory."

The colonel nodded.

He focused his attention again on Cooney, who Travis had let do all the talking since they'd arrived on the bridge a few moments before, their plan in place.

"You propose to use this transporter to beam a remote sensor to the manifold, and then—"

"It's very simple, Colonel," Cooney interrupted,

sounding exactly as exasperated as Travis would have expected him to, had their plan been genuine. "We beam out the sensor, and we take readings. No more, no less."

"And if it tells you there is a blockage in the manifold?"

"We deal with that then. We may even be able to use the transporter to deal with it, in fact."

Peranda nodded and turned to Travis.

"Providential you should think of this transporter, Mayweather. At precisely the time when we need it."

Travis shrugged, doing his best to sound—and seem—casual. "Can't tell you why it occurred to me. I suppose it's because we've used it to get out of a few sticky situations before."

Peranda nodded. Travis could tell he was still suspicious—of both them and their plan. He was counting on the colonel's obvious desire to stay in General Elson's good graces—by delivering *Enterprise* and its mysterious passengers on schedule—to overcome those suspicions.

"We're ready whenever you give the word, Colonel," he added.

"All right," the colonel said finally. "Let's try your plan."

Cooney nodded. "Yes, sir."

He and Travis left the bridge together.

Not surprisingly, two of the Denari soldiers rode the turbolift down with them.

The soldiers followed them to E-deck. The transporter lay at the end of an access corridor near engineering.

Without a word, he and Cooney got to work.

It was all part of their ruse, of course, as was nine-tenths of the equipment they'd picked up along the way from one of the science labs. All they really needed, in fact, was in the smallest container they'd brought, a square metal case a meter long and as thick as an old-fashioned dictionary.

Travis put that case to the side now, and continued assembling the sensor device they didn't intend to use.

Minutes passed.

The two soldiers had initially taken up positions along either side of the corridor, directly behind Travis and Cooney. Now they began pacing and talking to each other. Relaxing.

Travis glanced over at Cooney, who nodded imperceptibly.

It was time.

"That's a problem," the man said suddenly, sounding frustrated. "The slots don't align."

Cooney made a show of setting down the equipment he had in his hands harder than necessary.

"Now what?" he asked, glaring at Travis.

"You're the engineer."

"It's your ship. How do you usually do this?"

"It's not something we usually do." Travis snapped his fingers. "Wait."

He bent down and opened the square metal case.

And pulled out a pair of Starfleet-issue communicators.

"We could use these," Travis said, pulling them out. "Same circuitry."

One of the guards stepped forward. "Hold on a minute. Let me see those."

"Sure." Travis handed them over.

"These look like our communications devices." He handed one back to the other guard, who nodded. "What do you need these for?"

"Because they use the same interlocutal circuits as the sensors," Cooney said. "Here. I'll show you."

He got to his feet and held one out to the guard, who moved forward to take the communicator.

As his fingers closed around it, Cooney reared back and decked the soldier, who went down like a sack of potatoes.

The other guard brought his weapon to bear. Travis was already moving, though. He took hold of the barrel as it was coming up and used the man's own momentum to wrench it out of his hands.

He brought his knee up into the soldier's stomach, knocking the wind out of him with a rush. The soldier bent over double.

Travis brought the butt of the weapon down on the man's head, and he joined his companion on the floor.

"That went well," Cooney said.

Travis turned to him and smiled. "Interlocutal circuits? Where'd you come up with that?"

"What came out of my mouth. Believe me, no thought went into it." Cooney picked up the other guard's weapon.

"All right, kid," he said. "Go to it."

Travis walked to the console. He took a minute to gather the information he needed from *Enterprise*'s computer—the size and internal configuration of the ship he suspected was out there, in particular the amount of headroom above the seats. He made his calculations, took the best guess he could about its most likely position relative to the manifold, and punched in a set of coordinates.

He took the two communicators, reset their frequencies, and placed one on the transporter platform.

Then he stepped behind the console and sent it on its way.

As it finished dematerializing, he realized he'd almost forgotten something. Something very, very important.

He opened a channel to the bridge.

"Mayweather here. Sensor is away."

The Denari engineer's voice came back. "Yes. We can see that. But we're not picking up any telemetry. Please advise."

"Hold on. We'll be right back to you." He cut the circuit. He'd respond to them in a minute. But first . . .

Travis opened the communicator and took a deep breath.

He was about to find out if he'd guessed right about all this, or if he'd just set himself and Cooney up for several long, unpleasant sessions with Colonel Peranda and his shock rod.

"This is Ensign Mayweather. Is anyone out there? Please answer."

He waited. Nothing but static.

He heard a noise behind him, and turned.

On the ground, one of the Denari soldiers was stirring.

Cooney stepped up behind the man and dragged

him to his feet. He placed his weapon against the side of the soldier's head.

"Not a word. Or you're a dead man."

Travis lifted the communicator and spoke into it again.

"This is Mayweather. Over. Are you there?"

Nothing. This was not good. Had he guessed wrong? Had he simply beamed the communicator out into open space? Were the power fluctuations being caused by something else entirely?

The console beeped.

"It's the bridge," Travis said. He turned to Cooney. "What do I tell them?"

"Tell them we shut down the sensor so we can reboot it. Tell them it'll take . . . ten minutes to get a signal."

"Ten minutes?" That seemed like a long time to him. "To reboot a sensor?"

"Who's the engineer here?" Cooney shook his head. "All right, tell them five, then."

Travis reached out to open the channel—

And the communicator beeped.

"Travis, you there?"

He drew his hand back from the console and broke out into a big smile. He'd recognize that voice anywhere.

It was Commander Tucker.

"Sir," he said. "I can't tell you how good it is to hear from you."

"Same here. I was starting to think you wouldn't pick up on our signal."

"Sorry about that. It took a while for me to remember about the Xyrillians."

"That's all right. What's the situation there?"

"Not . . . perfect. Hold on a minute."

Travis closed the communicator and called the bridge. He gave the engineer who answered Cooney's story.

"A reboot shouldn't take more than a minute," the man answered.

"Uh . . ." Travis turned around to Cooney and gestured for help.

Cooney frowned.

"Tell him we had to jury-rig something together. It's not a standard-issue sensor."

Travis told him.

"That doesn't sound right. Let me speak to Cooney," the man said.

Travis turned around again.

Cooney shook his head. "I don't know. Let me think."

"You're both dead men," the soldier sneered.

"Shut up," Cooney said.

"Let me go," the soldier said, "and—"

Cooney clocked him in the jaw, and the soldier collapsed to the ground again.

"I told him to shut up."

Cooney strode past Travis to the console, and punched the channel open.

"What?" he said.

"Cooney?" the Denari engineer's voice came back.

"Cooney here. The reboot's going to take five minutes. I'll let you know when we've got a signal. Understood?"

Without waiting for an answer, he punched the channel closed.

"Best defense—good offense," he said to Travis.

"Let's hope so." Travis opened the communicator again. "Commander?"

"Right here. What's going on?"

Travis told him.

"Sounds like we don't have a lot of time."

"No, sir. Ten minutes at the most before all hell breaks loose."

"You better get us on board, then. Use your previous coordinates as a guide, take us one at a time. Start with me—in ten seconds."

"Yes, sir." Travis moved to the transporter console and set the coordinates. He called up Commander Tucker's profile and poised his hands over the controls.

He was, truth be told, a little nervous. Beaming a communicator from place to place was one thing. Beaming a person . . .

That was something else entirely.

The communicator beeped again.

"Travis?"

"Yes, sir?"

"I just remembered something. I don't recall you being trained on the transporter."

"Not formally, no, sir."

"Ah. You know about the different settings for molecular and quantum-state transport?"

"Uh . . . no."

"Oookay." Commander Tucker was silent. "Molecular level is what we use for cargo. That's the default. Quantum-state is what you have to use for living organisms. People."

"Oh." Travis's blood went cold. "Sir, I'm—I don't know what to say."

"It's all right," Tucker said. "We can do this. Access the operator screen. You got it?"

Travis did as he was told. "I got it."

"All right. Here's what you do."

The commander guided him through the process. Travis felt like an idiot every step of the way. He didn't know what would have happened if he'd beamed over Commander Tucker with the wrong settings—nothing good, he was certain of that.

It was a relatively simple adjustment to the controls. Travis started the countdown again, in his head.

At two, he began initialization of the primary energizing coils. At one, the targeting scanners began to verify the target coordinates—he had to override the automatic shutdown protocol, which kicked in when the scanners hit the cloaked ship.

At zero, he activated the matter stream transmission.

A nanosecond later, the outline of a man began to appear on the pad before him.

"Holy . . ." Cooney said, stepping slowly forward to stand with Travis at the console. "It really works. Son of a gun, Mayweather, it really works."

Travis shook his head. In the transport chamber, the man began to materialize completely. "Where did you think that communicator went?"

"A communicator's one thing, kid. A man—that's something else altogether."

Travis couldn't disagree with that—especially after the lesson he'd just learned.

The man finished materializing. A whip-thin, bearded man in a green-and-orange jumpsuit.

Travis barely recognized him.

"Commander?"

Trip stepped down from the platform. "I know. The beard. The clothes. Let's put it this way, Travis. It's been a rough few—"

The commander stopped in his tracks and stared at Cooney.

"Chief? The professor and I thought you might be here."

"Tucker?" Cooney said, as if he couldn't quite believe his eyes. "The professor? You mean Brodesser? What—"

Right then the console beeped. "Cooney? Mayweather? What's happening down there?"

That was Peranda. The mood in the room changed abruptly.

Travis turned to Cooney. "You should take it."

Cooney shook his head. "If I take it, he'll want answers. Maybe you can stall him."

"Go on, Travis," Commander Tucker said, stepping behind the console. "Talk to him. I'll get the others on board."

Hoshi came next. She wobbled a little as she came off the platform, but there was a smile on her face as she took in the ship, and Travis.

Trip knew how she felt. It was almost unreal, after all this time, to be back on *Enterprise* again. But they had no time to celebrate—Travis's talk with this Peranda had not gone well.

The colonel was sending two engineers down to see what was happening.

"He'll send more soldiers with them," Cooney

said. "We've got as long as it takes them to get down . . ."

His voice died out as Brodesser materialized on the platform.

Cooney looked at him, and shook his head.

"Professsor. Who else you got out there? Captain Duvall?"

"Hardly," Brodesser said. "It's good to see you, Chief."

"And you. It's like old home week around here," Cooney said as the two men shook hands.

"Not exactly." Trip set the controls to bring Malcolm over.

"Not exactly?" Cooney asked. "What does that mean?"

"It means—oh, never mind." Trip shook his head. They didn't have time to talk about parallel universes right now.

Reed stepped off the transporter platform. "I used the mooring clamps," he said, tossing Trip a phase pistol. "They should hold long enough for our purposes. We still pressed for time?"

"We have no time," Trip said. "We have to get control of the ship—now." He looked to Travis and then Cooney. "Engineering is just down the corridor. We'll—"

"I know where engineering is," Cooney snapped.

"Then let's go," Trip said, biting back a sharp retort of his own, realizing that whatever it was that had always set him and his universe's Cooney at odds, this man apparently had it as well.

"Trip," Malcolm said, stepping past him. "Please. You stay back, all right? Let me—"

Malcolm never finished his sentence.

Four Denari—two in uniform—turned into the corridor, directly in front of them.

Reed fired. One of the men in uniform went down. The other tried to backtrack, but Travis took him out. The other two Denari froze. Phaser blasts struck them as well, and both toppled.

The door to the engine room was straight ahead. Malcolm ran toward it. Trip and the others followed.

Malcolm paused at the engine room door.

"I'm going in first. I'll take out any Denari I see on the main level. Travis, you come in behind me, target the upper level. Hoshi, you do the same. Commander, you and the professor stay behind me, watch for stragglers. You"—he pointed with his weapon at Cooney—"secure this door."

"My people are in there too," Cooney said. "Make sure you don't hit them by mistake."

"I know who they are," Travis said.

"Okay." Malcolm nodded. "Let's go, then."

He flung the door open, and charged.

Eighteen

Taking control of the engine room was, well, not easy, but easier than Trip had thought it would be. They'd had a big advantage from the start: when the six of them burst in, they immediately shifted the ratio of human to Denari in their favor.

Part of that was because a big chunk of the Denari engineering staff had been on the bridge, as he learned afterwards, waiting for the "remote sensor" they'd put in the manifold to report back.

It was also because Ryan and Yee had gone on duty early, so the two of them were working right alongside Lieutenant Hess on the lower level when Reed opened the door and charged.

And this Colonel Peranda Travis and Cooney had been going on about—"smarter—a lot smarter than he seems at first"—had only posted half a dozen guards in the room—three on the upper level, three below.

Malcolm and Hoshi took out one each when they entered. Ryan smacked one with a spanner from behind as he was about to fire on the newcomers. One started down the gantry, firing as he went. He managed to clip Cooney in the shoulder, sending him skidding across the deck to land in a heap against the wall, out cold. Hess caught the soldier's ankles from behind and the man flipped head over heels down the gangway, smacking himself unconscious on the way down.

Trip got the fifth soldier himself, peeking out from behind the intermix chamber, and then there was only one left. Reed played a game of hide-and-seek with him for a minute, while Travis sneaked around the chamber and came up behind him. The man raised his hands in surrender, but Reed stunned him anyway. No time to deal with captives.

Trip jogged to the nearest control station and sealed the doors. He lowered the emergency bulkheads behind them.

Nothing short of a phase torpedo was going to get them out of here now.

All that was left was the easy part—at least, as they'd laid it out, during those hours they'd waited in the cell-ship. Having Hess here, and Yee and Ryan—that was a bonus he hadn't counted on then. He gave them the tasks he'd originally assigned to Malcolm, Hoshi, and the professor: Ryan at the auxiliary control panel with him, Hess and Yee at the life-support station.

"Reroute everything right here," he told the two junior engineers. "This panel. You two go from the armory on up, I'll do the bridge on down."

Behind him, he heard Hess and Yee hard at work as well.

The com began sounding a minute into their task.

"Engineering, this is Doctor En'hakar in the sickbay. We are experiencing difficulty with our diagnostics. Please advise."

"Engineering, Lieutenant Hava in the armory. I do not have control of ship's weapons. Please respond."

"This is Westerberg on the helm. Autopilot has engaged, and I can't reroute to manual control. Guys, what's going on down there?"

Westerberg. Trip smiled.

Brodesser, whom Trip had seen out of the corner of his eye, walking around the chamber, stepped up next to him and smiled as well.

"I told you he'd be here, didn't I?"

"Like old home week," Trip said, punching in a new series of control instructions to the helm—the last of the bridge stations he had to reconfigure. He saw Ryan and Yee were seconds away from being done as well.

He turned to the life-support station.

"Lieutenant?"

"Just a second," Hess said. "We're rerouting the last of the override circuits."

"Commander?" Travis was standing by the main entrance. "I can hear them out there."

Trip frowned. That was quick. Not that they could do anything out there, with the door and the bulkheads to get through, but still . . .

"All done here," Hess said.

Trip turned back to the auxiliary console.

"Ryan? We're waiting on you."

"Not any more, sir." He stepped back as well.

Trip looked around the room. Hoshi was with Cooney, who seemed to be coming around. Travis

213

was on the main door, Malcolm on the upper level, the rest of them right alongside him, ready to go to work.

"All right," he said. "Let's tell this Peranda of yours who's in charge of the ship now." He reached for a com panel.

"Commander?"

That was Reed, standing at the top of the stairs.

"I don't think we should contact him," Reed said. "I think we cut life support right now."

Trip frowned. "That wasn't the plan."

"We didn't know there were a hundred soldiers aboard when we made the plan," Malcolm said. "We start talking, we give him time to react. Who knows what he'll do? Sabotage the ship?"

"Your lieutenant's right." Cooney had drawn himself up to a sitting position. "Peranda's a snake. Believe me. Even if he agreed to surrender, I wouldn't trust him for a second."

"Gotta second that, sir," Travis put in. "The colonel strikes me as the kind of man who would stoop to anything. Booby traps. Sabotage. You name it."

Trip nodded. "All right."

It was hardly sporting of them, he felt like pointing out, to just cut the atmosphere off completely without warning. And there was Westerberg to consider. But the others had a point. Peranda had an overwhelming numerical advantage. Best give him no time at all to use it.

"Sir?" That was Yee. "One of the launch bay doors is opening."

"Close it."

"Already done."

Well. Peranda wasn't stupid. He wasn't going to sit around and wait for them to make a move.

"Airlocks on F- and G-decks opening."

"Shut them too. All right, Lieutenant," he said to Hess. "Let's do it. Cut life support."

Hess nodded and punched in the command.

Not more than five seconds later, the com sounded.

"Colonel Peranda to engineering. Cooney, Mayweather, whatever sort of stunt you have in mind—"

Trip punched into the transmission.

"This is Commander Charles Tucker, Colonel. Chief Engineer of *Enterprise*. This isn't a stunt. This is us kicking you off our ship. Don't worry, though—we don't intend for anyone to die. We just want you a little more . . . tractable."

There was a pause. "Tucker. I see I should have trusted my instincts more. Not let Cooney and Mayweather go off together. Well, what's done is done. Let's deal with the present situation."

"No deals," Trip interrupted. "In case you hadn't noticed, I'm in control of the ship now."

"Here is my deal," Peranda said. "You have five seconds to turn life support back on, or your Westerberg is dead. Starting now. Five—four—"

"Don't do it, Tucker!" Westerberg called out, his voice carrying over the com.

Trip looked over at Travis. "Is he serious?"

The answer was plain to see in the helmsman's eyes.

Trip ran a hand through his hair. "Colonel, I want to warn you that if—"

"Time is up, Tucker. And I see life support is still off." The sound of a phase pistol firing came over the com. "So Westerberg is dead."

Peranda's words echoed through the chamber.

"Son of a bitch," Cooney said.

Trip looked around and saw the same shock and disbelief he felt on every face in the room.

"Now," Peranda said, a hint of self-satisfaction in his voice that made Trip's blood boil, "my next action will be to destroy the helm console. I have enough firepower here to do that, I guarantee you. In five seconds. Five—four—"

Trip's mind raced. He couldn't think of a thing to do. Nothing. Except what Peranda wanted, and that wasn't acceptable.

"Damn it."

He stepped back from the console and slammed his fist into the hull. This was not in their plan.

He looked around the room. "Any ideas? Anybody?"

No one spoke.

"—and zero," Peranda said. Again, the sound of a phaser firing. Then a second, and the hiss of electric sparking.

And silence.

"From what I can tell from here," Ryan said quietly. "Helm is gone."

Trip swore again. All right, they could reroute helm function to another console. They'd lose some control, but Travis could handle it. But what—

"Next," Peranda said, and he was breathing heavily now. No surprise—they were all going to start getting a little light-headed soon. "I shall destroy every station on the bridge. Commander, I am not joking. I will take this ship down with me if you don't give—us—back—life support."

All at once, Travis was standing next to Trip.

"He has people on this ship—passengers he's ferrying back to Denari. They're important to him. Tell him he can take them when he goes."

Trip shook his head. "No, damn it. This guy just killed a man, and we give what he wants? No." The thought of it made him sick.

"Five," Peranda said.

"We lose the bridge, we lose control of the ship," Travis said.

Trip looked at Travis, and over at Malcolm.

"Do it," Reed said. "Give him what he wants. We'll deal with the consequences later."

"Three," Peranda said, slowly. "Two—"

What he wants. He'll kill all of us, his own people included, to get what he wants.

Bet those soldiers wouldn't necessarily like that.

Trip punched the channel open.

"Denari soldiers, you destroy the bridge, you destroy the ship. Peranda hasn't told you that, has he? You doom yourselves. Don't do it. Whoever's up there, holding those phasers. Don't do it. We promise—"

"Zero," Peranda said.

A phase pistol fired.

Trip heard voices in the background. Shouting. The channel went dead.

He spun around to Ryan. "Tell me something."

The ensign was frantically tracing a signal path on his console. "Looks like the weapons station is not operational."

"That's all?"

"That's all."

Son of a gun. Maybe . . .

"Tucker to the bridge. Colonel?"

No response.

"Sir?" That was Hess.

"What?"

"They still have emergency lighting up there. If I can cut that as well, they won't be able to see. They won't be able to hit anything."

Trip slapped himself on the forehead.

"I'm an idiot," he said. "Do it."

He punched open a channel again. "Tucker to the bridge. Don't panic. Don't panic. We will turn life support back on shortly and evacuate you. Do not panic."

Still no response. He looked back over at Ryan.

"All other stations still test out."

Trip exhaled in relief, and shook his head.

He looked up at Reed.

"I thought you said that would be the easy part."

"Best-laid plans, and all that." Malcolm shrugged, and started down the stairs to the main level.

"Come on, Travis. Let's get those EVA suits, and get to work."

They went through the ship one deck at a time, starting with the bridge. Reed and Travis, in EVA suits, disarmed all the soldiers, then brought them to the turbolift, where Cooney and Yee took over, ferrying the barely conscious Denari down three at a time first to the brig—they put the stunned Peranda in a cell by himself—and then when that filled up, to junior crew quarters as they could find them.

The last thing they did was take Westerberg's body and bring it down to sickbay.

They then cleared B-deck without incident and took access ladders down to C. There, near the upper-level entrance to engineering, Reed and Travis found a knot of soldiers clumped behind the bulkhead. They had been working at the emergency panel, obviously trying to raise it so they could get at the door beyond.

Travis and Reed each bent and each lifted a man to his feet. They began to drag them down to the turbolift.

"Hold it," Reed said, stopping in the middle of the corridor. He set his man down and drew Travis's attention to the left-hand wall, down near the floor, where a silver disk half the size of a man's hand was stuck to the wall.

A barely visible beam of pale blue light, the thickness of a human hair, extended from the disk across the corridor.

"What is it?"

"Not a doorbell, I can safely say." Reed knelt down next to it and held out a sensor. "A little present from the colonel, I believe. A nasty little explosive device."

"Sir, all I can say is, I'm glad you have good eyes," Travis said.

"It's my job." Reed shook his head and stood. "No way to disarm it. For now, let's just tread carefully."

Travis nodded, looked down at the man he held propped up against the wall. The soldier was dazed, and just this side of conscious. Deprive him of oxygen too long, and they would end up killing him. They'd have to deal with this little booby trap later.

Reed bent down and, with a grunt, slung his man over his shoulder, then stepped over the beam.

Travis followed suit.

But ten meters down, they found another disk just like the first.

Reed set down his man, hopped over the beam, and walked farther down the corridor.

"And again," he said, kneeling down. "There seem to be quite a lot of these, actually."

"Not going to be able to work like this," Travis said. Lifting a half-conscious man a foot in the air one time was doable. Having to lift that weight over and over again . . .

"No," Reed agreed. "We're not."

He opened a channel.

A few minutes later, Commander Tucker had joined them, wearing an EVA suit of his own and carrying a full complement of diagnostic tools.

"This idiot Peranda," Trip said as he worked. "Half his crew's gonna suffocate, and we're gonna get the blame."

He was using a portable sensor to scan the interior of the device, look at the circuitry inside, and see what he could use to disarm it. The more he looked, the less he liked. Nasty was the word for this thing, all right. It was a set-once, never-use-again explosive. There was no way to deactivate it electronically—any stray current would more than likely set it off. That was unacceptable—it looked like the charge was powerful enough to tear through the corridor wall, maybe even through the hull beyond.

He frowned.

"We're going to have to get in there and physically disconnect the wires."

"How do we do that?"

Trip reached back into his box of tools and pulled out a set of micropliers.

"Very carefully," he said.

It took him half a minute to disarm the first one. He got faster as he moved on. Still, by the time he'd covered the entire length of corridor between the bulkhead and the turbolift, a good five minutes had passed. Five minutes they didn't have.

He stood up, and saw both Denari were now unconscious.

There was another stretch of corridor past the turbolift. Trip pointed in that direction.

"I'll check down there," he said, pointing. "You get the rest of the soldiers onto the lift."

Reed and Travis handed off their unconscious charges to a waiting Cooney and Hess. Trip moved past them into the next corridor.

This wasn't exactly going the way he'd planned either. If they didn't work very quickly, a lot of people were going to die.

He turned a corner and frowned.

No booby traps that he could see, but four more soldiers lay stretched out on the floor before him. Unconscious, passed out directly in front of a single door. Unused crew quarters, if he was remembering right. Why were they here?

He approached the door. Locked. Why—

All at once he remembered. Peranda's passengers.

He opened a channel.

"Ryan?"

"Right here, sir."

"Do me a favor. C-deck, Cabin 428. Open it, will you?"

"Aye, sir. One minute."

Trip waited. How many people were in here? he wondered. Should they put them with the other Denari? Probably the safest move—keep them separate, but definitely under lock and key, until they knew who they were dealing with.

The door slid open, and Trip stepped through.

The room was dark. His eyes took a moment to adjust. Details of the room came to him—a table and two chairs, a couch behind it. The configuration of the walls was completely unfamiliar. Had Peranda actually gone into the superstructure and—

All at once, he remembered. Cabin 428, and 430 next to it—those had both been unused crew quarters. The captain had asked for more substantial guest rooms after the incident with the Jantaleyse ambassador. Trip had suggested joining two spare compartments together, gotten Archer's okay, and promptly passed the assignment along. At which point, he'd forgotten all about it. Well, not forgotten, it was on his follow-up list, but pretty far down that rather lengthy series of items. This was the first time he was seeing the end result in person.

All in all, a pretty good job had been done, he decided.

He'd save the detailed inspection for later, though. Right now the important thing was that 428 was empty. The adjoining door led him into 430, the converted sleeping quarters.

And this room, he saw instantly, was occupied.

A soldier, unconscious on the floor, just past the entryway. Two people on the bed, also lying still: a boy, farthest from him, who looked immediately familiar for some reason, and a woman, turned on her side, away from the door.

Even as Trip reached out a hand to roll her toward him, he realized whose face he was going to see. Who Peranda's passengers were.

Captain Duvall and her son.

As he touched her shoulder, began to move her, he saw he was right. He saw something else as well.

Duvall's eyes were wide open.

Even before Trip had a chance to absorb that information, she let out a scream and jumped up at him.

He stumbled backwards and tripped over the unconscious soldier. He toppled over on his back on the floor.

Duvall was on him in an instant. Trip tried to reach for his phase pistol, but in his weakened condition and inside the EVA suit, he felt like he was moving in slow motion. His arms wouldn't do what his brain told them to—not quick enough, anyway.

Duvall pinned his arms down to the floor with her knees and pulled his phase pistol out herself. She jammed it up against his face mask, square between his eyes.

Then her expression changed.

She lowered the pistol. "Tucker?"

The word was barely audible through the mask.

She stepped back and let him get to his feet.

Even as Trip rose, she was walking back to the bed and reaching under the pillow.

She came up with an emergency breathing mask, put it on, and inhaled deeply.

She looked up and said something to him.

Trip tapped on the side of his helmet—can't hear you.

"A good captain is always prepared," she said, speaking loudly and clearly.

Next to her, the boy sat up in bed. He had a breathing mask too.

Trip opened a channel.

"Malcolm?"

"Right here. The corridor all set?"

"It's clear. Four soldiers about ten meters down, another one inside Cabin 428, all right? And I've found Peranda's prisoners too."

"An unexpected bonanza."

"You could say that. Listen, make it quick with those four, all right? I'm gonna have Ryan turn life support back on in this section now."

"Will do. Reed out."

Trip piped in Ryan and told him what to do. All the while, Duvall watched him, wondering what he was going to do. Trip was wondering that himself.

A minute passed. Travis came into the room and got the soldier Trip had fallen over, who was struggling back to consciousness. He looked at Duvall and the boy, and shot Trip a question with his eyes.

"Not a word about this just yet, all right, Travis?" Trip said over the com.

"Aye, sir. Not a word."

Travis left. Trip took his helmet off. The air was stale, but he was able to breathe.

Duvall had her arm around her son. She looked up at him.

"Where's Jonny?" she said.

Trip frowned.

"Jonny?"

"Captain Archer. I want to talk to him."

"He's not here." Trip was puzzled. Jonny? Nobody called the captain Jonny—not that he knew of, anyway. And how did Duvall know that Archer had command of this ship?

Of course she knew, he realized. Sadir had known—he must have told her.

"Starfleet sent you, didn't they?" she said. "I knew this day would come. I'm prepared to explain my actions. I won't try and defend what I did, but I hope people will understand—"

"Captain," Trip said, and then stopped. He didn't know quite where to begin. What to say to Duvall. Was any of this his business, even?

"Starfleet didn't send us. We just . . ." He frowned. "It's a long story. And this is a complicated situation, ma'am."

"It is that," she said. "Sorry about before, but I thought you might have been someone else. Someone sent to hurt Lee."

The boy looked up for the first time then, and Trip got a good look at him at last. He had to be twelve, maybe thirteen—skinny as a beanpole, but looking at his shoulders, his hands, his face, you could already see he was going to fill out. Going to end up bigger than his father, from what Trip remembered of Sadir. A lot bigger.

He looked at the boy's face again, and decided that he didn't look anything like the general. Not at all. Trip could see a bit of Captain Duvall in him—the eyes, especially—but the set of his jaw, the brow, the basic shape of his face . . . this boy was going to be his own man, clearly. And soon.

Trip frowned.

That sense of recognition was back again. He couldn't place it.

"I can handle myself," the boy—Lee—said. "Besides, Peranda wouldn't have dared try anything."

Trip forced himself not to smile. Teenage bluster—except that the kid was so serious, Trip almost believed him. Probably thought people really were afraid of him. And no wonder—he'd gotten so used to having people do for him, jump for him, that he'd forgotten the real reason why they obeyed—who they really took their orders from. Kid was in for a rude awakening, and soon.

"I'll ask you to stay here," Trip said, "until we decide what to do."

That was part of the truth. He also had the feeling that if the *Daedalus* crew members found out their turncoat captain was on board with them, there would be a mighty ugly scene. Duvall might not get the chance to offer whatever explanations she had. He would have to trust her and Lee to keep to their cabin, though—he really couldn't spare anyone to keep an eye on them.

And he couldn't spare any more time here. He had to check the rest of this deck for Parenda's little booby traps, and then start on D and E as well. They needed the colonel and his crew secured, and then they needed to find the people who really belonged on this ship. *Enterprise*'s crew. Though Kairn would certainly be interested in Duvall and her son. Still, he would hold off contacting *Eclipse* until he had found the captain. He would leave it to Archer to decide what to do about these two.

Jonny. Trip smiled.

Something told him that in this universe, there had been a little more going on between the captain and Duvall than a case of hero worship.

Nineteen

THEY BEGAN SEEING the first signs of battle about half an hour after leaving the Belt behind them. A hunk of metal, a cube four meters square, drifted past them to starboard.

"Analysis confirms. That is the reaction chamber of a Stinger vessel," T'Pol said, studying her console. "I am picking up a trail of wreckage leading toward the site General Makandros marked for us."

Archer nodded. That trail was all that remained of the DEF's First Battalion—Makandros's ships that had been ambushed by Elson's forces. The general had asked them to come this way during their reconnaissance, to search for specific items among the wreckage: debris from PDC vessels—computer storage arrays, weapons systems, engine components—that might contain salvageable data, information Makandros could use in the coming days.

The captain guided the Stinger along the debris path now, marveling at the extent of destruction. Ships blown in half, ships with their hulls blackened and scarred by weapons fire, vast quantities of metal and plastic too melted or mangled to attempt to identify—it had clearly been a violent battle, and the wreckage itself told the story. The DEF, surprised, outnumbered, outgunned, communications suddenly jammed, retreating in close formation, instantly recognizing the battle as lost, trying to preserve an escape route for at least one of their ships to warn General Makandros of Elson's treachery.

The captain suddenly remembered the trick Makandros had used to capture them after their escape from Rava, when the general's computers had seized control of the Stinger's guidance system and weaponry. He wondered if the retreating Stingers of the First Battalion had utilized the same strategy to maintain such close formation in retreat.

"Considerable amounts of radiation in this area, sir," T'Pol said. "It is affecting our sensors, particularly long-range scanning ability."

"Let's not spend a lot of time here then," Archer said. "One quick pass through, see if we can spot what the general's after, and then we're on our way."

"Aye, sir."

Archer switched them onto autopilot, instructing the ship's guidance system to parallel the debris trail. Mentally, his focus shifted from the wreckage laid out before them to the next stop in their mission—Colonna Station, a DEF military outpost halfway between the Denari system and the interstellar void. While the outpost had reported no signs of PDC forces in their area, Makandros's greatest fear was another flanking maneuver by Elson's forces. If PDC ships surrounded the combined Guild/DEF fleet before they were ready to fight—before their logistics and supply units had fully integrated the two forces—the war would be over before it started.

A smear of blue and green in the far left-hand corner of the viewscreen suddenly caught the captain's attention—the anomaly. They would pass near it on their way to Colonna—near enough to get a good long look at the object. As he and T'Pol had discussed on resuming their stations first thing this morning, they planned to slow from full impulse during their closest approach, to allow time for the Denari sensors to fully map not just the anomaly, but the surrounding region of space. T'Pol also planned on thoroughly scanning the area for any artificial satellites—though Makandros and Kairn had been quite insistent that neither maintained such devices in the region, they had already passed a sufficient number of them on their journey to make Archer think it a chance worth taking.

The captain still had no idea how they were going to get the data they needed to return home. His sleep the night before had been fitful, his mind wrestling with the question until far too late in the evening. Only one idea of any real merit had occurred to him: Victor Brodesser. He'd learned from Kairn that the professor was with Trip and Hoshi, and in Archer's opinion, if there was anyone who could solve the impossible, it would be *Daedalus*'s designer.

"Captain?"

He turned to T'Pol.

"Picking up an energy source, sir. Headed straight toward us," she said.

"And there it is." That was Yamani, at the weapons

console. He was pointing to the main viewscreen, where a barely visible speck of light, at about ten o'clock relative to their current heading, glinted in the distance.

"What is it?"

"A ship, sir," T'Pol said. "Further telemetry coming in now."

A status indicator on Archer's console began blinking. Yamani had just put weapons on alert status. Archer nodded in approval. Though the odds of running into PDC forces out here were slim . . .

Better safe than sorry.

"Life signs?" he asked.

T'Pol shook her head. "The radiation is masking my readings."

"Try hailing them."

"I have been. No response."

"Let's take a closer look." He switched the viewscreen to magnification level five. Immediately the image jumped into focus.

It was a Stinger—exactly like their ship. It looked virtually undamaged, some scoring from weapons fire on the side hull. Its running lights were on.

"Reactor is on-line, obviously," T'Pol announced. "Core temperature slightly higher than nominal but within acceptable boundaries. Hull is intact. Major systems are still powered. No structural damage—"

"Still nothing on communications?"

"No, sir. One moment." She made a series of adjustments to the sensor control panel. "Still no life signs, either. Although, again, the radiation is masking a great deal of the incoming telemetry."

The captain frowned. If there were survivors . . . injured crew . . .

He turned around in his seat and looked through the cockpit entrance to the main cabin beyond.

"D.O.," he called out.

The young woman, stationed at the front-most starboard weapons console, looked up.

"Sir?"

"This ship has EVA suits?"

"Yes, sir," O'Neill replied. "One for each of us, two spares."

Fifteen, then. Archer thought a moment.

"I want you to prepare an EVA team," he told her. "Eight people. We'll bring our ship alongside the derelict, you'll board and search for survivors. Ferry over spare suits if—"

"Captain," T'Pol interrupted, "that will not be necessary."

He turned in his seat to face her.

"There is a rupture in the other ship's coolant line. The on-board atmosphere is contaminated."

Engine coolant. Archer sighed and shook his head. They were all dead, then.

"Is the ship salvageable?"

She nodded. "Once the gas is vented."

"Makandros will want to know. Transmit this location and our data to him."

"Aye, sir." T'Pol swiveled in her chair to access the controls.

The instrument panel before her exploded.

The ship pitched to starboard. Archer barely managed to stay in his seat.

"Two ships!" Yamani shouted. "At nine and three

o'clock, both firing projectile weapons. All weapons stations, return fire!"

Data streamed across the captain's console. Archer took a second to take in the smallest, most salient bits of it—the two ships were PDC, fighter class, small two-person vessels, directly to port and starboard, closing fast—then he disengaged the autopilot and took control of the helm. Set course: twenty degrees down from zero axis and straight ahead.

He punched engines, full impulse.

"Where the hell did they come from? T'Pol?"

There was no response.

Archer turned.

She lay still, head and shoulders draped across the com panel. He saw blood—green blood; he had never seen Vulcan blood this close before—streaming from a cut on her forehead.

"Medkit!" he shouted, turning his head. "I need a medkit up here, and I need someone on sensors. Kowalski! Get—"

Space in front of them flared bright white.

Archer raised a hand to shield his eyes. That and the fact that he was facing away from the viewscreen saved him from being completely blinded. He braced for the shock wave. It hit a nanosecond later, the same way the wave back in Sydney that had sworn him off bodysurfing forever had hit: like a bad-tempered Sumo wrestler.

He was shoved backwards in his seat. The ship shuddered. The captain could hear it—literally hear it—trying to shake apart. Metal groaned.

That was no projectile weapon.

"Ensign?" He turned to Yamani, the question in his eyes.

"Photon charges—about a half-dozen of them."

"They didn't come from those two little ships," Archer said.

"No, sir. Tracking their trajectory." Yamani frowned. "Sir . . ."

From the tone of his voice, Archer knew it wasn't good news.

"There's a third ship," Yamani said. "Much larger than the other two. It fired the photon charges."

Archer took a quick glance at the sensor panel and saw the ensign was right. The third ship was easily twice their size. And cutting hard to follow their change of course—moving at .75 light speed. The Stinger's impulse engines topped out at a max of .6 light speed.

Not good. Not only were they outnumbered, they were outclassed as well.

Time to get out of here, he thought, and reached down to engage the warp engines.

They were off-line.

He punched open a channel to the Stinger's engineering chamber just below the main deck.

"Sir, I—" It was Lieutenant Hess.

"I need warp drive," Archer said, not wasting any time on preamble. "Now."

"I can't give it to you. That first blast destabilized the reaction chamber."

"Stabilize it."

"That's what I'm trying to do."

"How long?"

"At least an hour."

"You've got ten minutes."

"Ten minutes to realign the crystals? It can't be done, sir."

"Make it happen, Lieutenant. Or we're all dead."

He closed the channel.

"You are being unrealistic, Captain."

That was T'Pol's voice.

Archer looked to his right.

His science officer was sitting up, holding a compress to her forehead with one hand, working the sensor console with the other. Kowalski stood over her with the medkit, frowning.

He breathed a sigh of relief. "You're all right?"

"I am fine. Ensign, you can return to your station. Captain, it normally takes a day to align the crystals in the reaction chamber. Ten minutes is an unrealistic time frame."

"In case you hadn't noticed, it's three against one here, Sub-Commander. Ten minutes is what we have—if we're lucky."

As if to prove his point, Yamani spoke up.

"Here they come again," the ensign called out.

Archer checked the console. The two smaller PDC ships were indeed coming hard on their tail, trying to herd them into the larger vessel's line of fire. Pincer formation—the captain recognized it once. Looked to him like the Denari had taken a few strategy lessons from *Daedalus*'s computer, as well as weapons and warp drive. The pincer formation was a textbook attack maneuver, right out of the Academy's first-year battle tactics course.

Which the captain had aced.

"Hold on to your stomachs," he said, and hit braking thrusters hard as he could.

The inertial dampers on the Stinger were good. Archer heard a minimum of cursing from the main cabin behind him.

The two PDC fighters shot past and just barely missed colliding with each other. The larger vessel, though, wasn't fooled. It adjusted azimuth in midattack, and fired photon charges again.

The captain hit full impulse as hard as he could, sent them screaming straight downward. Barely in time. The charges went off behind them. The captain rode the shock wave as best he could.

By the time he'd stabilized the Stinger, he saw the three PDC vessels were re-forming for another run. Delta formation.

Archer reversed course and made for the debris trail again. He had the idea of snaking in and out of the wreckage, using it to fool at least the smaller ships' sensors.

Twenty seconds into the maneuver, he could see it wasn't working.

"T'Pol," he said, gunning them up and away from the wreckage. "Please tell Lieutenant Hess she now has five minutes to get me warp drive."

"I am in contact with the lieutenant, sir. Again, five minutes is not a realistic—"

"Realistic is not an option at this point," Archer said. "Tell her to do the best she can."

"An incorrectly aligned crystal will destroy us as surely as a photon charge."

"I'm open to other options." Archer shook his head. The larger ship was coming for them now. He changed course, put one of the smaller vessels between the two of them. Elementary blocking tactic—it worked long enough to slow their pursuers. Temporarily.

"How the hell did we get into this mess anyway? Where did these ships come from?"

"I believe I have discovered a blind spot in our sensor grid, which the two smaller vessels took advantage of."

"What about the big ship?"

"It must have waited out of range until the attack commenced. As I mentioned earlier, the radiation surrounding the debris field has affected our long-range scanning ability."

That was something the PDC ships had no doubt counted on.

Archer suddenly realized something else. "The blind spot in our sensors—the PDC knew about it before they attacked."

"Yes, sir."

"So it's not just this ship that has it. It's all the Stingers. A design flaw. We should let Makandros know."

"I have been trying to send a transmission."

"Trying?"

"Our signals are being jammed."

Of course they were.

The ship shuddered again.

Near miss. He'd lost track of one of the smaller ships for a second, and it had come in firing at them. Projectile weapons only, but still—

One direct hit, and they were history. The Stinger had no hull plating to polarize, and few defensive weapons to speak of—not to mention those faulty sensors. At least the PDC didn't know about the general's little trick with the computers—

The captain sat up straight.

"Riley!" he yelled. "Get up here and fly this ship!"

"Sir?" T'Pol asked.

"Gonna even up the odds here a little, Sub-Commander." Archer hunched over the helm, bringing them around the debris trail again, searching. Ah. There it was.

He became aware of Riley standing over him.

"Take the helm," he said, getting to his feet. "Keep us in range of that vessel, all right?"

As she sat, he leaned over her shoulder and pointed at the viewscreen—at the Stinger they'd passed scant minutes ago, the ship with the coolant leak and its running lights still on.

"In range?" Riley frowned. "What does that mean?"

T'Pol responded before the captain could.

"It means keep us close enough to allow our computer's guidance signals to control that ship. The exact limit of that control is currently uncertain—unless you know differently, sir?"

Archer smiled. "No, I don't."

"I get it," Riley said.

The floor dropped out from underneath them—Riley dodging another projectile blast.

Archer clapped her on the shoulder and moved to T'Pol's station.

"So how do we do this?" he asked.

"I am accessing the Stinger's command-line interface. Instructions should be available to us there."

Her fingers flew across the console. Archer

watched her work and wished he'd asked Makandros for more details about how the computer tie-in worked, exactly. How far apart the two ships could be for the linkage to operate.

"Direct hit on the larger vessel," Yamani said, a note of satisfaction in his voice. "They're dropping back."

"Nice work, Ensign," Archer said, not lifting his eyes from T'Pol's console. He could see what she was doing—scrolling rapidly through an interface that listed all ship functions, breaking them down into menus, submenus, sub-submenus and so on, searching for the right one.

She just wasn't doing it fast enough.

He took the empty station next to her.

"I'll work from the bottom of the interface," he said, and brought up the same display she was looking at. Environmental systems function, atmospheric control function, exhaust flow control function—

The ship suddenly accelerated—Archer felt the impulse engines rumbling—and shot forward.

"Delta formation again," Yamani said.

"Roger that," Riley said. "Hang on."

They banked right. Archer felt a shock wave—another photon charge?—push them even harder in that direction.

He went back to the console.

Sensor control function, sensor storage function, sensor calibration function—

"Captain," T'Pol said suddenly. "I have it."

Archer looked at her screen. Weapons control function, remote guidance subsystems, interface protocol . . .

Bingo.

"System seems relatively straightforward. Instructions to the satellite vessel are routed through communications . . ." Her voice trailed off, and she looked over at the captain.

"Communications are jammed," he said.

She nodded. "Over a short distance, though, we should be able to insure signal integrity."

T'Pol brought up the system interface on-screen. She began punching in commands. A moment later, she frowned.

"No response from the other ship. It is either damaged, or we are not close enough."

All at once, they banked hard left—so hard Archer almost fell out of his seat.

He was about to remind Riley that a little advance warning was called for on maneuvers like that when he looked up at the viewscreen and saw they were right on top of the other Stinger again.

"Thank you, Ensign," T'Pol said. "Systems are now handshaking. Captain, we have control of the other vessel."

"Well done, everyone. Give me helm here," the captain said, leaning over his console. "Send weapons to Mister Yamani's station."

T'Pol did as he asked. The captain studied the control layout—exactly like this Stinger's. Excellent.

"All right." He checked the position of the three PDC ships—the two smaller ones were corkscrewing around the debris field, using it as cover, coming back for them. The larger ship had moved off. Archer saw why now. The hit that ship had taken had resulted in debris blocking a weapons port. Elson's people were probably clearing it out. It would take them a few more minutes to get back in the battle.

But the captain didn't have that time.

Too bad. The first attack with the other Stinger was going to come as a complete surprise. He would have liked to use it up on the ship that posed the biggest danger.

They'd get to her soon enough, though.

"All right," he said. "Let's see if we can't teach these ships a little second-year strategy. Ensign Riley, you know Rackham's back door?"

He heard her laugh. "Yes, sir. I do indeed."

"Mister Yamani?"

"Rodriguez and I were just talking about it the other day, Captain."

"All right. Let's do it. We're the decoy, obviously."

T'Pol frowned. "Rackham's back door?"

"It's an old Academy attack move. A little unorthodox," he smiled, "but that's exactly why it'll work."

"Could you be more specific?" T'Pol asked.

Archer smiled. "You might as well just watch."

The two fighters were bearing down in pincer formation again.

Riley punched thrusters, and drove straight at them.

At the last possible second, she dove. The PDC fighters fired—two misses, not even close—and then moved to follow, practically skidding to a halt in space and turning.

"Nice," Archer said.

He saw the corner of Riley's mouth turn up in a smile.

"Here comes the fun part," she replied.

The fighters had made long arching parabolas in space that brought them right up on the Stinger's tail. Now Riley cut forward thrust in half, which put them back in range of the PDC weapons. The captain could well imagine the smiles the pilots of those ships were wearing right now. They thought one of those last rounds of weapons fire must have gotten them, that their engines were going. That the chase was almost at an end.

The captain smiled.

They're right about that, he thought.

All three vessels passed the apparently disabled DEF Stinger.

And Archer activated that ship's drive.

"They see it, sir," T'Pol said. "They're veering off."

Too little, too late. Yamani already had the other ship's weapons stations on-line.

"Locked on target," Yamani said.

Archer smiled. "Fire."

Streaks of light—charged torpedoes—flew from the DEF ship toward the fighters. One dodged. The other didn't.

It exploded in a sudden flash of orange and white.

Riley punched thrusters and shot after the remaining fighter. It veered frantically from left to right, trying to escape pursuit.

The Stinger closed.

"At your discretion, Mister Yamani."

The ensign didn't waste a second.

"Charges away," he said, and a heartbeat later, the second fighter exploded.

Riley took them right through the hail of white and orange it left behind.

"Rackham's back door," T'Pol said. "Interesting."

"Not textbook execution," the captain said. "But it worked. Nice job, people."

He looked up at the viewscreen just in time to see a third explosion.

"What . . ."

"The other Stinger," T'Pol said, "has just been destroyed."

The big PDC ship, Archer saw, was moving toward them again.

Yamani's console flashed.

"Weapons lock!" the ensign shouted.

"Initiating evasive action," Riley said.

Archer was about to tell her to stay on course—they had momentum, they should use it.

But Riley's reactions were too quick. Even before he could open his mouth, she hit thrusters hard, veering them back toward the debris trail.

Mistake, the captain thought.

Space around them flared white.

Archer didn't have time to brace himself. The ship wrenched hard left, and he went with it, slamming into the cockpit wall. He stumbled and went to his knees.

His vision swam.

"Direct hit!" Yamani was yelling. "Aft hull plating. Weapons stations A and B disabled."

Archer blinked and looked behind him.

The main cabin was on fire. Half a dozen of his crew lay on the deck, stunned. O'Neill was bleeding, Rodriguez was rolling on the floor, crying out.

"Captain, I only have half thrusters."

That was Riley, right above him.

Archer grabbed on to the back of the nearest chair and pulled himself upright. Every muscle in his body was sore. He reached for the com, to respond to Hess . . .

And saw the main viewscreen was black.

"Lateral sensor array is off-line," T'Pol said. "Trying to compensate."

He nodded and opened the com.

"Archer to engineering. Report."

"Hess here. Not good news, sir. Got another ten minutes before the field collapses. We'll have to shut down before then."

Ten minutes of life left in the engine. Archer frowned.

He turned to the main cabin and called the first person he saw.

"Duel!"

The ensign, tending to one of his fallen comrades, looked up. "Sir?"

"Get those EVA suits down. Get them prepped and ready."

"Aye, Captain."

Archer spun back to the cockpit crew.

Riley was half turned around in her chair, anguish in her eyes.

"Sorry, sir," she said. "My fault. I should have—"

"Enough," Archer snapped. Her eyes widened in surprise.

If she was expecting sympathy, he didn't have time.

"Keep us from getting hit again. I know," he managed a smile, "you won't make the same mistake twice."

"No, sir. I will not," she said, and bent to her task.

The viewscreen came back to life.

The PDC ship was closing—fast.

"Mister Yamani, we still have starboard weapons?"

"Yes, sir."

"Ensign Riley, keep us starboard to that vessel. No matter what."

His mind ran through scenarios—Academy battle simulations, his own limited combat experience, stories he'd heard from other captains. Nothing.

"Anyone? Any thoughts?"

The ship shuddered again. Archer heard the crew behind him returning fire.

"Jettison the warp core," Yamani said. "Lure the PDC ship near it, and set it off."

"Target it with our weapons, you mean?" the captain asked.

"Either that, or a timed charge."

"Unlikely to be effective. Their sensors will easily detect it," T'Pol said.

"You have a better idea?" the captain asked.

"I am thinking," T'Pol said.

Her console sparked. The viewscreen went black again.

"Sensors are off-line," she said.

Archer punched the com.

"Engineering?"

"Reactor is failing, sir. Ten minutes may have been optimistic."

Archer frowned.

He didn't like Yamani's idea any more than T'Pol had, but he didn't see as they had any other options.

"Lieutenant Hess, I'm sending Ensign Yamani

down to engineering. We're jettisoning the warp core with timed charges attached."

"Won't be much of a bang, sir."

"What?"

"We pumped out most of the antimatter already. Just in case. I can activate the injectors again, but—"

"No," Archer said. "Never mind."

He looked at T'Pol.

"I don't see as we have much choice," he said. "Transmit our surrender."

She nodded and leaned over her console again.

A second later, she looked back up.

"Our signals are still being jammed. It appears the PDC are not interested in hearing what we have to say—under any circumstances."

He nodded, tight-lipped. There wasn't much left for them to do, then.

"Ensign Riley," he said. "Bring us around."

"Sir?"

He smiled grimly. "Let's take as many of these bastards as we can with us."

She nodded. "Aye, Captain."

T'Pol spoke again. "Perhaps I can reconfigure the targeting sensors to give us minimal scanning ability."

"Do it." The captain called Hess again.

"Lieutenant, does this vessel have a self-destruct circuit?"

She took a second before responding.

"Aye, sir. A ninety-second circuit."

"How late into the countdown can we abort?"

"Any time."

"Activate it now. Give me marks every ten seconds." Archer looked up and saw T'Pol had worked her magic. The viewscreen was live again, though the resolution was a fraction of what it had been, the images blurry and unfocused.

He could see one thing clear enough, though—the PDC vessel was closing fast.

He leaned over Riley's shoulder.

"At ten seconds, we're going to want to dive them."

"Aye, sir. A kamikaze run."

He nodded. "That's right."

"Seventy seconds, Captain." Lieutenant Hess's voice came over the com.

"Roger that," Archer said, and turned.

He looked out into the main cabin.

Circuits on the aft and port walls were still sparking—the consoles there were empty. O'Neill and Sanchez were leaned up against the engineering core, half-conscious. The rest of the crew was still working at starboard weapons stations.

The captain stepped through the cockpit door. All eyes turned to him.

"I'll keep this short, ladies and gentlemen."

"Not good news, is it, sir?" O'Neill asked.

"No. The PDC ship is not acknowledging our surrender."

His eyes went around the room quickly, making sure that each person understood the implications of what he'd just said.

"One minute." Hess's voice rang out behind him.

"We're going to try and take that last PDC ship with us," Archer said. "Self-destruct. Anyone who wants to abandon ship in one of those"—he nodded to the EVA suits that Duel had stacked in the center of the cabin—"is more than welcome. Go now, though."

He looked out among the sea of faces. No one moved.

"We're with you," D.O. spoke up. "Right to the end, sir."

Archer nodded.

"Thank you. Man your stations."

"Forty seconds," Hess's voice came back.

Archer stepped back into the cockpit.

The PDC ship was still closing.

"Is that another ship behind them?" Yamani asked.

Archer squinted. The ensign was right: a fourth vessel was now entering the fray—as if the PDC needed reinforcements.

"That's one big ship," Riley said. She was right: this vessel was even larger than the first, though that was all he could tell about the ship, with the limited sensor resolution they had right now.

"Thirty seconds, sir."

"Roger that." He frowned. "Ensign Riley, anyway you can think of to get us in range of both of them . . ."

"I'll be up for a commendation?"

The captain had to smile. "If I have anything to say about it."

She smiled back, and refocused her attention.

Archer's gaze came to rest on T'Pol. The two of them locked eyes a moment.

"Don't know if I can put in for a commendation for you, Sub-Commander. Seeing as how you're not officially Starfleet."

"I understand."

"Still . . ." He smiled. "I'll do what I can."

T'Pol seemed on the verge of a reply when all at once her station beeped.

"Second vessel is firing weapons, Captain," she announced. "Phased energy bursts. Not . . ."

Her voice trailed off.

The PDC ship behind them exploded.

Archer blinked. Either the big vessel had made a terrible mistake, or a miracle had just occurred.

"Twenty seconds."

"Incoming transmission," T'Pol announced. "It's . . . it's for you, sir."

For the first time since he'd known the Vulcan, T'Pol looked honestly surprised.

"What's the matter?"

She almost—and Archer thought he could see her straining to keep the expression on her face neutral—smiled.

"It's Commander Tucker," T'Pol said.

Archer thought he'd heard her wrong.

"Commander Tucker," she repeated, and put the signal on screen.

She was right. It was Trip.

What she hadn't mentioned was that he was sitting in the command chair on the bridge of the *Enterprise*.

Archer's chief engineer smiled and got to his feet.

"Captain. Sorry it took us so long."

Archer opened his mouth to respond, and couldn't think of a thing to say.

"Ten seconds," Hess called out.

The captain found his voice.

"Lieutenant," he smiled, "you can stand down self-destruct."

Twenty

A LONG, HOT SHOWER. A shave. A fresh uniform. A pot of strong coffee. Porthos curled up sleeping in his ready room. Archer was in heaven—or the closest to it he supposed he'd get in this life.

In other words, he was back aboard *Enterprise*, and all was right with the world. His world, anyway.

The Denari were still having trouble with theirs.

"You have my word, General," the captain told Makandros. Archer was in his command chair, Makandros's image on the main viewer before him. "We have no intention of leaving just yet."

And we may not be leaving at all, he could have added, but since he and T'Pol were still the only ones among the crew who knew that they lacked the sensor data that would enable them to return to their own universe, he kept silent on that score.

"I am glad to hear that, Captain. I would be gladder to hear you agree to my request."

"I understand that, sir. You'll understand that I must attend to the health and well-being of my ship and crew first."

"Of course," Makandros said, looking as if he did not, in fact, understand at all. "I will contact you again in a few hours. Let us say two hours, which should give you—"

"No." Archer shook his head. "I will contact you, General, once I've had a chance to discuss this with my senior staff."

Makandros glared. The captain felt certain that among the uncomplimentary thoughts rushing through the man's head this moment about Archer, foremost was regret at ever letting the captain and T'Pol off *Hule* once he'd had them there.

Archer couldn't blame him. The general was used to having his orders obeyed without question, not disregarded. Certainly while he was commander of the DEF, even more so now that was acting as commander of the combined DEF/Guild forces.

"Very well," Makandros said. "I will wait to hear from you." With a nod, he closed the circuit, and the screen cleared.

Archer sat back in his chair and looked around the bridge.

Every station was occupied. Every member of his crew, having been ferried back from *Hule* immediately on *Enterprise*'s arrival at the Guild/DEF rendezvous point, was hard at work, testing and retesting every circuit aboard the vessel, going over the repairs the Denari had performed—check that, the repairs Cooney and Hess had performed at the Denari's command—making sure all systems were back at nominal.

But there was one nagging problem they were still dealing with, a legacy this Colonel Peranda had left them: a series of booby traps located at several critical hall corridor junctures, and most seriously, a rather large explosive charge that had been planted in Launch Bay 2. While the booby traps were easy enough to disarm, the launch bay charge could not be removed without a code that Peranda possessed—a code the Colonel, currently cooling his heels inside *Enterprise*'s brig, had yet to surrender. Reed was down there now, trying to make the man see reason—much as Archer had done a few hours ago, on his way to the bridge.

Peranda had looked up at his entrance.

"Don't waste your time," he said. "I have nothing to say until you people are prepared to deal."

"There aren't going to be any deals."

Peranda remained silent.

"I'm Jonathan Archer, the captain of this ship."

"You know who I am."

"That's right. I know what you've done as well." Archer looked him in the eye. "I want the code to disarm that explosive in my launch bay."

"Are you prepared to deal?"

"I don't make deals with murderers." Trip had told him about Westerberg.

"Then we have nothing to say to each other."

Archer checked his anger. He would not let Peranda get to him.

"General Makandros is very interested in talking to you. Perhaps you'll speak more freely to him."

Peranda remained silent.

Archer had to give the man credit—he was playing the only card he had for all he was worth.

Archer wasn't going in on the game, though.

"I'll be back, Colonel. To see if you've changed your mind."

"I believe you will," Peranda said, in such a way that Archer looked him in the eye.

All at once, he had the feeling that the man had more tricks up his sleeve. The thought gave him pause.

Outside the brig, Reed was waiting.

"Nothing," Archer said. "I'll leave him to you, Malcolm."

"Aye, sir."

The captain had every confidence in his security officer and his team. He was certain they'd get not only the code from Peranda, but whatever other secrets the colonel was hiding.

He snapped back to the here and now, and glanced around the bridge. A lot of unfamiliar faces on the bridge at the moment—many of his officers were down in sickbay, getting a quick physical from Phlox. As everyone in the crew had been doing, in shifts, over the last few hours.

Those who had been most adversely affected by their time in the Denari environment were being confined to sickbay or placed on restricted duty—Dwight, Hoshi, Malzami, and Dingham so far, though Archer was certain that list would grow longer as Phlox saw the rest of the crew.

The captain himself felt back to a hundred percent, though he supposed a good part of that was psychological, a change in mood attributable to regaining control of his ship and his destiny. Now all that remained was to find a way back to their own universe . . .

And finish up the business that they had gotten involved in here. Which brought him right back around to Makandros's request.

Find General Sadir's son.

In the day he'd been gone, the DEF ships at Kota had won control of that facility. Elson had withdrawn his forces to Denari, to regroup there. The man was refusing all attempts at contact, at mediation.

A long, bloody civil war seemed inevitable.

"We must find the boy," Makandros had told him. "We could use your help. Your ship can—"

"I know what my ship can do, General. When it's at a hundred percent. Which we're not yet. Right now, we're piloting off an auxiliary helm station, there's a problem with our main sensor array, and we have booby traps scattered throughout the vessel."

"You'll let *us* know when *you're* ready," Makandros had said. Archer had said he would—once he talked it over with his staff, with Trip, in particular, who knew considerably more about the Denari political dynamic than he did—but the captain felt sure they'd honor the general's request. Help prevent the Denari from slipping into total war.

The com sounded.

"Engineering to Captain Archer."

Archer smiled. And speak of the devil . . .

"Trip. You have news for me?"

"Yes, indeed. Warp engines are back on-line."

"That was fast."

"Got more than the usual complement of qualified people down here," Trip replied. Archer knew he was referring to Cooney and the other *Daedalus* personnel, who were assisting him. "Sir, you got that minute for me now?"

His chief engineer had been after him for a moment in private from the second Archer had stepped back aboard the starship. The captain had put him off for the last few hours, to make sure the whole crew got settled and that the ship was in condition. But now . . .

"Sure. Come up to the ready room."

"Actually, Captain, I wonder if you'd come down here."

"Engineering?"

"Yes, sir. D-deck."

Archer frowned. Could the Denari have done something to the engines after all? Trip had said they were fine, but what if there was a problem he didn't want to discuss in front of the rest of the crew?

"Sure. Be right there," he said, and closed the circuit.

When the lift door opened on D-deck, Trip was waiting for him. But instead of taking him to engineering, Trip led him to an access ladder and started up it toward C.

"Hold on," the captain said.

Trip, halfway up the ladder, paused and turned around.

"What's going on?"

"Well—" He looked down the corridor in both directions to make sure no one was listening. "You know that request of Makandros's?"

"Find Sadir's son?"

Trip nodded. "Yeah. That's going to be a lot easier to do than you might suspect."

Archer looked over at Travis, who'd stayed silent the entire time, arms folded across his chest as Trip finished telling the captain who was inside the cabin behind them. At least he knew why he hadn't seen his helmsman the entire time since he'd been back aboard *Enterprise:* Travis had been here, guarding Duvall and her son.

"What does she know?"

"She thought we were sent by Starfleet," his chief engineer replied. "I told her that we weren't—not exactly. And we haven't discussed anything to do with our situation—*Enterprise,* parallel universes, all that. Nothing."

"I see." The captain was quiet a minute. "And the boy—he's in there too?"

"Yes, sir," Trip replied. "A little under the weather—something he ate yesterday. I'm thinking it's the same thing that's been happening to us, except in reverse. Doesn't seem too serious."

The captain nodded. Of course. The protein intolerance that had affected his crew here probably worked both ways. If the boy had eaten some of *Enterprise*'s food . . .

"Let's get Phlox up here to see him."

"I already spoke to the doctor. He said once he's through with the crew—"

Archer interrupted him. "As important as this boy is, let's keep him healthy. Tell Phlox—"

The door to Cabin 428 opened, and a woman—

slim, medium height, shoulder-length black hair, dressed in a simple black pantsuit—leaned out.

Captain Duvall. Monique Duvall.

In his mind, she'd been dead for fourteen years.

Now here she was, alive, in the flesh, looking exactly as he'd remembered her.

Maybe even better.

"Jonny," she smiled. "I heard your voice."

Archer blinked, and swallowed hard. He didn't know what to say. Jonny? The moment he'd hit puberty, he had insisted people stop calling him Jonny. Certainly not Monique Duvall.

"Captain," he managed. "It's good to see you again."

Except that "again" was wrong—he realized it as he spoke. He had never met this woman—this Monique Duvall—before in his life.

"And you," she said. "I've been waiting to talk to you."

"Of course. Give me a minute first, won't you?"

Giving him a look that mixed equal parts impatience, disappointment, and anger, Duvall nodded and disappeared back into the cabin.

Archer collected himself and turned back to his chief engineer.

"Get Phlox up here," he said again. "Tell him this is a priority."

"Aye, sir."

He turned and spoke to Travis.

"For the moment, let's keep on as you were, gentlemen. No one else finds out the two of them are here yet—all right?"

Both nodded.

"All right," Archer said, and turned toward the door to 428.

"Sir," Trip said. "One thing."

Archer stopped in his tracks.

"She's not the woman you knew, Captain. Even if she looks exactly the same—"

"I understand, Trip. Thanks."

Archer nodded then, and stepped through the door into 428.

For a second, he was disoriented—the room was dark, dimly lit, configured differently than he'd expected. No bunk, a low table, comfortable chairs around it, a kitchen area . . .

Right, the captain recalled. This is the suite we set up with 430, after that business with the Jantaleyse ambassador.

Duvall was standing in the kitchen area, pouring herself a glass of amber liquid from a clear, multi-faceted glass bottle.

She turned and smiled at him.

He smiled back.

Monique Duvall. Valedictorian of her Academy class. The best simulator pilot Archer had ever seen—and a pretty darn good one in real life as well. Helmsman on the *Harmony 2*, first officer on the *Constellation* prototype, captain of first the *Maximillian* and then, of course, *Daedalus*. He'd met her his first day of classes at the Academy—she was escorting her younger sister around, showing her the sights, renewing old acquaintances, having just returned from her first deep-space assignment—patrols in and around the new Centauri settlements, which were being harassed by Thlixian pirate vessels. Somehow, Archer had ended up alone with Duvall for fifteen minutes, quizzing her on what life 'out there' had been like. What a pest he must have been, he realized later. She'd put up with him good-naturedly until it was time for her to leave . . . at which point they'd shaken hands and said good-bye.

It was the beginning of the most serious schoolboy crush of his life.

Duvall had been in and out of the Academy for that entire year, alternating studies with patrol assignments. The captain remembered scheming up ways to spend time with her—preparing for conversations the two of them might have, practicing jokes he would tell her, pumping her little sister for information on her likes and dislikes . . .

The effort had been almost entirely for naught. He'd seen her only a handful of times over those next few months, and then they'd lost touch completely, until the *Daedalus* project was announced. Then they'd renewed their acquaintance, become friends . . . though the captain never quite got over feeling just a little bit like a nervous schoolboy in her presence. Tongue-tied, almost.

He felt a little of that right now.

"Honest-to-God scotch. I never thought I'd see this again." She finished pouring her glass and held out the bottle to him. "You want some?"

"No, thanks."

She shrugged and set down the bottle.

"Cheers," she said, and bolted half her glass in a single gulp.

"We need to talk," Archer said.

"I know." She looked him in the eye and frowned. "You don't seem happy to see me. Why is that?"

He couldn't help but smile. "Oh, I am, believe me. It's just that—"

"When I heard that a Starfleet vessel had been captured and that you were the captain . . ." She set her glass down on the counter. "Fourteen years, Jonny. I swear to God, I've thought about you every single day."

Archer flushed.

He had to set her straight this instant as to who he really was, and why he was here, because if calling him Jonny hadn't been enough of a clue, the look she was giving him right now . . .

This universe's Jonathan Archer and Monique Duvall had been close—very, very close indeed.

"You're in a tough position," she said. "I understand. You're Starfleet here, and after what I've done—"

"Captain—"

"Monique, Jonny. You haven't forgotten my name, have you?"

"No, of course not. But, please, let's sit down and talk."

Duvall wasn't listening.

"Everything I did, I did for him. For Leeman." Tears filled her eyes. "It was Lyatt's choice—his father's name. I went along. I didn't think it would be a good idea to insist on Henry. But in my mind, that's how I thought of him. Just like we talked about, Jonny."

Archer looked at her, and heard his heart pounding in his chest.

"What?"

She nodded toward 430, and managed a smile. "He's right in there, Jonny. Our son."

The captain blinked.

Words failed him.

Three surprises awaited Trip in sickbay.

Phlox had finished with the crew.

He was examining Ferik.

Neesa was with them.

She standing on one side of the diagnostic scanning chamber, her back to Trip. She turned reflexively at the sound of the door opening, and their eyes met.

For a second, Trip didn't know how to react. In his mind, he hadn't decided whether or not he should try and see her, or anyone aboard *Eclipse*, for that matter, again. The way he'd left before had felt like good-bye. A final good-bye. He didn't want to stir up emotions—hers or his—all over again.

But the instant he laid eyes on her, those thoughts went right out of his head. And a broad smile broke out on his face. She returned it.

"Neesa."

"Trip."

He went to her then, and they embraced.

"I wasn't sure if I was going to see you."

"I wasn't sure if it would be a good idea."

Trip became aware that Phlox was staring at them. He was also aware that he really didn't care about that in the least.

Up until this instant, he hadn't even thought about whether or not he should tell the captain about his relationship with Trant. Now he realized he would—moreover, he realized, there was no reason to hide that relationship. Not that he'd have a lot of time to spend with her over the next day or so, or however much longer they were here, but still . . .

He wanted to squeeze in whatever moments he could before good-bye.

She eyed him closely. "I miss the beard."

"Not regulation, sorry."

He held her at arm's length, unable to wipe the smile off his face, barely able to keep from taking her in his arms and kissing her. Instead, he looked over her shoulder toward Ferik, who was now entirely inside the scanning chamber.

"What's happening?"

Phlox, leaning over the chamber read-out screen, answered instead of Trant.

"I am running a detailed series of scans on Mister Reeve's neurological functions," he replied without looking up, sounding—to Trip's ears, at least—somewhat peeved.

"Your doctor," Trant said, "thinks he can cure Ferik."

For a second, Trip was so stunned, he didn't know what to say.

"Cure is perhaps the wrong word, Doctor," Phlox said. "I can repair the underlying physical damage done to the higher brain structures. The degree to which that will actually "cure" Mister Reeve's problems is entirely unknown at this point."

"It's a cure as far as I'm concerned," Trant said. "Short-term memory formation has never been the problem—it's the recall process itself that's been disrupted. If we can get that operating again—"

"How much of Ferik's previous memories remain intact is still a question," Phlox said.

"I know they're in there," Trant said.

"Based on what evidence?"

"I've been with Ferik for fourteen years, Doctor. Those memories have surfaced from time to time."

"And they may continue to do so. I only mean that a full recovery may not be possible."

"I'll work with him."

"You cannot train memory recall, Doctor. As I'm sure you know."

"But there is evidence—as you may or may not know—that the formation of neural signal paths can—"

"Hey, hold on." Trip looked from Trant and to Phlox. "This is good news, any way you look at it. No need to argue."

"I was not arguing," Phlox said. "I was simply—"

"Doc," Trip said, a note of warning in his voice. "Let it go."

"Of course."

"It is good news, and I am very grateful to you, Doctor, for agreeing to examine Ferik in the first place," Trant said.

Something in her voice gave Trip pause. She didn't sound entirely happy about this latest development. He wondered if he was the reason why.

He'd have to try and figure that out later. Right now, he had other business to attend to.

"Doctor," he said, more formally. "I need to take you away for a minute. Captain Archer needs you."

"Is it an emergency?" Phlox asked, hunched over the diagnostic screen.

"I guess you could say that."

"It either is, or it isn't. Is a life at stake? Permanent injury?"

"No, but the captain said—"

"It will have to wait," Phlox said curtly. "Interrupting the treatment at this point will force me to start all over—an hour's worth of work."

"How much longer do you need?"

"Fifteen minutes, perhaps. Half an hour at most."

"All right," Trip said reluctantly. He didn't like going back empty-handed, but he didn't see as he had much choice. "But please, as fast as you can."

"What's the problem?" Neesa asked. "Maybe I can help."

He was about to tell her she couldn't when he remembered that Trant knew as much, if not more, than Phlox about this particular issue.

"Maybe you can," he said to her. "Come on."

Archer had that drink after all.

And then he sat Duvall down and made her listen to him.

It took a long time to convince her he was telling the truth. He thought in the end her decision to accept what he was saying might have had more to do with the way he was acting toward her—or rather, not acting—than the words he was saying.

"You are . . . different," she said at last. "I can see that."

The captain felt himself blush again under her scrutiny. He felt oddly inadequate, after hearing about the relationship the woman in front of him and his—doppelgänger, for lack of a better word—

had enjoyed. Lovers for more than three years. On the verge of marriage until *Daedalus*. Planning to have a child together.

Duvall, in fact, had been pregnant when the ship had attempted to launch.

Now, at last, he had an explanation for her actions fifteen years ago. Stranded, defenseless, she'd done what she had to in order to save the child growing within her. By turning over *Daedalus's* technology to Sadir, she had insinuated herself in the general's good graces. And she had convinced him *he* had fathered the child she was carrying.

The Monique Duvall he'd known would never have been capable of doing all that implied.

But he had to remember what Trip said. This was not *his* Duvall, placed in different circumstances. This was another person, a complete stranger to him. He'd have to treat her that way, keep her at arm's length until he found out where she stood on a number of things—most importantly, on the incipient war.

No time like the present to start finding out.

The two of them were seated on the couch in C-428. Archer stood now and began pacing the room.

"I have some questions," he said brusquely. "I hope you don't mind answering them."

"No. Go ahead."

"You've been in contact with General Elson," he said. "You're on your way to see him. Why?"

"Not my choice," she responded instantly. "If you'd come here a day ago, you would have seen the guards on our door. Four of them."

"Elson kidnapped you?"

"No, not exactly, though he certainly wasn't going

to let us—let Lee—wander about freely once Lyatt was dead."

"So how did you get on board *Enterprise?*" he finally continued.

"When word first came to us, back on Denari, about the capture of a Starfleet vessel, I was contacted. Naturally."

"Naturally."

"Lyatt asked me to help look over the ship. The new technology, the weapons . . . he had it brought back to Denari, where Lee and I boarded."

"And then you went to Kota?"

"That's right. Where we were when the news came. Lyatt was dead, and we were suddenly prime targets. Elson wanted us with him on Denari." She shrugged. "The rest you know."

He did indeed. Elson's goal was the same as Makandros's—the Guild's. Control Leeman Sadir, the heir to the throne.

Who wasn't even his father's son.

If word about that ever got out . . .

Archer wondered, suddenly, how strong the resemblance between him and the boy was.

"What are you thinking?" Duvall asked.

"I'm thinking this is a complicated situation. You know about what's happening out there now," the captain said, gesturing to the space visible through the cabin window.

"A little."

The captain told her about Elson's attack on the DEF, Makandros's subsequent alliance with the Guild, the terrible destruction on Denari.

She was silent a moment after he'd finished.

"I'm afraid the fighting has just begun."

"I want to help stop it before it goes any further." He looked at Duvall. "Makandros and Lind are looking for you too. For your son."

"I have no doubt about that."

"They want him to lead the Council."

"Out of the goodness of their hearts?"

"Out of a desire for peace."

"He's thirteen years old, Captain. They don't want him to lead. They want him to be their puppet."

Archer managed a smile. "I suspect they'll have a hard time doing that with you around."

"I'm not so sure. When Lyatt was alive . . . perhaps. But by myself . . . I'm human, not Denari. Not one of them at all."

She looked vulnerable then. For a second, Archer felt sorry for her.

Then he remembered what the *Daedalus* crew—Cooney, Brodesser, all the others—had gone through because of her actions, and his sympathy vanished.

"Your son's human too," he pointed out. "Who else knows about that?"

"No one."

"Not Sadir?"

"No."

Archer frowned. "He never suspected?"

"Not that I know of." She smiled. "Lyatt kept his own counsel. From the day I told him I was pregnant, I can tell you that he never treated Leeman as anything but his own."

Archer nodded. "What about anyone aboard *Daedalus?* Anyone here you confided in?"

Duvall shook her head. "No. Doctor D'Lay knew I

was pregnant, but he died in the . . . when Lyatt took over the ship."

"And the boy? Does he know?"

She smiled. "Leeman, Captain. His name is Leeman."

"Leeman, then," Archer said, and was about to repeat his question when a sudden noise from behind made him turn.

There was someone standing in the shadows, in the doorway between the two cabins.

"Lee?" Duvall called out. "Is that you?"

The figure stepped into the light.

Twenty-One

"PENNY FOR YOUR THOUGHTS?" Trip asked.

Neesa looked up at him. "What?"

"Another Earth saying, means tell me what you're thinking." The two of them were on D-deck, heading up the gangway to C-428/430. Since leaving sickbay, their conversation had been very subdued. Neesa hadn't put together a complete sentence yet—just a series of monosyllabic answers to his questions. She had a lot on her mind, obviously.

"What I'm thinking? Nothing tremendously important."

"Can I guess?"

She managed a half smile. "Sure."

"You're thinking about Ferik."

"In a way." She looked over at him. "I'm thinking about Ferik the way he used to be. Wondering if he'll be that way again."

"He won't."

"When did you get a medical degree?"

"You don't need a medical degree to figure that one out. It's been more than a decade. A lot has happened to him. There's no way he can be the same person."

"I suppose you're right. I guess, more than that, I'm wondering if things will be the same between us."

"You know the answer to that," Trip said, more gently this time. "They can't be."

She paused a moment. "So what do I do?"

"What do you mean?"

"If he recovers—fully recovers—do we stay together?"

"Well, on Earth, that's how a lot of people do it. Stay together no matter what. They make a vow—till death do them part, the saying goes."

"Is that how you're going to do it?"

He looked at her. "Sometimes, that's what I think I'll do. Sometimes . . . I have absolutely no idea."

"Leave it till you meet the right person?"

"I think I will."

She smiled. "I wonder what you're like here—the Tucker in this universe."

"I wonder what the Neesa in mine is like."

They stopped walking. They kissed.

"Do you know where Negatta is?" she asked. "How far away?"

He frowned. "Negatta? What does Negatta have to do with anything?"

The com sounded.

"Reed to Commander Tucker."

Trip walked to the nearest com panel.

"Tucker here. What's up, Malcolm?"

"We've got a problem."

"I hate it when you say that. Go on."

"Carstairs took apart one of Peranda's little booby traps. They're on timers."

"Say that again?"

"They're on timers. Random timers. They switch on and off, automatically."

"Oh. That's great." It was in fact, just the opposite. They'd swept the ship for those traps using sensors set to detect the ultraviolet beams the bombs used as a triggering device. If the beams weren't active . . .

"Better sweep the ship again. Use sensors set to the bomb's composition this time."

"Going to take a lot longer that way."

"I know. Better get to it. I'll let the captain know. You inform the crew."

"Will do."

"How is Peranda?"

"Silent as the grave. Which is where I'd like to put him."

"I'm with you on that. Stubborn bastard."

"Sooner or later, we're going to need that launch bay."

"Sooner, probably." Trip frowned. *Enough's enough,* he thought. He wondered if Archer would authorize the use of a little . . . chemical persuasion. "Let me talk to the captain. See what I can do."

"Right. Keep me posted."

"Will do. Out."

Trip turned back to Neesa.

She was smiling.

"What now?"

"I was thinking, you need a little sodium dipentothal. That would loosen his tongue a bit."

He smiled back. "You're a woman after my own heart."

One thing the Archers had always been good at—taking pictures. Digital stills, home movies, old-fashioned photographs—there were boxes and boxes of them in the attic in his parents' old house, waiting alongside the other boxes of their possessions, waiting for the captain to decide what to do with them.

Right before the Broken Bow incident, a few days before *Enterprise*'s launch, Archer had gone back to that house for the first time in more than a year. A sudden desire to see old friends, old places—he'd wondered, in retrospect, if part of him had known somehow that he wouldn't be going back that way again for a long, long time.

It had been that same something, perhaps, that had led him up to the attic and into those boxes, where he'd spent a good hour looking at pictures from his childhood and, eventually, from his father's. Pictures of Henry Archer as a baby, a boy on his first day of school, as a gangly, awkward teenager, and finally, as a young man, on the day of his marriage.

Those images had stayed with the captain. He'd brought some of them along, in fact, digital captures stored on the workstation in his quarters. They'd also remained in his memory for the last two years while *Enterprise*, powered by the engine his father helped design, made its way through the galaxy.

Looking at Leeman Sadir, standing in the doorway between cabins C-428 and 430, was like finding one of those photos—a picture of his father that he'd never seen before, Henry Archer at twelve, maybe thirteen, still gangly and awkward, not a boy any longer, not quite a teenager . . .

About the same age as the boy he looked at now, who, no matter what name he was going by, was most definitely an Archer.

"You should be in bed," Duvall said, getting to her feet.

"I'm not dying." The boy looked directly at Archer. "This is him?"

Duvall nodded. "That's right. This is Captain Archer. Captain, this is my son Lee."

Archer looked the boy over and, for the second time in less than an hour, had trouble finding his voice.

Seeing Lee was like seeing the road not taken—the road that he frankly wasn't sure he'd ever take—in physical form before him. In some ways, as close to a son as the captain would ever have.

"Pleased to meet you," he said, holding out his hand.

The two of them shook.

"And you, sir," the boy said, loosing his grip. "I've heard a lot about you."

"Really? Good things, I hope."

"Oh yes."

Both his grip and his voice were firm, confident, self-possessed beyond his years.

He was, however, a little green around the gills.

"Lee," Duvall said, a note of warning in her voice. "Don't overexert yourself. Please."

"I'll go back to bed in a minute." He looked at the captain. "You're here to take us to General Elson?"

"The situation has changed," Duvall said. "We were just talking about it."

"What's happened?"

"Elson hasn't been entirely truthful with us, apparently," Duvall said, and repeated what Archer had told her, albeit in a somewhat abbreviated form. Lee listened with a seriousness that belied his age. Again, the captain was struck by his calm demeanor.

Whatever faults Sadir and Duvall possessed, his first impression was that they'd raised a fairly impressive kid.

"Makandros has allied himself with the Guild?" The boy frowned. "That doesn't seem possible."

"You can see for yourself shortly," Archer said. "They want to meet with you."

"The Guild?" The boy looked to his mother. "They're . . . we can't trust them."

"Times have changed. And if Elson has really done the things he stands accused of—destroying the plant at Charest—he's the one we can't trust."

"I can't believe he'd do that. Father always said . . ." The boy, all at once, looked uncertain—a child again, not the young man he was striving to be. Archer did the math—thirteen years old. Lee still had a lot of growing to do.

"Your father knew how to adapt, Lee. We'll have to do the same. In the meantime . . ." Duvall put her hands on his shoulders and spun him around. "Let's get you back in bed. The doctor should be here soon."

Duvall was right, Archer realized. Where was Trip? More than enough time had passed for him to return with the doctor.

And just then, the door sounded.

"Who is it?"

"Trip, sir."

"Come on in," the captain said, freeing the lock.

His chief engineer entered the room.

Doctor Trant of *Eclipse*, dressed in a green-and-orange Guild uniform, followed a step behind.

Archer took one look at her and frowned.

She took one look at Duvall and the boy, and her eyes widened in surprise.

"You're Sadir's wife," she said.

"You're with the Guild," Duvall said. She turned to Archer. "What's going on here?"

"That's just what I was wondering." He turned to Trip. "Commander? I thought I asked you to bring Doctor Phlox."

Trip stopped in his tracks and groaned softly to himself.

He'd made, he suddenly realized, a terrible mistake.

He should have cleared Trant with the captain. Why he hadn't thought of that down in sickbay or on the way up here . . . Stupid. Too caught up in seeing Neesa again, too surprised by Phlox's announcement regarding Ferik, too anxious not to return empty-handed—

"Sorry, Captain," Trip said. "Doctor Phlox was busy. I should have double-checked with you about bringing Trant."

"You should have."

"Is there a problem with my being here?" Trant asked. "I'll leave."

"No, it's all right, Doctor," the captain replied, but Trip could see that even though the frown on his face was gone, Archer was still angry. His voice, however, betrayed none of that emotion as he spoke. "Captain Duvall, Doctor Trant has been treating my crew for a variation of the same problem your son is suffering from. I've trusted her with their lives."

"I don't know that I'm willing to trust her with my son's."

"Captain," Archer pointed out, "may I remind you, the Guild has no interest in seeing Lee harmed. Just the opposite, in fact."

Duvall frowned, considering. Behind her, the captain saw Lee doing the same.

"I always have exactly the same interest, when it comes to my patients," Trant said. "Helping them get better."

"You say you've treated this same problem before?" Duvall asked.

"It sounds like the same problem, from what Commander Tucker was telling me," Trant corrected. "I won't know, of course, until I examine your son."

Duvall nodded reluctantly. "All right." She gestured towards 430. "There's a bed in there. Probably the best place to do the exam."

"I agree," Trant said. "Shall we?"

The three of them left the room.

Archer watched her go a minute, then shook his head.

"You were right, Trip. She's a different person."

"Yes, sir."

"I suppose I'm a different person here too."

"I suppose. Don't know that we'll ever know that for sure."

"Let's hope not." The captain looked directly at him. "We have a problem."

"Yes, sir." Trip prepared himself for that tongue-lashing.

But Archer's next words surprised him.

"It's about the boy."

"Sadir's son."

"No."

Trip frowned. "Is there another boy?"

"No." The captain hesitated a moment. "Only one. But the thing is . . . he's not Sadir's son."

"Oh." Trip didn't understand. Had he missed something? "Well, then, whose . . ."

Archer looked directly at him, and all at once, Trip knew why the boy had looked so familiar to him before.

"Oh boy," he managed. "Could be a problem is right."

"You see a resemblance?" Archer asked.

"Now that you mention it . . ."

"Will others?"

"Hard to say. Depends on how often they've seen you. If they see the two of you together . . ."

"We can't let that happen, then," Archer said. "Denari's future rests with that boy. No one can even suspect he's not Sadir's son."

"Agreed."

"I'm going to have to lie low for a while. You've had the most experience with the Denari. Anyone needs to talk to *Enterprise,* for any reason, they talk to you."

"Yes, sir." Trip suddenly remembered what Malcolm had told him. "Something I need to talk to you about, Captain. Peranda's little booby traps."

"We got all those, didn't we?"

"We thought so. But we just found out they work off timers. There may be some on board that haven't armed themselves yet."

"Wonderful."

"We're going back over the ship again, top to bottom. We'll find all of them."

"Be easier if Peranda would tell us where they were."

"He's still not talking."

"We're going to have to do something about that. A little truth serum, perhaps?"

"Just what Doctor Trant and I were thinking. She's already volunteered to help us administer it."

"I see."

Archer studied him a moment, and Trip could see the question in his captain's eyes: What, exactly, was the nature of his relationship with Trant?

Trip was ready to answer that when the entrance to 430 slid open, and Trant herself appeared in the doorway.

"Some interesting results," she said, turning to talk over her shoulder to Duvall. "I'll let you know."

She turned back to the door then, scanner in hand, and saw Trip. A smile crossed her face.

Later, he would recall every second of what happened next in excruciating detail, as if it had all happened in slow motion.

Neesa smiling. Behind her, in the bed, the boy, sitting up. Duvall turning away from her son, taking a step toward the door as well.

At that instant, Trip, for some reason, looked down.

A pencil-thin beam of blue light stretched across the bottom of the doorway, at ankle height. One of Peranda's bombs. Trip traced the beam back with his eyes. The bomb was fixed to the back of one of the table legs along the same wall as the door. He wouldn't have spotted it in a million years.

He took in all that in an instant, and pushed the captain away.

"Stay there!" he yelled to Neesa. "Don't move!"

He tried to wave her back with both hands.

For a fraction of a second, her expression changed. But whatever she thought then, whether she intended to act on what he was saying or not, it was too late.

Her foot was already moving forward.

The last thing Trip saw was it break the thin blue line of the beam.

Then, for a split second, everything turned a brilliant, bright white.

Twenty-Two

ARCHER BLINKED and opened his eyes.

He was in sickbay, on one of the beds. Trip and Phlox were leaning over him.

His head hurt like the dickens.

"What happened?" he croaked, his voice sounding thick and harsh with disuse.

"An explosion," Phlox said. "You're quite all right."

"Peranda." Trip's face was grim. "One of his little going-away presents."

Archer remembered then: the two of them talking, Trip suddenly pushing him toward the door . . .

Then nothing.

"How long have I been here?"

"Almost a day."

"You're all right?" he asked Trip.

"Except for this." Trip touched the side of his face and turned his head to the right. He had a black and blue bruise that stretched from his temple all the way down to his jaw. "You and I were blown clear across the room, along with that new couch in there. Protected us from the shrapnel."

"Almost all the shrapnel," Phlox corrected. "You had quite a nasty head wound, Captain. A bit of a concussion as well."

"What about the others? Duvall? Lee?"

"Kid's all right, sir. A few bruises. Nothing serious."

"Some potential hearing loss," Phlox added. "And his digestive system is still functioning at less-than-optimum efficiency. But he is basically fine."

The captain nodded.

He noticed Trip hadn't said a word about Duvall.

"Commander," he repeated. "What about Duvall?"

Trip shook his head.

"She didn't make it, sir. I'm sorry."

Archer groaned and closed his eyes.

In his mind, he went back to that instant in the brig, when he'd looked at Peranda and known that the man had something else up his sleeve. Another trick. The bomb.

"I saw it," he said softly. "I saw it in his eyes, and I didn't do anything. I could've saved her."

"Not all your fault, Captain," Trip said. "Travis was warning me not to underestimate him. I did it when we first took over the ship, and Westerberg died, and I did it again when—"

Trip's voice broke.

Archer opened his eyes and saw his chief engineer blinking away tears.

He suddenly remembered there had been someone else in the room, too.

Doctor Trant.

"Trip?"

"Sir."

"Not Trant too? She's not . . . ."

Archer's voice trailed off. Trip hadn't responded then, but he didn't need to. Archer saw the answer in his eyes.

"Ship took a beating," Trip said, and actually managed a laugh. "We're going to need new guest quarters, too."

"It's all right." He sighed heavily. "For what it's worth . . . I'm sorry, Trip. I guess the two of you were pretty close."

"Yes, sir. We were."

Phlox stepped forward. "You should be resting, Captain. Your injuries are not severe, but you have lost a considerable amount of blood."

Archer nodded. He did feel weak. And hungry.

And anxious to know what had been happening while he was unconscious.

"A minute, Doctor. Trip, can you fill me in? What's been happening?"

"Strategic situation is status quo. Makandros and Lind are anxious to talk to you, and the boy."

"They know he's here?"

"They do. A mix-up after the bomb went off. When we gave them the news about Trant, we ended up telling them about the boy as well."

"Understandable," the captain said. And no great disaster, considering they were about to tell the general and Lind about Lee anyway.

"Yeah. But Makandros isn't happy."

"What a surprise."

"We do have some good news, though. Launch Bay Two is operational again."

"Peranda talked?"

"With a little help." Trip smiled thinly. "Gave us

the location of every device on the ship, and the codes to disarm them. Sneaky bastard. He put one in your quarters too, sir."

"You're sure he was telling the truth?"

"It would have been physiologically impossible for him to do otherwise," Phlox said, "considering the amount of serum we put into his system."

"He hasn't stopping talking yet. We may be able to get some valuable information about General Elson's intentions from him," Trip said. "Provided he doesn't get too sick."

"It's nothing serious," Phlox added. "Just . . . uncomfortable."

"Good." Archer felt exactly zero sympathy for the man.

"Captain." Phlox stepped forward again. "Please. You are running on adrenaline right now. Your system needs rest."

"I'll rest in a few minutes." He looked up at the doctor. "Right now, I need to talk to Commander Tucker. Alone."

Phlox frowned. "I really would prefer—"

"Doctor, give us a moment."

Phlox nodded reluctantly, and left.

"Have you talked to anyone else about what I told you? About Lee?"

Trip shook his head. "No, sir."

"Good. Let's keep it that way. A lot depends on him, poor kid." Archer frowned. "He knows about his mother?"

"He never lost consciousness. We couldn't keep it from him."

"And how's he handling it?"

"Not too well, frankly. I tried to talk to him a little, but . . ."

"Maybe I'll have better luck. He knows me—or thinks he does, anyway, from what Duvall told him. I'll try in the morning."

"Yes, sir."

Archer looked in Trip's eyes. "You going to be all right?"

"Yes, sir." Trip nodded. "I'll be fine. Soon as I stop beating myself up for not forcing that information out of Peranda before."

"I'll be doing a little of that too, later, I suspect."

Trip managed a laugh. "That'll make three of us. You should have seen Malcolm."

The captain could only imagine. He smiled to himself—

And then remembered something else he needed to talk about with Trip. The anomaly. Their nonexistent way home. Not just Trip—he wanted to alert all the department heads. A staff meeting.

Then a wave of exhaustion washed over him, and Archer decided that too would have to wait till morning. He said good night to Trip, and lay back on the bed.

He saw Trip and Phlox enter one of the isolation wards. The captain wondered, briefly, who the doctor was treating in there.

And then sleep took him. An uneasy, dream-filled sleep, with scenes from his first year at the Academy, places and times he'd shared with his Duvall, mixed in with fantasies of the life this universe's Jonny and Monique had shared.

Incongruously, a young Henry Archer kept popping in and out of his dreams.

Archer called that long-overdue staff meeting for the next morning, in his ready room, after Phlox reluctantly dismissed him from sickbay. He kept it small and private: himself, Trip, Reed, and T'Pol.

"Just us?" Malcolm asked, leaning up against the far wall near the small cabin's sole port.

"That's right," Archer confirmed. He and Trip stood side by side, backs to the inner bulkhead, while T'Pol sat in front of his workstation. "What we discuss in here, stays in here. Understood?"

Heads nodded.

The four gave him a status update then, on the extent of the damage suffered by the ship and crew—minimal, the status of repairs—almost complete, and the crew's overall health—supplemented by a brief com link with Phlox).

And then Archer took a deep breath and told T'Pol and Reed the secret he'd brought them there to hear:

Who Leeman Sadir's father really was.

The two of them were silent a moment after he finished talking.

"That's unbelievable," Reed said. "So there's a strong resemblance between the two of you?"

"Strong enough," Trip said.

"Which is why Trip will be our liaison with the Denari. So no one spots that resemblance."

"Captain," T'Pol said. "May I speak frankly?"

Archer nodded.

"You are concerned for the boy. That is understandable. You may also feel a degree of responsibility for him—kinship, even. That is understandable as well. However—"

Despite his best efforts to stay calm, the captain felt his cheeks flush.

"I know what you're going to say, Sub-Commander. And I appreciate your concerns. But I'm well aware that the boy is neither my kin nor my responsibility. I simply want to do what I can to help him—and the Denari—avoid a cataclysmic war."

"And how far are we willing to go to do that?" T'Pol asked. "If General Elson cannot be convinced to stand down—or his men convinced to defy his orders—what then? Will we use *Enterprise*'s weapons to force his surrender?"

Before Archer could reply, Trip spoke up.

"I'm not even sure that would be possible. If Elson stays in the Kresh, it's going to take a lot more firepower than we have to get him out of there. Even with help from Makandros and the Guild . . ."

"We're not getting directly involved in the war—if there is one," Archer said firmly. "That would be compounding the mistake Captain Duvall made."

"But here we are, in the middle of one side's battle group. Perhaps we should have a contingency plan in place, sir, just in case," Reed said. "I wouldn't need to consult with DEF or Guild liaisons—simply determine the required force levels, and if the need arose—"

Archer shook his head. "I don't think so, Malcolm."

"What if Elson attacks us, sir?" Reed asked.

"We have the ability to outrun any potential attack," T'Pol said.

"As long as we see it coming." Trip turned to the

captain. "Sadir knew all about the Suliban cloaking device. It's possible his people were working on ways not just to detect it, but build one of their own."

Archer frowned. "How possible?"

"Not very," Trip admitted. "A long shot."

"Then let's set that aside for a moment. We have more important things to worry about." He turned to T'Pol. "Sub-Commander, could you bring these two up-to-speed on our other problem?"

Trip and Reed exchanged puzzled looks.

"Other problem?"

The Vulcan leaned forward in her chair.

"We may not be able to get back through the anomaly," she said, and then explained.

"No," Trip said when she'd finished. "There has to be a way to get at that information."

"We're open to suggestions," Archer replied.

"The helm," Trip said instantly. "A record of course instructions, thruster firings . . . We pull data from the console—"

"The one Parenda destroyed?" Reed asked.

"The data might be salvageable."

"The data does not exist," T'Pol said. "Helm was off-line as well when we transited."

"Okay." Trip frowned and thought a moment. "We need a record of our course through the anomaly, is that right?"

"Correct," T'Pol said.

"An outside observer. The Denari have to have records."

"We thought of that," Archer said. "We need data from the other side of the anomaly as well—from our universe. That's our real problem."

Everyone was silent a moment.

"What if . . ." Trip said hesitantly. "The orbital platform—the one the Denari in our universe were building. Would that have what we need?"

"If they spotted us, I suppose it might," T'Pol said. "A rather large 'if,' considering we were trying to remain hidden. And even supposing the platform's instruments do contain the data we need, how do we get at it? We are, literally, a universe apart."

Trip smiled. "The mine got through. What if a communications signal could as well?"

"You're proposing we contact the Denari back in our universe from this one?"

"Yes, sir."

"It is an . . . interesting idea." T'Pol nodded to herself, and Archer could see her mind working as she spoke. "The anomaly has many of the same characteristics as a subspace field node. It is theoretically possible that a properly modulated signal could be transmitted through it. We could not be certain of reaching the correct universe, but . . ."

"Possible?" the captain asked. "How long would it take to find out if the idea would work?"

"Couple of days," Trip said. "Modify the carrier signal, try and isolate the Denari outpost . . ." He looked to T'Pol. "Sound right?"

She nodded. "At a minimum."

"Captain," Trip pointed out, "Professor Brodesser might be able to help out on this."

Archer nodded. "I was thinking the same thing. Why don't you ask him?"

"I would if I could find time. Makandros keeps calling every half hour. He's contacted us twice this morning already about seeing the kid. Took a good deal of persuading to keep him from coming over here personally."

"Is that a yes?"

Trip threw up his hands in defeat. "Yes. I'll talk to him."

"Good." Archer smiled. "And I'll go talk to Lee."

T'Pol frowned. "Lee?"

"The boy. Sadir's son. That's his name."

She nodded.

Archer felt her gaze on him, weighing his intentions.

He felt it on him, in fact, all the way down to the boy's quarters.

The boy was still on C-deck, halfway around the saucer from where he'd been, in an unused crew cabin. Yamani was on guard duty. Archer nodded to him as he stepped up to the door com and pressed it.

"Who is it?"

"Captain Archer, Lee. Can I talk to you?"

Silence.

"I want to be alone."

"I can understand that. I just want a minute of your time."

There was no answer. Archer was about to try again when the door opened. He entered.

Lee was sitting in a chair, staring at a blank workstation screen, a blanket wrapped around his shoulders. Again, the captain was struck by his uncanny resemblance to the young Henry Archer. Then he noticed something else: the bed behind him hadn't been slept on.

"You've been up all night?"

"I'm not tired." The boy continued to stare at the screen, his expression unreadable. There were big, dark circles under his eyes.

"Phlox tells me you haven't been eating either."

"I'm not hungry. My stomach still feels a little queasy."

"You need to eat. What happened to you before—Doctor Trant explained what the problem was, didn't she?"

The captain knew for a fact she had: Phlox had told him so. The doctor had also told him that Lee had a firmer grasp on the theory—quantum mechanics, parallel universes—than Phlox himself did.

Gets that from his paternal grandfather, a little voice inside his head said.

Archer squashed it.

"She did."

"So that if you stick to eating the foods Colonel Peranda brought over—"

"I understand. I'm just not hungry."

"Lee . . ."

"I'm fine, Captain."

"No food, no sleep . . . you won't be for long." Archer sat down on the bed near him. "If you want, I can have the doctor prescribe something to help you rest."

"Drugs?" The boy shook his head. "No. My father used to say it was important to face your problems, not hide from them."

"My father used to say the same thing. But in order to face your problems, you need a clear head.

And for that, you need to rest. Let me get you some medicine."

"I understand. I appreciate your concern," Lee said, sounding like he couldn't give a damn about Archer's concern. Or anything else, for that matter. And who could blame him, really?

"A lot of people are concerned about you, Lee."

The boy shook his head.

"They don't care about me. They care about who I am. Do you understand? They used to say they wanted to be my friend, but what they really wanted was to use me to get close to my father."

"Not everyone is like that."

"The people I know are."

"I'm sure you had friends—people your own age . . ."

The boy shook his head. "I didn't."

"From school—"

"I didn't go to school. I had tutors. They were my friends. Doctor Oav. Maj Wooler. General Elson."

Archer blinked.

"Elson was one of your tutors?"

The boy nodded. "For military history. Strategy. But he taught me other things too. How to watch the people around me, how to judge what they were really thinking. We played it like a game."

And he taught you how not to trust anyone, Archer thought but didn't say. He wondered if Elson hadn't been planning something like this coup he was attempting for a very long time.

Makandros and Lind had their work cut out for them.

"They want me to turn against him now, don't they? The Guild, and General Makandros."

"They want to stop a war from breaking out."

"But sometimes you have to fight. It's a leader's responsibility to decide when. That's what my father told me. He said that was the hardest decision of his life—deciding that he had to fight the Presidium. Take over from them."

The boy looked up at Archer, his eyes fierce, determined.

"He was a great man, my father. Everything I am, I owe to him. I hope I can be worthy of his memory someday."

The captain held his tongue. Not exactly the picture of Sadir that Trip had painted for him, but then, what did he expect, given the source?

"If he fought to bring peace to your world," Archer said, choosing his words carefully, "then don't you owe it to his memory to try and keep that peace? However you can?"

"I'm not going to turn on my friends just because they say so. They're all I have left."

His voice broke on the last word. A tear trickled down his cheek.

"Sorry," he said, sniffling. He wiped his nose with the back of his hand.

At that moment, he looked more like a kid than at any time since the captain had met him. A lost, lonely, frightened kid.

"That's all right, Lee. Let it out."

"I can't stop thinking about her. And about my father. What I'm going to do without them around."

"Maybe I can help you."

The boy looked up at him again, but remained silent. After a few seconds, the captain went on. "I know you don't really know me, Lee, but I'd like to be your friend. No ulterior motives."

"You're not going to make me talk to the Guild?"

"I'm not going to make you do anything you don't want to," Archer said. "That's a promise."

The boy nodded. "If I did go see them—the Guild—would you come with me?"

Archer sighed heavily. "I can't."

"Why not?"

"Because . . ." He couldn't make the lie he'd told Makandros—that he was still weak from his injuries—come out. And he couldn't tell him the truth, either. "I just can't, Lee. I'm sorry. Commander Tucker will go with you, though. Okay?"

The boy nodded. "Okay."

But it wasn't. Archer could see it in his eyes. The connection he'd just made with the boy was slipping away.

And all at once, Archer had an idea.

"Hold on a second," he said, smiling. "I'll be right back."

And he was, a few minutes later. But not by himself. Porthos trotted into the room alongside him.

Lee was sitting on the edge of the bed. The boy's eyes widened when he saw the dog.

"What is that?"

"This," he said, smiling, "is Porthos."

As if on cue, the animal bounded into bed alongside Lee, and tried to lick his face. The boy pulled back, frightened.

Of course. He'd never seen a dog before.

"Down, Porthos," Archer commanded. "Get off that bed."

The dog paid him no mind.

Archer pulled a treat out of his pocket and held it up.

"Porthos," he called. But the dog's sense of smell had already picked up the new scent. Porthos leapt down and bounded back to the captain, tail wagging happily.

"Sit," Archer said, holding the treat higher.

Porthos sat.

Lee looked on, fascinated.

"He's trained."

"Barely." He gave Porthos the treat. The dog wagged his tail and barked.

"Another?"

Porthos barked again, in agreement.

"You'll have to perform." The captain caught Lee's eye and smiled. "Roll over."

Porthos looked at him quizzically.

"Go on," Archer said, motioning with his hand. "Roll over."

Porthos barked again.

The captain laughed. "Close enough. Good boy," he said, and gave Porthos another piece. The dog lay down on the floor and began munching away. Archer knelt down next to him and scratched behind his ears.

Lee padded over, barefoot, and stood by the captain.

"He likes it."

"That's right."

"Can I try?"

"Sure."

He showed the boy where Porthos liked to be scratched. Lee had it in no time flat.

The captain had a split second of wondering if the protein intolerance would make the boy—or the dog—allergic to each other before he remembered Trip and Trant, and realized that if physical contact was capable of causing those problems, his chief engineer would have said something about it.

"Why does his tail move back and forth?"

"That means he likes what you're doing."

"His name is Porthos, you said."

"That's right."

"That's a strange name, isn't it?"

"An old-fashioned name. It's from a book—a famous Earth book, *The Three Musketeers.*"

Lee looked at him blankly.

"It's in the ship's library. You can access it from the workstation later, if you like. Right now, though, you really should get some rest."

"Okay." The boy stood, and for the first time, gave Archer an honest-to-goodness smile. Archer smiled back.

Porthos jumped up on the bed again.

"Hey." Lee frowned. "That's my spot."

"Come on, Porthos. Get down."

The dog whined.

"I think he likes it up there," Lee said.

Porthos turned in a circle and settled himself down on top of a pillow.

"He'll stay there all day, if you let him."

"Can he?" The boy's eyes shone with excitement.

"If you like."

The boy nodded and climbed into bed. Porthos

made room for him—barely—then licked his face and settled back down.

"Don't be afraid to push him away when he does that."

"I won't," Lee said, stifling a yawn.

"Good. I'll be back in a few hours. We can talk some more then."

Archer turned for the door, the smile still on his face. If he'd been a betting man, he would have laid odds that Lee would be fast asleep by the time it closed behind him.

No sooner had it done that, though, than the com sounded.

"Bridge to Archer."

The captain opened a channel.

"Right here, Trip. What's going on?"

"Better get up here, sir. All hell's breaking loose."

Twenty-Three

Trip stepped aside and let the captain take the command chair.

"Let me see the recording first," Archer said.

Trip nodded to Carstairs, on communications, who brought up the transmission they'd received not ten minutes ago. Elson's image filled the viewer.

Now, as before, one word came to mind when Trip looked at the general: patrician. Elson had silver hair, sharp features, and a reasoned, calm manner. A born leader.

Probably just what he was counting on.

"Citizens of Denari. In light of the attacks by Guild forces on our planet and in the outer system—in particular, their capture of our base at Kota—it becomes necessary for me to convene the Council of Generals here in the Kresh, and ask them to grant me a temporary appointment as overall force commander. I do this in the interests of our planet, in the interests of justice, and in memory of those brave citizens who have given their lives in this struggle—those who have made the ultimate sacrifice to help defeat anarchy and chaos, in the form of the Guild and their allies. I ask for your support in this endeavor, and your prayers. In moments such as these—"

"Stop it there," Archer said. On-screen, Elson's image froze. "What's that mean? Overall force commander?"

"Elson's taking control," Trip said. "Eliminating the opposition. At least, that's what Makandros was saying." Along with a number of other, more choice turns of phrase, which Trip didn't feel the need to share with the captain right now. "Sir, they're getting pretty anxious about the kid."

"I'm working on it," the captain said. "He's not exactly a prime candidate for conversion to their cause right now." Archer filled him in on what the boy had said regarding General Elson.

"Makandros won't like hearing that."

"Which is why we're not going to tell him," the captain said. "I'm going to let the boy sleep a bit. He was up all night. Maybe he'll feel differently after some rest."

"Maybe." Trip frowned. Let the kid sleep? At a time like this?

He wondered if there wasn't something to what T'Pol had said before, about the captain regarding Leeman Sadir as both kin and responsibility. That would only make their job even harder.

As if on cue, the com system sounded.

"It's the general, sir," Carstairs said.

"Tell him to hang on a minute." Archer stood. "Go on, take it. I'll listen in the ready room."

Trip waited until the door had closed behind the captain before giving Carstairs the signal.

The general did not look happy.

"Six hours," Makandros said without preamble. "That's how long we have now, Tucker. I thought you might want to know that."

"Sir?"

"Six hours until the Council meets and hands all power to Elson. Once that happens, there's nothing anyone can do to prevent all-out war. Not even Leeman Sadir."

Trip nodded. "I understand, General. Thank you for keeping us apprised of the situation."

Makandros's eyes were cold fire. "That's all? 'I understand'? When countless thousands are poised to die, and you hold the one person who could save them hostage on your ship? 'I understand'?"

"He's not a hostage," Trip said.

"Then why won't you let me talk to him?"

Trip struggled for an answer. Com noise came over the channel for a second. Then another voice sounded.

"This is Captain Archer, General. You'll be able to speak to the boy in a few hours."

"Archer?" On-screen, Makandros frowned. "Where are you? I have no visual."

"None is being transmitted at the moment," the captain said. "The boy is still recuperating from his injuries. He'll be able to speak to you soon."

"Soon? Didn't you hear? We have six hours—less, as a practical matter. Once the other Council members enter the Kresh, they're in Elson's power. There'll be no changing their minds then."

"I understand."

"You and Tucker—*so* understanding." Makandros's glare returned. Trip could hear the anger in his voice, hear him barely holding that anger in check. "You have no right to interfere in our affairs like this. Leeman Sadir is Denari."

"And human," Archer said.

More human than you know, Trip thought.

"Besides," the captain continued, "as I recall, you interfered with us in the first place. Or have you forgotten that?"

There was silence for a moment.

"I cannot waste time like this any longer," Makandros said. "We have plans of our own to make." He closed the circuit without another word.

Trip frowned at the blank screen.

That went just about as poorly as he'd feared.

Archer appeared in the ready room doorway.

"Looks like Lee's going to have to learn to do without sleep."

"Why should he be any different than the rest of us?"

Archer managed a small smile. "I'm going to give him a couple hours."

"Cutting it close, sir."

"No sense in waking him if he's going to act the same way," the captain replied, a slight edge to his voice.

Trip nodded. "Yes, sir. A couple hours."

He supposed that made sense.

It clearly wasn't anything Archer was going to change his mind about, anyway.

* * *

Eclipse had contacted *Enterprise* as well, almost immediately after Elson's announcement had been broadcast. On a far less contentious matter than Leeman Sadir.

It was that matter that brought Trip to sickbay now, to the isolation chamber at one end of the bay and the man who lay unconscious within it. Ferik Reeve. He had been recovering for the last twenty-four hours, healing from the treatment Phlox had given him. He was sleeping peacefully, his features arranged into a small smile, his face unlined, worry-free.

Trip didn't want to be around when he woke up. He didn't want to see that face change, to see Ferik have to absorb the tragic news about Neesa. Part of it was a genuine concern for the man's emotions.

Part of it was that he didn't think he could go through that all over again himself.

He thought of her now, as she'd been the first time he'd seen her, back aboard *Eclipse*, in the decontamination chamber. On the command deck, after his initial, failed attempt to repair that ship's reactor. The first time they'd kissed, in his quarters. Their aborted kiss in the launch bay. He missed her. He'd said good-bye once, and managed it not at all well. He'd hoped to do better the second time around.

But he'd never had the chance.

Trip had been the one to pull her from the rubble of C-430—knelt there, holding her hand, feeling the warmth seep out of it, as Phlox tried desperately to restore the spark of life. He'd sat with her awhile longer, even as the doctor gave up, moved on to Duvall, and then Lee.

He'd walked with the gurney all the way down to

sickbay, and stood by her side even as he received news about the captain, and the boy, and the ship, and the first angry communication from Makandros when the general learned Duvall and her son had been aboard *Enterprise*.

Malcolm had finally pried him away from Neesa's side some hours later, gotten him back to his cabin, and handed him a stiff drink.

Trip had talked, then. Reed had listened—until very, very late in the evening.

"Initial signs are encouraging."

Trip looked up. Phlox had entered the chamber. The doctor pointed to a schematic on the diagnostic screen concerning Ferik, a schematic that for all the sense it made to Trip, might just as well have been in Greek. "You'll note here, and here"—Phlox gestured—"the increasing percentage of C-ketolin, which is indicative of memory formation."

"So when's he going to wake up?"

"Well." Phlox folded his arms across his chest. "The brain is an unbelievably complex organ, which we have spent the last two days traumatizing, albeit to therapeutic ends. I can assure you there is no obstacle to his regaining consciousness, save his own body's healing processes."

"So, you don't know?"

Phlox frowned. "I believe that is what I just said."

Just then, at the other end of the room, the sickbay doors opened. Lieutenant Royce from *Eclipse* entered.

Royce had been a frequent visitor to *Enterprise*

the last two days, to see Ferik. Now he was here to bring the man back home.

"Tucker. Doctor Phlox," Royce said, entering the chamber. "How is he?"

"He is well." Phlox frowned. "I would still recommend leaving him here for at least another twenty-four hours, though. To be sure the tissues have healed sufficiently."

"We don't have twenty-four hours, Doctor. No one does." He cast a particularly meaningful glance at Trip.

Phlox frowned. "Perhaps I am not expressing my concerns candidly enough. I don't feel it's wise to move Ferik at the moment. Not wise as in dangerous. Potentially lethal."

"So is life." Royce again looked meaningfully at Trip. "Especially since it seems like we're about to go to war. Absent any last-minute miracles."

"Is that a reference to the boy?"

Royce smiled. "If you like."

"Don't give up on him yet."

"It's not him we're giving up on, Tucker."

Trip rolled his eyes. "You can't honestly think we'd deliberately prevent you from talking to him."

Royce's silence was answer enough.

Trip sighed. There was no point to this argument.

"Let's get you a gurney to move him," Phlox said. "From what you're saying, Lieutenant, this area could well become a war zone in not too short a time."

Trip nodded, then moved to follow—

And a hand closed on his wrist. He almost jumped clean out of his skin.

The commander looked down and saw Ferik, eyes wide, staring up at him.

There had been no miraculous transformation.

It wasn't as if the Ferik who listened, sitting gingerly on the edge of the diagnostic cot while Phlox examined him, while Trip and Royce explained what had happened to Trant and him, was a completely different person. Just as Trip had thought, just as he'd told Neesa herself barely two days ago, the man who woke seemed, in speech and manner, to be much the same as the one he'd been at the start of Phlox's treatment.

But there were differences, subtle but telling ones. In his eyes—the way they stayed focused on whoever was speaking to him. In his facial expressions—the way he reacted instantaneously to what was being said. And in his voice, when he spoke after the three of them had finally finished asking their questions and relaying the tragic news.

"I can't believe it." Ferik looked up at Trip. "How could this happen?"

"I wish I had an answer for you."

"The answer is war, Ferik. We're at war." Royce put a hand on the man's shoulder. "How do you feel? Can you walk?"

"Easy, Lieutenant." Phlox frowned. "I do not want to put too much stress on Ferik's system."

"No," Ferik said. "Let me try."

And before Phlox could say another word, Ferik hopped down from the bed and took a few steps. Awkward ones, at first, with a hint of the somewhat shambling gait he'd had before the procedure.

He reached the far end of sickbay and turned.

And as he started back toward them, his stride smoothed out, his back and shoulders straightened, and he smiled. It transformed his face. Trip, for the first time, saw a hint of the man he must have been fifteen years ago. The man who Trant had fallen in love with.

"Satisfied, Doctor?" Royce asked.

Phlox frowned. "No." He picked up a hand scanner and ran it over Ferik. He studied the results a moment, then nodded.

"All things considered, you seem in good health. I would urge prudence, however, in your physical activities over the next few days. And, here." Phlox handed him a flimsy. "This is a summary of the procedures I performed, with some suggestions on medications that may aid the healing process."

"Thank you, Doctor."

"You're welcome." Phlox bowed slightly. "I am sorry for your loss as well, sir. Doctor Trant seemed to me an excellent person, as well as an outstanding physician."

"I . . . appreciate that." The man's words were still hesitant, Trip thought, but now it seemed a hesitation born not of confusion, but consideration—the difference between a mind searching for a word temporarily misplaced, rather than one whose meaning was lost entirely.

Ferik turned to Trip.

"I remember you. We were friends, I think."

"We were." Trip held out his hand. "Good-bye, Ferik."

"Good-bye . . ."

305

"Trip. My friends call me Trip."

"Trip, then."

They shook.

"I'll stick with Tucker." Royce stuck out his hand to Trip. "Good-bye. For real this time, I suspect."

"I think so too. Take care, Royce. Tell the marshal thanks again from me and Hoshi. For everything." He met the man's eyes. "And tell him not to give up on the boy yet."

Royce nodded, then turned to Ferik. "Ready?"

The man gave his assent, and the two of them started across sickbay.

Just as the corridor doors were opening, Phlox called out from behind Trip.

"Lieutenant Royce, one moment."

The doctor retreated into his office and emerged a moment later, a carryall in one hand. He crossed sickbay and handed it to Royce.

"What's this?"

"Doctor Trant's effects. I intended to give them to you the other day, and quite forgot."

"You should have these." Royce passed the carryall to Ferik, who opened it. Trip caught a quick glimpse of what was inside—a bracelet, a belt, her medical scanner—before Ferik closed it up again.

All at once, something tugged at Trip's consciousness.

It kept tugging, all the way out of sickbay and into the turbolift.

It took him until the lift doors opened to deposit him on the bridge to realize why.

He stood there, unmoving, for a long moment.

Picturing the items in the carryall again. The bracelet, the belt . . .

The scanner he'd given Trant.

Then he pictured her, in the last few seconds of her life, as she turned away from Leeman Sadir, lying in bed in cabin C-430, and spoke.

"Some interesting results."

Those were her last words, as she studied the scanner she'd just used to examine the boy, giving him a complete, thorough physical. The results of which might very well still be in that scanner's memory. The results of which just might include a detailed genetic work-up.

"Commander?" Carstairs was looking up from his station, looking across the bridge at him. "Is everything all right?"

"I don't know," Trip said, and headed for Archer's quarters.

Twenty-Four

"YOU'RE SURE ABOUT THIS?" Archer asked.

"That they've got the scanner—absolutely. Whether or not they'll look at the data, whether it has the kid's genetic work-up . . ." Trip shrugged. "No way to know."

The captain couldn't believe it. All the trouble he'd taken to make sure no one would spot the resemblance between himself and Lee . . .

And now Trip was telling him that the Guild had incontrovertible proof that the boy was one hundred percent human in their possession.

He felt like screaming.

"Damn it." The captain turned to his chief engineer. The two of them were in Archer's quarters, Trip sitting in the chair next to the captain's workstation, Archer now pacing the small room.

"Worst-case scenario," he said. "The data's there, and they find it. What happens next?"

Trip shook his head. "These are good people, sir, the Guild. I spent a lot of time with them. But . . . they've been fighting for almost a decade.

Barely staying alive. You can bet if there's a way that information can help them, they'll use it. Kairn more so than Guildsman Lind, maybe, but—"

"I understand." Archer didn't know that he wouldn't do the exact same thing in their shoes: use the fact that Lee was human to discredit him in front of the rest of the Council. Except . . .

"They won't do anything yet. Even if they have found the data. Because right now, they need the boy to use against Elson," Archer said, thinking out loud. "But after that . . ."

"Exactly," Trip nodded. "After that they won't need him at all."

And if it suited their purposes, they'd expose him. Force him out. Or, what was even more likely, the captain realized, they'd blackmail him. Threaten him with exposure, but keep him in power. Make him their puppet, just as Duvall had feared.

"And we have no way of knowing if any of this'll come to pass," Archer said.

"No. And it ain't like we can ask 'em about it, either."

Both men were silent a moment.

This changed things, Archer realized. Complicated them tremendously. If the boy did what they were asking him—met with Makandros and Kairn, took his father's place on the Council—he could be walking right into a trap. A potentially deadly one. The captain couldn't let Lee charge down that path blindly.

"Sir?"

The captain looked up to find Trip staring at him questioningly.

"You're not thinking about telling him, are you?"

"You read my mind."

"You can't do it, Captain. Learning that he's not Sadir's son—that could send the kid into hiding. Running away from everything—Makandros, Kairn, the Council—entirely."

"Isn't that his decision?"

"Not right now, sir." Trip looked him in the eye. "Right now, it's yours."

Archer sighed.

Trip was right, of course. A war was brewing—a system was at risk. Stopping that war, saving lives, had to take priority over the truth. Even if it meant sacrificing the boy.

Didn't it?

The com buzzed.

"Archer here."

"Carstairs, sir. It's the *Hule* again."

Archer turned to Trip. "Let's play it safe. You remain the liaison for now."

"So we assume they haven't found the data."

"That's right."

Trip nodded and keyed open the channel. "Tell the general I need five minutes."

"Five minutes, aye, sir. Bridge out."

His chief engineer stood.

"Makandros isn't going to sit around forever, waiting for the kid to make up his mind."

"I know," Archer said. "See if you can stall him just a little while longer."

Trip nodded and left. The captain took the chair he'd vacated. Ship's status reports were still up onscreen—he'd been in the middle of reviewing them when Trip had arrived with this latest bit of bad news. There was a list of completed systems checks, and next to it, a second list of those that remained to be done. Everything was on or ahead of schedule—a few more hours of work, and *Enterprise* would be back to full readiness.

Not that they had anywhere to go at the moment. And that reminded him . . .

Archer keyed in a quick series of commands. The workstation monitor cleared, then filled with an image from one of the science labs—T'Pol, Brodesser, and two of the crew from *Daedalus* whose names he hadn't gotten, all gathered around a table on which rested a partially disassembled subspace beacon.

Archer opened a channel.

"Hard at work already, I see," he said.

At the sound of his voice in the lab, everyone looked up. T'Pol said something to Brodesser and moved closer to the screen.

"Captain, I assume you are interested in learning what progress we have made."

"Guilty as charged."

"We are about to begin modification of the beacon's carrier wave. In addition, an examination of our computer records has already provided the Denari outpost's transmission frequency. I would estimate within another twelve to fourteen hours, we will be capable of sending a test signal."

"Which will be your universe's Hubble Constant," Brodesser called out, without looking up from the beacon. "That'll go a long way toward determining whether or not you're talking to the right Denari."

"Sounds like you're making progress."

"We are," Brodesser replied.

"Indeed." T'Pol lowered her voice, leaning closer to the screen and obscuring the others behind her. "Captain, I am still uncomfortable being away from the bridge at such a critical time, particularly given your absence as well. Professor Brodesser is fully capable of supervising—"

"T'Pol." He cut her off quickly. "What you're doing down there is at least as important as what happens on the bridge. Maybe more so." Being safely back on *Enterprise* had certainly lessened the sense of urgency about returning home—the ability to eat, drink, and breathe without feeling sick was a big plus—but their supplies weren't going to last forever. "We have to find a way to get that sensor data."

She nodded with obvious reluctance. "Yes, sir. However, if anything arises that requires my presence—"

"I promise we'll contact you. In the meantime . . ."

"Yes, sir. Back to work."

"That's right."

He smiled, and closed the channel. At almost that same instant, the screen's status bar began blinking.

It had been two hours to the minute since he'd left Lee to get some sleep. Time to wake the boy up and get a decision out of him.

One way or the other.

Trip drummed his fingers impatiently on the armrest of the command chair.

"I have the *Hule* for you now, sir," Carstairs said, looking up from the com station.

"Put 'em through."

Trip rose and waited for Makandros's face to appear on the viewscreen before him. He'd had a hard time reestablishing contact with the Denari vessel— a lot of com activity going back and forth between *Hule* and the other ships in the DEF/Guild fleet, Carstairs had said. *Maybe so,* Trip thought, but he wouldn't be surprised if at least part of the delay was Makandros giving him a little bit back, a little taste of what it felt like to sit around waiting.

Trip sympathized with the general. He was a little tired of waiting around himself. Not that he didn't have sympathy for the captain's position too—it had been hard enough for Trip to deal with a Brodesser who wasn't really Brodesser; he couldn't imagine what Archer must be going through—but he was anxious to have this over with, one way or the other. *Enterprise* was keeping a whole armada of ships waiting on them. And speaking of waiting . . .

Where was Makandros, anyway? The viewscreen was still dark.

"Ensign?" Trip asked, turning to Carstairs.

"Sorry, sir. They said a few seconds. Let me—"

Right then, the screen came to life, showing him *Hule*'s command deck.

But Makandros wasn't there. Instead, the center chair was occupied by a woman Trip had noticed in the background during his previous conversations with the general.

"Where's General Makandros?"

"He is otherwise occupied. I am Colonel Briatt, in temporary command of *Hule*."

"Colonel. Commander Tucker, in temporary command of *Enterprise*."

"I know who you are. What do you want?"

"What do I want?" Trip frowned. "The general tried to contact me before."

"No doubt to inform you that the fleet is breaking up. Consider yourself hereby informed."

"Breaking up?"

"Re-forming into smaller, more maneuverable squadrons. In the event we are attacked, this will give us greater tactical flexibility in our response."

Trip's gaze went to Ensign Duel at the science station.

"Confirm that, sir," Duel said quietly. "The Guild/DEF fleet is moving apart."

"You should move your ship as well, Commander Tucker. This many vessels, bunched so closely together—we have most certainly drawn the notice of General Elson's fleet."

"Thanks for the advice. We'll take it under consideration," Trip said.

"I suggest you do. Now if there's nothing else . . ."

"There is, actually. Leeman Sadir—the general wanted to talk to him. You can tell him the boy should be waking soon."

"I'm sure he'll be interested to hear it. *Hule* out."

And before Trip could say another word, the viewscreen went dark.

"Huh," he said, sitting back down in the command chair.

He didn't know what to make of that—Briatt cutting him off so quickly. On the one hand, it wasn't entirely unexpected. Like he'd told the captain, Makandros wasn't going to sit around forever. The general had told them before that he had plans of his own to make, and Trip supposed he'd done just that. Even so, not to be interested in talking to the boy at all? That was a little extreme. There had to be something else going on.

He wondered if he could find out what that something else was.

"Carstairs," he said, turning to Hoshi's replacement at the com. "See if you can get me Marshal Kairn, aboard the *Eclipse.*"

The young man nodded and bent to his station.

Trip, meanwhile, opened a channel of his own.

Twenty-Five

Archer frowned.

"Get Briatt back on the com. I want to talk to her."

"*Hule*'s moved out of range, Captain. In fact, except for a few transports and one of the Guild ships that's under repair, we're the only vessel left here."

Archer frowned. He couldn't believe Makandros had all at once given up on talking to the boy. Trip was right. Something else was going on.

"Keep trying to contact them—Kairn and the general," he said. "Let me know the second you do. And let's take Briatt's advice. Move us well away from the rendezvous point. Out of the Belt entirely, in fact."

"Yes, sir," Trip replied over the com. "Captain—"

"Yes?"

"Not to be a pest, sir, but it has been two hours. That's how long you wanted to let the boy sleep before—"

"I'm standing in front of his cabin right now."

"Ah."

"Apology accepted." Archer smiled. "I'll keep you posted, Trip. Out."

The captain stepped back from the com panel. He nodded to Yamani, on guard duty, who then unlocked the door for him.

Archer entered the dimly lit cabin. Rather than switching on the light, he let his eyes adjust to the semidarkness.

The first thing he saw was the bed, and Porthos sprawled out across it, right where Archer had left him. Sound asleep.

Not Leeman Sadir.

The boy stood at the far end of the cabin, staring out the room's sole window port. He turned and offered Archer a half smile.

The captain returned it.

"Still having trouble sleeping?"

"I woke up right after you left. Couldn't fall back asleep. Unlike him," Lee said, nodding toward Porthos, who suddenly sat up in bed and barked once.

Archer smiled. "An ion storm couldn't disturb his beauty sleep."

"I'd like to change places."

"You've got a lot more to think about than he does."

"Yes," Lee said. "That's true."

The boy seemed about to continue, but instead turned back toward the window, his gaze fixed on the stars outside.

"You hungry? Thirsty?" The captain nodded toward the refrigerator in the corner. "I don't know if they told you, but there's food in there for you."

Lee shook his head. "No, thanks."

Okay, the captain thought. *So much for small talk.*

"There've been some developments," he said, and then told Lee about General Elson's proclamation, his decision to convene the Council and, in effect, ask them to make him absolute ruler of Denari. He watched the boy as he spoke, waiting for some reaction. But Lee's face remained impassive.

"I know you're still taking it all in, Lee. And I meant what I said before about not forcing you to do anything you don't want to. But this puts us under the gun now. If you want to present a united front—"

"I'll do it," the boy blurted out. "I'll talk to Makandros and the Guild."

"Good." Archer nodded. "I'm glad to hear it."

Which he was, except that he couldn't help thoughts of the scanner Ferik had in his possession, the information on it, and what it could mean for the boy's future from intruding just then. There was indeed a part of him that wanted to tell the boy everything.

Archer set it aside, and smiled.

"Now all we have to do is find them," the captain said, explaining the fleet's break-up. "But we should get you up to the bridge, so that—"

"There's something else," the boy said, all in rush. "Someone else, actually, that I need to talk to."

The captain, who'd already taken a step toward the cabin door, stopped in his tracks.

He didn't like the slightly hesitant, slightly defiant tone that had crept into the boy's voice just then.

"Oh?"

"Yes," Lee said. "General Elson."

Archer sighed.

"Lee—"

"We only have other people's word for what he's done, Captain. No proof."

Archer shook his head. "I saw Makandros's fleet. The ships that Elson's forces ambushed."

"It could have been the other way around. You weren't there. Who's to say how it really happened?"

"There's more than that, Lee," Archer said gently, resisting the urge to tell the boy not to ignore the obvious. "Colonel Peranda was his man."

"I know that," the boy said quietly.

"Peranda is responsible for your mother's death. For almost killing you."

"No." The boy shook his head. "I don't believe General Elson would have ordered those things."

"I know you were close to him, Lee, but—"

"Captain."

The boy turned to face him directly for the first time.

The circles underneath his eyes, Archer saw, were even bigger and darker than before.

"All I want to do is talk to him. My father always said if you were going to judge a man, you had to be willing to look into his eyes. Hear his side of the story."

The captain couldn't help the look of exasperation that crossed his face then. "Lee," he began. "You—"

"Captain, if I'm going to turn against the general, I need to make sure that it's the right decision. You can understand that, can't you?"

Archer sighed again. What he understood was that there was going to be no talking the boy out of this.

"All right. Let's get up to the bridge then, so you can have that conversation."

In the turbolift, Archer tried to talk strategy with the boy. The captain stressed that whatever explana-

319

tions Elson had for his actions, it was important for Lee not to take them at face value. That he had to probe the general not just for words, but reactions. See what Elson thought about Lee's taking his father's seat on the Council, what the idea of a meeting between the boy, General Makandros, and the Guild provoked. By the time the lift doors opened, the captain was beginning to think that Lee's conversation with Elson was, in fact, a good idea, if for no other reason than that it might reveal the general's thinking to him.

Trip, however, didn't share that belief.

When Archer told him what Lee wanted to do, his chief engineer all but exploded. The captain had to take him by the arm and drag him off to his ready room, leaving Lee in the custody of Ensign Yamani, who'd accompanied them to the bridge from his quarters.

"Commander," Archer said as the ready room door closed behind them. "You need to calm down."

"Calm down? Captain, did I miss something here?" His chief engineer shook his head. "Everybody forget about those nuclear bombs already? The attack on Makandros's fleet? What happened right here, on *Enterprise?* You remind the kid that his mother's dead because of Elson? Peranda was taking orders from him, if you remember."

"I told him," Archer said. "All that and more. This is something he needs to do."

"And we're going to let him?"

"If we want his cooperation, we don't have any choice. Relax, Trip."

His chief engineer took a deep breath. Archer

gave him another few seconds to get fully under control before speaking again.

"Talk doesn't cost us anything right now. Especially since we haven't heard anything from Kairn or Makandros. At least, I assume that's the case."

"It is." Trip nodded. "We think they must have moved deep inside the Belt, that they're setting up defensive positions there. Carstairs is working on boosting our signal so we can reach them."

"Look at it this way. This'll give him time to do that."

Trip frowned.

"I still don't like it, Captain."

"I don't like it much either. But we're trying to stop a war here. Whatever we have to do to make that happen . . ."

"Yes, sir." Trip shook his head. "I'd still rather he talked to Kairn and Makandros first. You know the first thing Elson's going to do is try and poison the kid's mind about them."

"I know. Which is why you're going to be in on that conversation too. Making sure Lee gets both sides of the story."

"I'll do my best."

The com sounded.

"Bridge to Captain Archer."

"Go ahead."

"I have the Kresh, sir."

"Thank you. Commander Tucker will be right there."

Archer closed the channel and turned to Trip.

"Show time."

* * *

"Just stand here," Trip said to the boy, placing Lee directly in front of the command chair. "Look at that screen, and speak right at him. That's all. He'll see you."

"I don't understand." Lee looked around him to the ready room door. "Where's Captain Archer?"

"Something came up," Trip lied. "Don't worry. He'll be out as soon as he can. Now you remember what the two of you talked about?"

"I remember."

"Just don't let him avoid your questions. Make sure—"

"I remember," the boy said, more sharply.

Trip threw up his hands. "Okay. I hear you."

He stepped back and nodded to Carstairs. The ensign keyed in a series of commands at his console, and the viewscreen came to life.

General Elson—looking exactly as he had two hours ago when they'd heard him issue his proclamation to convene the Council, not a hair out of place, not a sign of stress or doubt on his features—glanced up at the screen and smiled.

"Lee. You're all right. Thank God."

The boy cleared his throat.

"Yes, sir. I'm fine," he said.

"After we lost contact with the ship, I was worried."

Elson had shifted locations within the Kresh, Trip saw. He was in a different place than he'd broadcast from earlier. Behind the general now, Trip caught glimpses of a huge, high-ceilinged room, and dozens of people milling around. More than dozens, in fact. Hundreds. A lot of them soldiers, who, judging from their posture and the way people who came near them reacted, were there on duty. Elson's soldiers, no doubt. He could guess the reason for their presence as well.

They were there to make sure the coming Council meeting went exactly as the general intended it to.

"Who are you?"

Trip looked up to find Elson's gaze had shifted to him.

"Commander Charles Tucker, temporarily in command of the *Starship Enterprise.*"

"One of the Starfleet officers. Lee is your prisoner then, I take it?"

"He's our passenger. Our guest."

Elson's gaze shifted back to the boy.

"He's right, General. I'm fine. These people are my friends."

Elson nodded thoughtfully.

"You're very understanding, Commander. After what was done to your ship and crew—"

"Which you had nothing to do with."

The general's eyes narrowed.

"That's right. I had nothing to do with it. The attack on your ship was led by General Makandros. I was in charge of arranging your vessel's transfer to Kota, but other than that . . ."

The general smiled disingenuously, first at Trip, and then at Lee. Playing to his audience for all he was worth.

Trip had to give it to him. The man was smooth.

"We need to talk, Lee," Elson said. "A lot has happened in the last twenty-four hours. I need to bring you and Captain Duvall up to speed." The general's eyes scanned the bridge behind the boy, and he frowned. "Where is she, Lee? Where's your mother?"

The boy blinked and shuffled unsteadily on his feet.

"She's . . ." he began, and cleared his throat. "She's not . . ."

"Captain Duvall is dead," Trip said, stepping forward, giving the kid a moment to compose himself. "An explosion, aboard *Enterprise.*"

Elson's reaction was immediate, and just as theatrical as Trip would have expected.

The man closed his eyes tightly and shook his head slowly back and forth.

"Oh no. God, no."

"There was a bomb," Trip went on. "A booby trap, apparently set by an officer under your direct command. A Colonel—"

"Peranda," Elson snapped. "That idiot. Where is he now?"

"In custody."

"I want him." The general's eyes darted to the boy and stayed there. "His orders were to transport you and your mother safely to the Kresh. That's all. He won't get away with this, Lee. I promise you."

The boy nodded.

"Commander," Elson continued, talking to Trip now but still looking at Lee. "I'd like to make arrangements to have the colonel transferred to our control, whenever is convenient."

"You'll have to talk to General Makandros about that," Trip said. "Peranda and his men are with him now."

Elson's expression froze.

He turned back to Trip.

"Is that so? Makandros? After what he did to your crew, you're on speaking terms?"

"That's right," Trip said. "We're on speaking terms."

He left it to the general to imagine what exactly they were speaking about.

Elson nodded thoughtfully.

"You should be aware he is an insurrectionist. Fomenting trouble within the border settlements, collaborating with sworn enemies of the Denari people—"

"Is that why you attacked his fleet earlier?"

Trip had hoped to provoke more of a reaction with that question, but Elson must have seen it coming. The general only set his jaw and nodded again.

"Precisely. I also have proof he's been collaborating with the Guild, our government's sworn enemy. That he may have helped them mount terrorist attacks right here on the planet's surface."

"You're talking about Charest?"

Elson smiled thinly. "You're very well informed about what's been happening on our world, Commander Tucker."

"We're on speaking terms with the Guild too," Trip said. "They tell a different version of that story."

"I imagine they do." Elson's words were for Trip, but his gaze remained focused on the boy. "I assume you've heard these stories as well, Lee."

"Yes, sir," the boy said. "To tell you the truth, I don't know what to think."

"The investigation of the incident at Charest is ongoing," Elson said. "Perhaps you would like to talk to the man in charge. One moment."

Without waiting for a response, he turned to one side and said something the com couldn't pick up.

Elson's image disappeared and was immediately replaced by a head-and-shoulders view of another man. A man with darker skin than Trip had seen on any Denari previously, his head completely shaved, wearing a uniform exactly like the general's.

Seeing the man, Lee, for the first time since Trip had met him, broke out into a big smile.

"Maj," he said, taking an unconscious step toward the screen before he got control of himself. "It's . . . it's good to see you."

"And you, young one." The man had one of the deepest voices Trip had ever heard. "I'm so sorry about your mother. You're all right?"

"I'm fine."

"These Starfleet officers are not mistreating you? Because if they are . . ." The man's gaze shifted and locked on Trip.

The two stared at each other a second.

Hard to tell over a com link, of course, but the concern Trip saw in this man's eyes seemed fairly genuine.

"I told you, I'm all right," Lee said. "I'm more anxious to find out what's been going on down there. Charest. The general says—"

"It was an attack," the man said, his face suddenly grave. "We have evidence the Guild was involved."

"What sort of evidence?" Trip interjected.

"I will be happy to share it with you when you arrive, Lee," the man said. "How far off are you?"

The boy's eyes darted to Trip.

"I—I'm not sure," Lee managed.

"You are coming to the Council meeting, are you not?" the man asked. "General Elson needs your support."

Before Trip or the boy could respond, the man's image disappeared, and Elson's face filled the screen again.

"I should have mentioned that earlier, Lee. I have convened the Council. We need to present a united front against the threat the Guild represents."

"Yes, sir. I . . . I was aware of the meeting."

"I see. And were you planning on attending? Taking your father's seat?"

"I . . ." The boy hesitated, looking all at once entirely lost, and far, far too young to be involved in the conversation.

Trip spoke up again.

"Seems to me that maybe your war council is a little premature, General. We're on speaking terms with the Guild, after all. With Makandros. And you. If we can do it"—he smiled and locked eyes with Elson—"maybe you all can do it as well. Get together. Find a way to avoid this war."

Elson shook his head. "The Guild would like that, wouldn't they? If we stopped harassing their ships— gave them time to regroup, plan new, even deadlier attacks . . ."

"So you won't negotiate with them?"

"I see no point."

"General, perhaps . . ." Lee had found his voice and stepped forward now. "The Guild has asked to speak to me, sir. Let me do that at least, before you—"

"Lee." Elson said, his eyes wide in what to Trip

was clearly feigned surprise. "Talking to the Guild? What would your father say?"

The boy blinked, looking lost again.

Trip's lips tightened in anger. "That's a low blow, General."

Elson turned back to Trip and for the first time allowed some of the anger he no doubt felt to seep into his voice.

"I fail to see what business this is of yours, Commander. Any of it."

"I don't like seeing people die for no good reason."

"Noble sentiments," Elson snapped. "But some things are worth fighting—and dying—for. Your father knew that, Lee."

The general's eyes fastened on the boy one final time.

"The Council meets in three hours. We'll be waiting for you."

Elson nodded, and the screen went dark.

Twenty-Six

"You know what's going to happen as well as I do, sir." Trip shook his head and kept pacing. "The second Elson gets his hands on that boy, it'll be the last time anyone ever sees Leeman Sadir."

His chief engineer, who'd joined the captain in his ready room was worked up all over again.

Trip had good reason. The general may have talked a good game, but the captain's assessment of the situation was pretty much the same as Trip's: Elson had gone after Makandros and Dirsch because they threatened his position, and he was going to do exactly the same to Lee. If not to kill him, as Trip thought, then to neutralize him in some other way. They couldn't deliver the boy into his hands.

Unfortunately, that was exactly what Lee wanted them to do.

"What if I do go? Take my father's place. Elson has to listen to me then." Lee had said, the instant Trip had brought him into the ready room.

"It's not a good idea, Lee," Archer had said.

"What do we lose by trying?"

"You, I suspect," Trip interjected.

"He's not going to do anything to me in front of the entire Council."

"No," Trip said. "He'll find a nice, secluded area to kill you in."

"Commander," Archer said, a note of warning in his voice. "Let's take a step back. Lee, who was that other man you were talking to? Maj—"

"Maj Wooler. Colonel Wooler. Another of my tutors—weapons, unarmed combat. I've known him my whole life."

"He seems a little more trustworthy," Trip said. "If a bit misguided in his allegiance."

Lee shot the commander an angry look. But the captain agreed with Trip. Wooler's feelings for the boy had seemed genuine.

"What's his role in all this? Why's he the one investigating what happened at Charest?"

"Colonel Wooler is—was—head of my father's security force."

Archer and Trip shared a glance.

"He's got men under his command? His own men?" Trip asked.

"Some. A couple dozen."

Enough to protect the boy, at least initially.

"Is there a way of contacting him without letting Elson know about it?"

The question had been meant for Lee, but Trip answered it.

"Doubtful, sir. I've been inside the Kresh. The way they have that place wired up . . ."

"Not that I know of," Lee added.

Archer sighed. They couldn't just send the boy in

there willy-nilly. Trip was right. That was a suicide mission. And the captain did not think there were enough phase pistols aboard *Enterprise* to send down an adequate security detail—the chamber Elson had been broadcasting from was crammed full of soldiers. He was not going to put his people in the line of fire. Bottom line: as much as he wanted to help Lee—help the Denari avoid war . . .

This was not their fight.

"We need alternatives," the captain said.

"We need more time," Trip said.

"Let me go, sir. I'm willing to take the risk."

Archer shook his head. "No. I'm sorry, Lee."

"Captain—"

"It's not just your life you risk by going. It's your planet's last chance to avoid war."

The com buzzed.

"T'Pol to Archer."

He opened the channel. "Go ahead."

"We need to talk, sir."

From the tone in her voice, she did not have good news.

"One minute, Sub-Commander." The captain turned to Lee. "I want you to go back to your quarters with Ensign Yamani. I'll join you in a few minutes."

"Captain," Lee said. "Maybe if I can get to Colonel Wooler first—"

"Not now, Lee. Please."

"When? We don't have a lot of time."

"Lee, this ship can do warp five. That means we can get from here to Denari in about two seconds, all right? We have time."

"It's going to take more than two seconds to convince the Council not to attack."

Archer sighed.

"You said you wouldn't force me to do anything I don't want," Lee went on. "Well, I don't want to stay here on this ship any longer. Not when there's a chance that I could stop a war."

"I understand. We'll talk about it. Just not right now."

"You can't keep me here."

Archer didn't respond.

Without saying another word, the boy spun on his heel and left the ready room.

The captain sighed.

"Kid's right, sir. We can't keep him here forever."

"I know that. One thing at a time, though." Archer keyed open the circuit to the science lab. T'Pol's face filled the screen.

"Sorry about that, Sub-Commander. Go ahead."

"We are aborting the project, sir."

Archer let out an exclamation of disgust. More good news.

"What's the problem?" Trip asked, leaning over the captain's shoulder.

"Further analysis of the gravitational flux within the anomaly reveals far more powerful EM distortion than we'd previously detected. We will be unable to maintain the carrier signal's integrity long enough for it to transit the dimensional gateway."

"What about redundant carriers?"

"You could have a shipful of carriers and not get a signal through that beast." Brodesser had stepped forward and now stood just behind T'Pol. "It's not going to work, Trip."

"So that's it?"

"That's it," Brodesser said. "For what it's worth, we're using the signal to map out the strength of the gravitational flux within the anomaly. That may be of some help to you."

"The professor is being unreasonably optimistic," T'Pol said. "Such a map will not prove useful."

"And your Vulcan is being a tad too pessimistic," Brodesser said. "That map will enable your ship to pass through the flux without being torn to pieces."

"As a practical matter, we will still be unable to return to our own universe, sir."

Archer nodded. "All right. Thank you both for your efforts, in any case."

"You're welcome," Brodesser said. "And we'll get you that map, Captain."

"And I will join you on the bridge, sir. With your permission."

"Of course. We'll see you in a minute. Archer out." The screen went dark.

The captain spun in his chair to face Trip.

"Got any more ideas?"

"I'm fresh out at the moment. Captain, don't you think it's time you let the rest of the crew in on what's happening?"

"Yes. Probably past time." And speaking of time . . .

Archer glanced back at the status bar.

Less than three hours to the Council meeting.

Lee was right, they didn't have that long to act. Not if they wanted to stop the war. Makandros had said it too: once the generals were all in the Council chamber, they were effectively under Elson's control. It would be close to impossible for them to go against him.

"Where are they?"

"Sir?" Trip asked.

"Makandros and Kairn—where are they?"

"I wish I could tell you. Carstairs can't seem to find them."

"Where's Hoshi?"

"Still confined to quarters. I don't know that she could be doing anything more, sir."

"Well, let's find out." He keyed open a channel. A second later Hoshi's face filled the screen. She looked about a million times better than she had the last time the captain had seen her—still thinner than usual, but there was color in her cheeks now, life on her face.

And a fork in her hand. He'd caught her in the middle of eating.

"Ensign, sorry for the interruption."

"That's all right, sir. Were my suggestions of any help?"

Archer frowned.

"Suggestions?"

"Ensign Carstairs had contacted me about alternative signaling methods—to try and locate *Eclipse?*"

"Ah." Archer nodded. Of course he had. "No, I'm afraid not. Still no sign of either vessel."

"I'm sorry to hear that. If I think of anything else, I'll be sure and let him know." She frowned. "Why were you calling, sir?"

"Just checking in," the captain replied quickly. "When are you back on the duty schedule?"

"Tomorrow, hopefully. Doctor Phlox wants to see

me get back another few pounds before he clears me." She smiled and shook her head. "I don't know how much more I can eat, though. Not without getting sick all over again."

The captain saw a stack of dishes behind her and what looked like the bone from a very thick porterhouse.

"I didn't know you ate steak," he said.

"I don't, usually. Doctor's orders."

"Well, we'll let you get back to it then."

Hoshi nodded. "Good luck, Captain. Commander."

Archer closed the channel.

"Okay," Trip said. "They don't want to talk to us. But can we find them somehow? Force the issue?"

"What are you thinking?"

"Modify the sensors. I can take a pretty good guess at *Eclipse*'s hull composition. Feed that data in . . ."

Archer nodded. "Sounds like it's worth a try. Let's check status with Malcolm." The captain opened a channel. "Reed, status on sensors."

"Another hour or so till all units are on-line again, and at full strength," Reed said. "We can try the modification then, sir, although, if they're deep inside the Belt, we still might not have much luck."

"An hour or so." Archer shook his head. "That's cutting it too close."

"Sir?" Reed asked.

Archer filled Malcolm in on everything that had happened. In the middle of his explanation, T'Pol entered. The captain started over, and got her up to speed as well.

"I hesitate to point out the obvious, Captain," she said the instant he'd finished. "But—"

"This is not our war. I know that."

"Our safest course of action is to do as the boy asks. Let him join the Council. That was our original intent."

"We thought he'd have Makandros and Kairn with him, though," Archer pointed out.

"Captain, I don't know that I'm comfortable bringing us that close to the Kresh anyway," Reed said. "I've seen specifications on the armament they have on that building. For us to approach the planet, with Elson in control of those weapons—it doesn't strike me as the most prudent maneuver."

"Perhaps we could locate an alternative drop-off point, another Denari outpost nearer our present position, to leave the boy at."

"We're not abandoning him—or our effort to stop the war," Archer said. "Not just yet, anyway."

The com buzzed.

"Bridge to the captain."

That was Carstairs.

"Archer here. Go ahead."

"I've got them sir. Marshal Kairn and General Makandros."

For the first time in what felt like forever, the captain smiled.

"Good work, Ensign."

"Not my doing, sir. They contacted us."

"In any case, we'll be right there."

He closed the channel and turned to Trip.

"Let them know the boy's ready to talk. Tell them what we learned from Elson, and see if they know this Colonel Wooler. Malcolm, you get hold of Yamani, tell him to get Lee back up here right away.

T'Pol, let's get one of the shuttle pods prepped and ready to go. If there's going to be a meeting between these people, it needs to happen soon."

His command staff hustled through the door. Trip stopped on his way out and turned back with a smile.

"Think we might just pull this off, sir?"

"We might at that. On your way now."

Archer watched the door close behind them, then went back to his workstation and activated the bridge monitor. He saw Trip enter the bridge and gesture to Carstairs. The viewscreen filled with the side-by-side images of Makandros, transmitting from what looked like the pilot's seat of one of the Stingers, and Kairn, standing on *Eclipse*'s bridge.

"Commander Tucker," Kairn said. "We need to talk."

The marshal held up something in one of his hands—gleaming metal, about the size of an old-fashioned hardcover book. Archer didn't recognize it.

Trip did.

"That's Doctor Trant's scanner," his chief engineer said.

The captain felt the blood drain suddenly from his face.

"That's right," Kairn replied. "Would you like to know what information we've just discovered on it?"

"Sure," Trip said, his voice sounding surprisingly, unnaturally calm to Archer, whose own heart was racing. "I'm listening."

Twenty-Seven

"THE BOY IS A FRAUD," Makandros said, speaking up for the first time. "Not Sadir's son at all. Human."

Trip had a split second to decide how to play it. Lie, or admit the truth. He wished that he and the captain had covered this eventuality in their discussions, that Archer was here instead of him right now, and then decided there was no point in lying. They were all on the same side here.

He hoped.

"That's something," he said, choosing his words carefully, "that we recently discovered ourselves."

"Really?" The expression on Kairn's face was cold enough to freeze coffee. "And were you intending to share this information with us?"

"We were talking about that as well."

"And were you going to decide before or after we installed a human as ruler of our world?"

"Like I said, we were talking. And that was not our intention at all. Our intentions are the same as yours. Stop the war."

"I would have hoped," Kairn said, "that the time

we'd served together would have counted for some-thing with you, Tucker. That you would have de-cided you owed us the truth."

"I'm sorry, Marshal. I really am." Trip paused a second. "Of course, it would have been impossible for us to contact you if we had decided to share that information. Considering that we had no idea where you'd gone off to."

Makandros spoke up. "We had plans of our own to make, Tucker. As I informed you earlier."

"Well, now that we are talking"—Trip didn't know if he shouldn't suggest this or not, considering that it would be precisely the worst-case scenario he and the captain had discussed earlier, but he was flying by the seat of his pants here—"why don't I go get the boy, and you talk to him as well?"

Makandros snorted in disgust. "The boy is useless to us now."

"He's still the only way you have to get Elson to stand down."

"We're finished here," Makandros said. "Good-bye, Tucker."

He turned his head to the side. Trip knew he was about to give the order to break contact.

"Wait."

Both men turned to look at him.

Trip's thoughts raced frantically, trying to find something else to say.

Meanwhile, Archer had Yamani on the com.

"Keep the boy in his quarters," he told the ensign.

"Sir?" Yamani replied. "I just spoke to Lieutenant Reed, and he said—"

"These orders take precedence."

"He's a little restless."

"Walk him around the ship, then. Just don't let him up here."

In the background, Archer heard Porthos barking and suddenly had an idea. "In fact, Ensign, take them both for a walk. Cargo Bay D-2."

"D-2. Yes, sir."

Archer closed the channel. Yamani had been to D-2 with Porthos before. He should be able to keep the boy occupied there for at least the next few minutes.

Until the captain could figure what they were supposed to do now.

On the viewscreen, Trip was doing the best he could, trying to convince Kairn and Makandros to reconsider their decision. Archer had mixed feelings about his chief engineer's argument, mostly because of his concern about the boy. Lee really had no place safe to go now.

And a very, very hard truth to face.

The com buzzed.

"Captain."

That was Malcolm.

"Go," Archer replied, trying to divide his attention between Reed and the scene still unfolding on the bridge.

"Makandros and Kairn. I've fixed their positions, sir. They're leading twinned battle groups, just outside the Belt. And, Captain, extrapolating their trajectories, relative velocities—I think I know what they're planning."

"Cut to the chase, Malcolm."

"They're on an attack run, sir. Headed straight for Denari."

The captain sat up straight. Reed had his full attention now.

"Show me."

Malcolm sent the data to his screen. Archer took one look at it and saw his tactical officer was right.

"Hell," the captain said, and stood up.

He walked out of the ready room, and into the middle of a heated argument between Trip, Kairn, and Makandros.

"Captain Duvall assured us," Trip was saying, "she was the only one who ever knew that Sadir wasn't the boy's father. Talk to the kid. He didn't even—"

"These two men have no desire to talk. They've already made their decision. To go to war," Archer interrupted, looking up at the screen. "Isn't that so?"

Now it was Makandros and Kairn who were surprised. Only for a second, though.

"Captain Archer," the general said. "All recovered from your injuries, I see."

"Don't ignore my question, General."

"We owe you no answers. Our plans are of no consequence to you."

"We're trying to help you."

"Your concern is noted."

"Don't be this way, General. You know how many people are going to die if you attack."

"And how many people are going to die if we don't?" Makandros shot back. "There are times, Captain, when war is the only option."

"There are. But you have another right now. Leeman Sadir."

Makandros shook his head. "The boy is useless to us. As I've just finished explaining to your commander. Now if there's nothing else—"

"I thought you wanted peace."

"We want peace more than anything else, Captain. Believe me." Kairn leaned forward in his command chair. "But a lasting peace—not one negotiated under false pretenses. Not a peace that could degenerate into an even bloodier conflict than the one we face now."

"If you don't want blood spilled," the captain said pointedly, "then break off your attack."

"Our intent is not to spill blood," Kairn said. "Our intent—"

"Excuse me, Marshal," Makandros interrupted. "As I told you earlier, Captain—our plans are none of your concern."

"I'm trying," Archer said through clenched teeth, "to help you—"

"Your help is not wanted," the general said. "Do not attempt to interfere with our plans. Otherwise, I'll be forced to attack *Enterprise* a second time."

All at once, there was silence on the bridge.

The captain let it hang for another few seconds before responding.

"That would be a very, very stupid idea," Archer said. "You're not dealing with a crippled ship anymore."

"And you would not be dealing with a general under orders to capture your vessel intact."

The two men locked eyes a moment.

"I trust we understand each other," Makandros said.

The screen went dark.

"They've cut the signal, sir," Carstairs said.

Archer nodded, and sat down in his command chair.

Trip stepped up alongside him. "What's this about an attack?"

Archer gestured to Malcolm, who filled Trip in.

"Doesn't make any sense," his chief engineer said. "Going after Elson in the Kresh? They might have a lot more ships than us, but there's still no way that's anything but a suicide run."

"Maybe they're hoping his forces will have their guard down while the Council meets," Archer said, realizing even as he spoke that just the opposite would in fact be true. The PDC ships would be on high alert, with so many VIP's in the Kresh.

"Or maybe," he said slowly. "They're not going to attack the Kresh at all."

"Sir?" Trip asked.

Archer turned to his chief engineer. "Tell me about Denari. Assuming Makandros and Kairn aren't foolish enough to attack the Kresh, what else could they be trying to do?"

"The planet has two continents. The Kresh is on the smaller one. The bigger one is where most of the population is." Trip frowned. "I don't know about targets there."

Archer nodded, thinking.

Our intent is not to spill blood, Kairn had said. So what else could they be trying to do?

"The other continent is where those explosions were," he said out loud.

"Charest," Trip filled in.

"Right."

"General Dirsch," his chief engineer said. "I remember—Kairn said that he was one of the most powerful members of the Council. Maybe he survived. Maybe they found him."

"And they're going to join forces?" the captain asked.

"Could be."

"Or," Malcolm spoke up now, "they could be trying to establish a base there."

Archer nodded. "Give themselves a supply line."

"God knows the Guild can use supplies," Trip said.

"Excuse me." T'Pol stepped down from her station into the main bridge area. "Captain, this conversation is entirely academic, of course. Our efforts should now be focused elsewhere. Don't you agree?"

Archer locked eyes with his science officer.

T'Pol was reminding him that they had other concerns—specifically, finding a way back through the anomaly to their own universe.

Except the captain wasn't quite ready to give up on this one yet.

"Maybe," Archer said. "And maybe not."

He stood and headed for the turbolift.

"Sir? Where are you going?" Trip called after him.

"Cargo Bay D-2," Archer said. "Commander Tucker, you have the conn."

On a long mission such as *Enterprise*'s, massive storage space was required. Not just for food and other perishables, but for spare parts, specialized equipment, repair materials, and the like. *Enterprise* had multiple cargo bays to serve those purposes, one of which was bay D-2, located, not surprisingly, down on D-deck. During the first few months of the ship's mission, it had been utilized primarily for items intended for trade with new species they encountered—replicas of art, artifacts, and other pieces of cultural significance. As those pieces were moved out, the idea had been to replace them with cultural artifacts from the civilizations they encountered.

For one reason or another, however, that sort of swapping had not taken place. Archer had found himself, instead, leaving items behind and receiving nothing in return. This had resulted in an almost completely empty bay D-2. It was a long, narrow room, shaped somewhat like an old-fashioned squash court, with a two-deck-high bulkhead facing the entrance. A perfectly flat wall, perfectly suited for bouncing a ball off. A room perfectly suited for letting a dog run wild in.

That was exactly what Porthos was doing when the captain arrived: running wildly after the tennis ball that Leeman Sadir had just thrown. His paws skittered on the hard metal surface as he chased after it, barking madly the whole while.

The boy was laughing. Yamani, a step behind him, was smiling too. Neither had heard the captain come in.

The captain gave them a few seconds more to enjoy the moment. Then he cleared his throat and spoke.

"Lee."

The boy turned, and the smile disappeared from his face.

"What's happening?" he said. "What did you decide? The Council meets in—"

345

"Less than two hours. I know." Archer turned to Yamani. "That'll be all, Ensign. Thank you."

The man nodded and left the bay. The captain turned back to the boy. His face must have given him away.

"What's the matter?" Lee asked. "Is something wrong?"

The captain sighed. "We have to talk."

"About what?"

Archer didn't even know where to start. How to start.

Porthos had caught up to the ball. He picked it up and bounded back over to Lee, dropping it at his feet. The boy ignored him.

"Captain?"

"Come with me," Archer said, making his decision.

"Where?"

"My cabin," the captain replied. "There's something I want to show you."

Archer bent, picked up the tennis ball, and led the way out of D-2, the boy and the dog following on his heels.

He sat Lee down and explained it in as few words as he could. Then, while the boy was still shaking his head, the captain activated his workstation and brought up a picture on-screen.

A picture of Henry Archer as he'd been at fourteen years old. A fishing trip somewhere, a pole slung over his back, in overalls and waders both two sizes too big for him.

Lee stared at it a good, long time. Continuing to

shake his head, and then, at last, stopping, and just sitting motionless.

"It's true," the boy finally said. "I look just like him. Like you."

"More him than me."

The boy stood then, and began to pace.

"I don't know why I never saw it before. My mother had pictures of you, and I looked at them, and I never once thought . . ."

"Not of me," Archer said.

"I know. The you here, in this universe. Not that it matters. They lied to me." He looked right at Archer. "So did you."

The captain sighed. "I'm sorry, Lee. Believe me, I wish I didn't have to tell you the truth now."

"It doesn't matter," the boy said. "None of it matters."

He sat down heavily on the captain's bed.

"So you're giving up?"

"What do you mean? What choice do I have? Makandros and Kairn want nothing to do with me."

"You were willing to go to the Council without them before. Stand up to Elson."

"That was before. Now I'm not . . . I'm nobody. I have no right there."

"You have every right. You're General Sadir's son."

"He was not my father."

"Maybe not by blood, but you said it yourself, Lee. Everything you are, you owe to him."

The captain let his words hang there a moment while he considered the irony of his defending the memory of a man who had murdered thousands of people.

"You wanted to be worthy of his memory," Archer added gently. "This is your chance."

"I understand that," the boy finally said. "But Makandros and Kairn . . . what if they contact the Council? Tell them that—"

"I don't think they will. Not in the middle of a surprise attack. Besides, even if they do, aren't people likely to believe they're simply trying to turn the Council against you?"

"Maybe." Lee still looked uncertain.

Archer leaned closer. "They've already turned their backs on a chance to make peace, Lee. Do you want to do the same?"

The boy shook his head. "No, I don't. But what happens afterwards? Even if we can stop the war, people will find out about me."

"They might. But that's afterwards. You have to decide what to do now."

"You're saying, put my life at risk."

"If that's what has to be done."

"That's easy for you to say. You wouldn't be the one walking in there."

"And if I went with you? Would that make a difference?"

"I don't know. What does it matter? You can't, right? People might see a resemblance."

Archer frowned. That had been his thinking before, but now . . .

If he really had talked Lee into risking his life to stop this war, could the captain do any less?

The com sounded.

"Bridge to Captain Archer."

The captain turned and cleared his father's picture from the display. He brought up the bridge monitor.

Trip's face filled the screen.

"Thought you'd want to know, Captain. Council meets in an hour."

Archer nodded. Behind Trip, he saw Malcolm and T'Pol talking, heads bent together over the tactical station. Probably tracking Makandros and the Guild.

"Sir?" Trip asked. "Are you—Have you talked to the boy?"

"I have. He's right here."

"So he knows."

"That's right."

"And? What are your thoughts now, Captain? Your plans?"

Archer frowned. *I'm not sure,* he was about to say.

At that moment, T'Pol straightened up at the sensor station. The captain's eyes went to her, and all at once . . .

He had an idea.

Twenty-Eight

SOMEONE LET OUT a long, low whistle.

Trip couldn't tell if it was Malcolm or Travis. Both of whom stared up at the viewscreen with expressions halfway between shock and amazement.

They were looking at the Kresh, courtesy of *Enterprise*'s sensors, rigged for maximum magnification.

Not that the Kresh needed magnifying.

"I told you it was big," Trip said.

"You, ah, weren't kidding," Travis replied.

"I've seen smaller planets," Malcolm said. He glanced down at his sensors. "Five minutes till we're in range."

"Transporter range, you mean?" Trip asked.

"Yes. Four and a half minutes till firing range. Their firing range. We can reach them from here with torpedoes, though I doubt we'd be able to do so with any real accuracy."

Trip nodded grimly. "Well, let's hope it doesn't come to that. Any word yet?" he asked, turning toward Carstairs.

"Nothing, sir. They had to have picked us up by now."

"They have. They're just not quite sure what to do about it, is my guess." Trip had an image in his mind of the command center above the Kresh, dozens of black-clad soldiers scurrying about, scrambling to man the gun emplacements in the cap atop the massive structure.

No. Dozens of soldiers was wrong. Hundreds. And within the Kresh itself, even more.

"Does anyone else," he said, shaking his head slowly, "think this is a really bad idea?"

Lee was still staring at him, just as he'd been from the instant the captain had joined him on the transporter platform.

"It's me," Archer said. "I promise."

The boy shook his head. "You don't—I mean, I can barely recognize you."

"That's the whole point, isn't it?" The captain smiled and turned to Ensign Duel, who was manning the transporter controls. And staring at him as well.

"You have our coordinates, Ensign?"

The man blinked and then looked quickly down at his console. "Yes, sir. Locked in, and waiting for a signal from the bridge."

For a signal from Trip, who had been sitting with Duel and Lee for the last half hour, going through the layout of the Kresh based on his memory and the boy's, and what sensor readings they'd been able to pick up from a distance. Enough information, his chief engineer felt, to enable them to beam in with a reasonable degree of accuracy.

Archer, of course, had been elsewhere. With Doctor Phlox. Getting altered so that spotting a resemblance between him and Leeman Sadir would be well-nigh impossible. Now, if there was anyone on board *Enterprise* the captain looked like . . .

It was Sub-Commander T'Pol.

He felt the tips of his ears one more time. Strange. Archer had had prostheses before, but there was something about wearing this particular makeup . . .

He could swear it was affecting his thinking. He felt a little more . . . logical.

"Bridge to transporter room."

That was Trip. The captain nodded to Duel, who opened the com.

"Archer here. Go ahead."

"Just heard from the Kresh, sir. We have thirty seconds to turn around, or they will consider our intentions hostile and act accordingly."

"And how long until we're in transporter range?"

"Longer than that."

"Prepare for evasive action, then."

"Travis is on it already, sir. Got a few tricks up his sleeve. Modified version of Rackham's back door that should buy us a couple minutes, at least."

"Good."

"Captain," Trip said hesitantly. "Are you sure—"

Before Archer could tell him yet again that he was indeed quite committed to the plan they'd come up with, the ship shook suddenly, violently beneath him.

That was no modified Rackham's back door.

That was weapons fire.

"Was that thirty seconds already?" Archer heard Trip yell. "Damn. Sir—"

"Go," the captain said.

"Good luck," Trip replied hurriedly, and then broke contact.

The captain turned to Lee, who was looking at him anxiously.

"They're firing on us."

"Nothing we can't handle." He felt the ship surge beneath him, and offered Lee what he hoped was a reassuring smile.

Modified Rackham's back door, Archer thought. Maybe modified so they boomeranged around the orbital platform above the Kresh, and came right back in at their target. That's how he would have done it anyway.

He thought about calling the bridge and suggesting it, and at that instant, T'Pol turned the corner and headed down the corridor directly toward them.

"Sub-Commander. Come to see what kind of Vulcan I make?" Archer asked, trying to lighten the mood.

As always, with T'Pol, it was wasted effort.

"No, sir."

"You're not going to try and talk me out of this again, because—"

The ship shuddered once more, not a weapons explosion but a different kind of stress altogether. Even with the inertial dampers on full, as Archer knew they were, he felt the hull strain to keep up with the maneuvers Travis was demanding of it.

"One minute," Duel called out.

"Not that either, Captain," T'Pol said. "I know that once you have set your mind on a course of action, your resolve is unshakable."

"I'll take that as a compliment," Archer said. "So why are you here?"

"To discuss certain . . . eventualities."

"Oh?"

"Should you fail to return—"

"Oh no." Archer shook his head. He did not want to talk about this sort of thing in front of the boy— Lee was nervous enough already. "I'm coming back. You can count on it."

"I of course anticipate your mission will be successful. But we must be realistic, sir. If something disastrous does occur—"

The ship, of course, chose that moment to shudder again, even more violently. More evasive maneuvers. Not explosions, thankfully, but the boy didn't know that, and suddenly looked another shade paler to the captain.

"Thirty seconds," Duel said.

"We can't talk about this now," the captain said, casting a meaningful glance toward Lee.

T'Pol frowned. "There is, obviously, no other time we can talk about it, sir. Now as I was saying . . ."

Archer sighed. There was no stopping her, clearly.

"If you do not return, and we do not recover the data we need, I wish your permission to proceed to the nearest Vulcan outpost and use their facilities to search for ways back to our own universe."

The captain considered her request a moment.

"Sir?" she asked.

"We'll talk about it later," he said.

"Later? Sir, as I said previously, there is no—"

Archer caught Duel's eyes then. The ensign nodded.

"Later," he said firmly, and then stood stock-still as the transporter beam took him.

To Archer's satisfaction, they had successfully calculated to within a meter: they materialized in the very back of the huge hall Elson had spoken to them from earlier.

It was even bigger than the captain had thought, from his brief glimpse of it on *Enterprise*'s viewscreen. A vast dome, hidden somewhere inside the heart of the Kresh. Within it, several dozen rows of stepped horseshoe-shaped desks, each occupied by black-clad soldiers, Elson's forces, and other men and women dressed in what he took for civilian clothes, the powerless delegates of the Presidium.

Those in power sat not in the hall, but at the very front of the chamber. Fourteen of them, on a raised dais, facing outward toward the others. The Council.

There was a fifteenth chair as well, at the center of the dais, that stood empty. Sadir's old chair, Archer guessed.

Just in front of the dais was an elaborately carved wooden podium, visible as well on three huge video monitors, each easily twice the size of *Enterprise*'s main viewer, suspended high above the chamber floor.

As Archer and Lee watched, General Elson rose from one of the fourteen seats, stepped up to the podium, and began to speak.

"My fellow officers. Members of the Presidium," he began. "You do me great honor by your presence here today. Your strength is my strength. Together, we will lead our planet to peace. As General Sadir would have wanted."

Applause—muted, polite applause—greeted his words. Among those clapping, Archer saw Colonel Wooler at the far end of the dais. The man's face was impassive—the captain couldn't read him at all.

He hoped they'd judged him correctly, or he was going to wish he'd talked things out with T'Pol while he'd had the chance.

"Go," the captain whispered to Lee.

Two soldiers flanked the aisle Lee had to walk down to reach the front of the chamber. At the sound of the captain's voice, they turned.

"Who are you?" one said, stepping forward. "What are you doing . . ."

His voice trailed off as he recognized Lee.

"Go," Archer said again, before the soldier had a chance to react.

The boy started to walk. He got a good four meters before the first head turned to look at him. Another meter before the whispers started.

By the time he was halfway down the aisle, the entire chamber was buzzing. On the screen, Elson faltered momentarily. He looked up, saw Lee, and for a split second, his expression darkened. Then he broke out into a broad smile.

"My friends," he said. "A miracle. Leeman Sadir."

The general threw his arms wide and stepped off the dais toward the boy.

He was the first—but not the only one—to embrace him. It seemed as if everyone in the chamber, soldiers and Council members and civilians alike, wanted to touch Lee, see him, assure themselves that the boy was really there with them. The boy himself was smiling, his eyes moist, as he accepted their greetings. Wooler had maneuvered himself next to Lee, was almost holding him up as the crowd continued to gather around him.

Archer's eyes scanned the room, and he saw that Elson, who'd stepped back from the crowd, was now talking to one of his soldiers, his hand cupped over the man's ear. Plotting.

The captain began to circle around the back of the huge hall, keeping his gaze fixed on the man Elson was talking to, trying at the same time not to draw attention to himself.

Elson resumed his position at the podium and raised his arms for quiet.

"Everyone, please," he said, as the delegates took their seats. "I suggest that in light of Leeman's return, we postpone our decision for at least—"

The boy, who was still standing just below the dais, engaged in conversation with Colonel Wooler, took a sudden step up. It put him right alongside Elson.

The general, all at once, looked uncomfortable. He tried to cover by embracing Lee again.

The boy stiffened and broke his hold.

Here we go, Archer thought, and opened his communicator.

"Archer to *Enterprise.*"

"Right here," Trip's voice shot back. "Captain, where the hell have you been? We've—"

"We cut it a little closer than we thought. You getting this?"

"Loud and clear, but—"

"Start transmitting," Archer said. "Let's hope they hear."

"Aye, sir," Trip said.

Leaving the channel open, Archer looked to the podium again. Lee had started to speak.

"With all due respect, General," the boy said, "I believe it imperative that the Council continue this session. That we take up the issue of war—or peace—immediately."

It was Elson's turn to stiffen.

"Lee," he said, trying to maintain the smile on his face. "I can only guess what you've been through these last few days. Let us postpone the session— postpone only, mind you—and give you a chance to recuperate. A few hours. That's all."

A few hours, during which Leeman Sadir would no doubt meet with some sort of accident. Or simply vanish into the vastness of the Kresh, never to be heard from again.

Lee shook his head. "No, sir. With all due respect, we have a brief window of time here—a chance to make peace. We have to seize it."

Elson sighed. "Lee, we talked about this before. After Charest, there is no making peace with the Guild."

"I don't believe the Guild was necessarily responsible for what happened there."

"I have evidence." That was Wooler, who was approaching the podium. "I've told you this, Leeman."

"I'd like to see it. I'd like to know what kind of evidence it is. Hard evidence or someone's word?"

Archer smiled, hearing his own words come back to him.

He smiled a second time at the obvious discomfort he saw on both Wooler's and Elson's faces as they listened to the boy.

"Before we start a war on someone's word, we should talk to them. That's all I'm saying."

"Talk to the Guild?" Elson almost spat out the words. "Never. They are not to be trusted."

"What about General Makandros? Is he not to be trusted as well?"

"This is not what your father would have wanted, Lee."

"All due respect—no one can know what my father would have wanted, General. He's dead. The rest of us—we just have to carry on as best we can."

The hall fell suddenly, eerily silent as the two—General Elson and Leeman Sadir—faced off at each other, the empty fifteenth seat on the dais behind them.

"I have every confidence in General Makandros," the boy said. "In the Guild as well, for that matter. They, above all else, desire peace. I place my fate in their hands gladly."

More of Archer's words, coming back to him. Words that were hopefully reaching other ears at this moment.

"We'll talk about this later," Elson said. He nodded toward the soldier he'd spoken to earlier, who stepped forward now and took Lee's arm.

That answered the only remaining question Archer had about Elson.

If the general couldn't achieve his desired goal peacefully, he had no qualms about using whatever force was necessary to get what he wanted. Whatever mess resulted from that force . . .

He'd clean it up later. Or not.

Archer walked forward calmly then, drawing his

weapon and talking into the communicator at the same instant.

"Trip," he said.

"Sir?"

"The nearest Vulcan outpost," the captain said. "That's where you need to go if we can't get that sensor data. T'Pol—"

Archer stopped in mid-sentence, because on the screen, he saw Lee try to shrug free of the soldier's grasp. The man grasped his arm harder and began to drag him physically away from the podium.

Wooler stepped in front of him.

"Release the boy," the colonel said. "Now."

"Hold him." Elson stepped between the two men, drawing his own weapon then.

Wooler looked from the General to Leeman Sadir, and then at the soldier holding the boy.

At that instant, static crackled over the assembly hall's com system.

"This is General Makandros," a voice sounded, from everywhere and nowhere at once. "I wish to address the Council—immediately."

Archer smiled as the excited buzz of conversation broke out once more in the chamber. Trip had done it—managed to reach the Guild/DEF fleet and broadcast what was happening down here to them, courtesy of his communicator.

Elson's face, up until that second the image of stoicism, cracked.

"Leeman Sadir is right to trust the Guild," Makandros's voice boomed out. "Because—"

Who moved first then, Archer could never be sure. Elson, realizing that all his plans were about to come to naught, or the soldier he'd tasked with dragging Leeman Sadir away from the assembly. Both men, all at once, had their weapons pointed directly at Leeman Sadir.

There was no question, though, about who moved fastest.

Wooler was a blur on the dais.

He drew not one, but two weapons, and fired.

Elson and his lackey both crumpled to the ground.

So much for last-second rescues, Archer thought, and holstered his own weapons again.

"Is anyone there?" Makandros's voice filled the chamber again. "What's going on?"

Wooler stepped to the podium, and pressed a button there.

"One moment, General."

Wooler turned to Leeman Sadir then, and exchanged a look with the boy. Then he walked to the empty fifteenth chair, and pulled it out for him.

As Leeman Sadir sat, the Council first, and then the entire assembly, broke out into applause.

"Sir?" Trip's voice came over the communicator. "Everything all right down there?"

Archer's eyes sought out—and found—those of Duvall's son. For a second, the two shared a smile.

"Right as rain, Commander," Archer said.

Epilogue

BRODESSER SHOOK his head and straightened.

"I could spend a year with that drive," he said to Trip, gesturing toward the cell-ship. "And at the end of it, I think I still might not have any better idea exactly how it works."

"We've had almost that long already, and haven't even gotten as far as you." Trip was less surprised at this than the professor—after all, he knew it was the product of twenty-fourth-century technology. Brodesser didn't.

Makandros had sent a Stinger for the professor and the rest of the *Daedalus* crew. They were leaving *Enterprise* now, on their way to assist the survivors of the Charest explosion, who included General Dirsch. Makandros and Kairn had made contact with him earlier, as Trip had suspected, and had been planning to join their forces with his. To confront Elson, and hopefully force him if to not surrender power, then at least to abandon his plans to extend it.

None of which mattered now.

What mattered was getting supplies and medical

assistance to the wounded and dying at Charest. Phlox had released a number of stores—those that closely mirrored the native *pisarko*—which now lay stacked alongside the Stinger.

Among those supplies was also the subspace beacon Brodesser had begun modifying earlier, during their failed attempt to broach the anomaly.

Now they intended to use it to contact Starfleet. *Their* Starfleet.

"Good luck working with that, anyway," Trip said, nodding toward the beacon.

"That is technology we understand," the professor said. "I don't think it'll take long at all to modify it in such a way that we can reach Starfleet." He smiled. "Any bets on which ship answers our signal?"

Trip returned his grin. "If it is *Enterprise*, treat me kindly, sir."

"Of course. Good-bye, Trip."

"Good-bye, sir. It was good to meet you."

"And it was good to see you again, Commander."

The two men shared a smile, and shook hands.

"I see," the captain said, staring at the woman on the screen. "Well, you can let him know I was trying to reach him. I will try again later."

The woman nodded, and without so much as a word of farewell, closed the circuit.

The captain leaned back in his chair and frowned.

Archer was in his ready room, where he'd come after the Council meeting—after a short stop in sickbay to have his prostheses removed. The captain had spent the last few hours talking privately with his senior staff, and with Makandros and Kairn, and attempting, when he could find time, to reach Lee-man Sadir. None of those attempts had been successful.

The boy was very busy indeed. Trapped in the third special session of the Council the captain knew of. That was, Archer supposed, a good sign.

It meant that Makandros and Kairn had kept their promise—a promise they'd given to Archer after Elson's death, a promise not to expose the boy as human, to see that those under their command who knew did not betray that knowledge either.

The captain knew, of course, that the truth would come out. Sooner, rather than later. He only hoped that the general's fears proved misplaced, that the revelation, when it came, would mean little.

Lee also seemed to be aware that his days as General Sadir's "son" were numbered. He had already taken Colonel Wooler into his confidence, a conversation the captain had been present at. To his—and Lee's—relief, the man had taken the news stoically. As he seemed to take everything.

"Blood matters," Wooler had said. "But you have been your own man now for some time, Lee. This changes nothing."

It certainly didn't change how the man treated him. Archer only hoped others would follow suit, when the time came. Thankfully, Lee was too busy with other matters to concern himself overly with the future now.

And speaking of other matters . . .

The captain had some of his own to attend to as well.

* * *

It was time—past time, in fact, as he'd told T'Pol earlier—to bring everyone on *Enterprise* up to speed on the dilemma facing them: the lack of sensor data that would enable them to return safely to their own universe.

Archer decided to share the knowledge with his junior officers privately, making them responsible for communicating it to their respective departments—passing it along as a problem to be solved, not a pronouncement of doom, as he feared a ship-wide announcement would be interpreted.

He found a few of the people he was looking for—Lieutenants Hess and O'Neill, Chief Lee, and to his surprise, Hoshi, who he'd thought was still confined to quarters—in the mess, eating a late dinner.

As he approached the table, backs straightened. All eyes went to the captain.

"Mind if I join you for a minute?"

Without waiting for a response, he pulled up a chair and sat, launching into an explanation of their problem—the missing data. About the failed attempt to communicate with the Denari back in their universe, how he now wanted any and all thoughts from them and their subordinates about ways to obtain the information they needed.

"Something occurs to me right away," Hess said when he'd finished. "We ought to make certain that the sensors themselves—and not the relays indicating their status—actually failed."

"Good point," the captain said. "Have second shift get on it."

"I'll take charge of that, sir," O'Neill volunteered. "Put my shift on it right now, in fact."

Archer nodded again. That would certainly make things go quicker.

"Excuse me—Captain?"

"Hoshi?"

She set down her fork, and shifted uncomfortably in her chair. "Sir . . . I have a way to get that data. I think."

"You do?" Archer frowned.

"Yes Captain." For some reason, Hoshi was blushing.

"Well? What is it?"

"The cell-ship."

"The cell-ship?" The captain frowned. "What about the cell-ship?"

"I . . ." She looked down at her plate. "While we were prepping for launch, I accidentally switched on the sensors. The data we need is in there, I'm sure of it."

"Wait a minute." Archer wanted to make sure he understood what she was saying. "The cell-ship's sensors were on?"

She nodded.

"Before you launched?"

"Yes sir," she replied, and then, all in a rush. "It's kind of embarrassing, sir. I made a stupid mistake while I was hooking up the com relay, and I know by now I should—"

"Whoa. Hoshi." Archer held up a hand. "Please. Don't apologize. This is the best news I've had all day."

Hoshi went on as if she hadn't heard him. "I'll definitely spend a little extra time with Commander Tucker on basic interface design, sir, so that this kind of thing doesn't happen again. Even though it is good news sir, I know I shouldn't—"

"Extra time?" Archer shook his head. "Oh no. On the contrary, Ensign—take the rest of the day off."

Everyone around the table laughed. Except Hoshi, who didn't realize he was making a joke.

"Take the day off? Stay in my cabin?" She looked horrified. "Do I have to sir? Can't I go back on duty?"

Archer stood then, and clapped her on the shoulder.

"Ensign, as far as I'm concerned . . . you can work as hard as you want for the rest of this voyage."

Leaving behind a slightly-puzzled looking Hoshi, the captain walked straight to the nearest companel, and punched open a channel.

Trip was on his way up to the bridge when he got the news. He turned the turbolift right around, and went right to the cell-ship.

Damned if Hoshi wasn't spot on. Damned if those Suliban sensors hadn't picked up every detail of their accidental trip through the anomaly.

It took him all of five minutes to set up the interface and download the data to the ship's computer.

When he got back to the bridge, Archer was just finishing up a conversation with Leeman Sadir. He was sitting at the head of a long, black table somewhere in the Kresh, looking for all the world like he belonged there.

Makandros, Kairn, Guildsman Lind, and—to Trip's surprise—Ferik Reeve were among those who surrounded him.

"Absent a few final details," the boy was saying,

"we are fairly well agreed. A transition over the next few years—"

"The next two years," Lind interrupted with a smile on his face.

"Over an as-yet-to-be-finalized period of time, during which power will gradually pass from the respective military units to the Presidium itself."

"It sounds like you have things well in hand, then," Archer said.

"I think we do," the boy said. "And all of us"—his gaze took in the table—"know how much we have you to thank for that."

"You're welcome," Archer said. "Now speaking of transitions . . ."

"I understand. We need to get back to work as well." The boy smiled. "Good-bye, sir. And thank you again."

Archer closed the channel and turned to Trip.

"We're all set?"

"Ready as we'll ever be." Trip turned to the viewscreen, where the anomaly beckoned.

And all at once, he smiled.

"What?" Archer asked.

What he'd been thinking about was that the anomaly represented a gateway, one that led to all possible universes. Including one where Neesa was still alive. One where there was no such thing as a mirror-image molecule, where the two of them had stayed together, and . . .

What? Remained on *Eclipse?*

He pictured himself as engineer aboard that ship, and frowned. That would have been more like a lifetime of repair work. So Nessa would have come on board *Enterprise.* Except this ship already had a chief medical officer. So what would they have done?

No, he suddenly realized. He was thinking about this in entirely the wrong way, because everything that he could imagine them doing together, they were doing. Had done. The theory demanded it. So in one reality, he was aboard *Eclipse*, in another she was on *Enterprise*, and in a third . . .

Trip smiled. In a third, even now, at this very second, the two of them were—

"If it's not that important," Archer said, interrupting his thoughts. "Then . . ."

"Right." Trip punched a few keys on his console. "Course calculated and transmitted to helm."

"Laid in and awaiting your command."

"Impulse and warp engines on-line."

"Then let's do it," Archer said. "Travis . . ."

"Aye, sir. Initiating course and speed—now."

The ship slid smoothly forward toward the beckoning anomaly. Trip looked into the spinning whirl of color and smiled.

"Home sweet home," he whispered under his breath. "Here we come."

ACKNOWLEDGMENTS

Thanks this time go to . . .

Everyone at Pocket Books and Paramount Licensing, especially Paula Block, Margaret Clark, Donna O'Neill, and Scott Shannon.

Rick Berman, Brannon Braga, and Connor Trineer, for the Trip I held in my mind while writing.

Leave us not forget Janet Holliday and the real Kevin Ryan. Nor kids, wife, dogs, or Dolby 5.1.

And *Star Trek* fandom, much-maligned at times, but an indispensable component of any successful *Trek* novel.

As many as 1 in 3 Americans
have HIV and don't know it.

TAKE CONTROL.
KNOW YOUR STATUS.
GET TESTED.

To learn more about HIV testing,
or get a free guide to HIV and
other sexually transmitted diseases.

www.knowhivaids.org
1-866-344-KNOW